ICE QUEEN

ICE QUEEN

FELICIA FARBER

PYRAMID PRESS

Copyright ©2020 by Felicia T. Farber

Library of Congress Control Number: 2020900593

ISBN: 978-0-9964708-3-4 (Hardcover)
ISBN: 978-0-9964708-4-1 (Paperback)
ISBN: 978-0-9964708-5-8 (E-book)

Published by Pyramid Press

Printed in the United States of America

To Isaac, forever a teen.

Foreword

Through an engaging, flowing, credible, and authentic teenage story, Felicia Farber—an experienced trial attorney, among her many hats—tells a persuasive tale of how a common and presumably innocent online activity almost ruins the lives of two intelligent, accomplished, and promising young persons. This activity is known as "sexting."

Today's teenagers travel a rough road. Social media and other enhanced communications can complicate and endanger their lives creating—as they do in this book— potentially dangerous situations extending to criminal activities and charges. The goal, responsibility, and task of teenagers' parents, caretakers, teachers, other school authorities, community and law enforcement workers, and virtually everybody else in teenagers' lives, are to point out and guide them through life's pitfalls. But as in the case of this valuable and admirable book, and in the words of Mark Twain, "There's more than one way to skin a cat."

I have no doubt that attempting to present a convincing and persuasive opus to teenagers about the dangers of sexting and cyberbullying through scholarly treatises and PowerPoint presentations would be just as destined to fail as would trying to convince crusty old adults. That is where *Ice Queen* works its magic. Through the use of this intriguing tale of teenage angst, Ms. Farber deftly combines her creativity, captivating writing, and legal prowess to succeed in reaching teens with the novel's critical messages and dramatic plot.

Now, it's been a long time since I've been an adolescent, but I thoroughly enjoyed this fast-paced, compelling story packed with twists and turns reminiscent of a hit teen drama series. All the while, this engaging book underscores the seriousness of the often inept and inadvertent social media practices of naïve contemporary teenagers and of the criminal legal troubles these practices can cause these unsuspecting "perps."

As a forensic and clinical mental health professional myself—academic, clinician, and teacher of psychiatry, forensic psychiatry, epidemiology, and addiction medicine—I have worked with my share of well-meaning, naïve, and intelligent teenagers, otherwise "terrific kids," who have had serious emotional and behavioral health issues resulting from cyber activities like those of the protagonists of this novel, Blair and David. I have witnessed firsthand the severe toll the fallout from common online practices such as sexting and cyberbullying can have on a teenager's mental health, from depression and anxiety, to trauma-related disorders and suicidal ideations. That is why, from my perspective, this particular literary work is of such great significance.

Added benefits are the sixteen "Discussion Questions" about the social and criminal/legal aspects of sexting and child pornography, followed by a "Glossary of Terms," provided at the novel's conclusion. These features serve to increase the relevance and usefulness of this book, both for its intended audience—teenagers—and for others interested in and concerned about the topics and issues raised.

For the forgoing reasons, I recommend this book as a cautionary tale to teenagers and their parents, caretakers, teachers, school administrators, and the like, in order to raise the awareness of these enhanced communication problems to all of these individuals. They can all benefit from it!

In a word, Felicia Farber's *Ice Queen* is an exceptional book which succeeds in its principal goal of providing an innovative platform for teens to learn the all too real consequences of sexting and cyberbullying. Everybody who is, who has ever been, who works with, and who otherwise has an interest and investment in the health and well-being of teenagers should read it.

Daniel P. Greenfield,
MD (UNC), MPH (Harvard), MS (Harvard)
Clinical Professor of Neuroscience (Psychiatry)
School of Health & Medical Sciences, Seton Hall University
Attending Physician, HMH / JFK Medical Center
Licensed to practice medicine in NJ, NY, CT and MA

Preface

The modern teenager lives in a digital world where over half the teenage population engages in sexting[1]—the sending, receiving, or viewing of anything considered sexually explicit over cell phones or electronic devices. Most teenagers do not understand the risks they face when sexting due to antiquated laws.

With increasingly sophisticated technology emerging at a dizzying rate, some of our laws regarding the creation and distribution of electronic content have been left trailing in the dust. The inadequacy of these laws in dealing with the online activities of today's teens is of particular concern, because behavior that seems normal to teens can have major legal ramifications.

Under most legislation, anyone underage who sexts— sends a nude/partially nude photo or video—can be considered to have committed sex crimes and be prosecuted under child pornography laws. Even sexting between consensual teens is unlawful if they are minors, giving common teen behavior the potential to be criminalized for millions of unknowing adolescents. Teens need to be educated before they find themselves in trouble, which can easily happen in today's world of instant multimedia communication.

Ice Queen is a work of fiction intended to create an entertaining mechanism for teens to learn that sexting and cyberbullying can have chilling effects. Ordinary adolescents who don't think they've done anything wrong can find themselves in similar situations to this book's characters, facing serious consequences. Since adolescents make up over 13% of the US population (approximately 42 million people,)[2] and the vast majority have smartphones, computers, or access to them,[3] teenage sexting and its dangerous repercussions are critical contemporary issues.

I believe this topic is so relevant, I have spoken and written about it for the legal and medical communities (see: www.feliciafarber.com) and am now writing for the most vulnerable, our teens. Teen victims of nonconsensual sexting are not only at risk for serious problems with the law, they also face an increased likelihood of mental health and physiological problems.

Sexting needs to be talked about at home, in school, and through a national dialogue. As technology continues to outpace our laws and terms such as revenge porn, vindictive sexting, and sextortion have become mainstream, closer attention needs to be paid to ensuring that teens are protected. Until our laws further evolve and it is universally recognized that teen sexting is not child porn, our teens are legally vulnerable.

This novel is intended for teens, but adults will find that it creates an excellent forum to discuss this very important topic. Thought provoking questions are provided at the end to facilitate discussion.

[1] Strohmaier, H., Murphy, M. and DeMatteo, D. Sex Res Soc Policy (2014), 11: 245. https://doi.org/ 10.1007/s13178-014-0162-9.

[2] Current Population Survey, Annual Social and Economic Supplement, 2014. United States Census Bureau, http://www.census.gov/cps/ data/cpstablecreator. html

[3] Anderson, M. and Jiang J., Teens, Social Media & Technology, Pew Research Center (2018), https:// www.pewinternet.org/2018/05/31/ teens-social-media-technology-2018/

CHAPTER 1

The Gatekeepers

I'm having serious second thoughts as my mother's Ford Explorer approaches the Cedar Woods Community Clubhouse. The allure surrounding this must-go-to pool party suddenly evaporates and I clutch my stomach as intense surges of panic stab at my insides like sharp little knives. Drawing a deep calming breath, I try to shake off the doubts rattling around my skull:

What if no one talks to me? What if they all stand around whispering and laughing at me like in school? My best friend Kayla's warning haunts me: *You think they're not going to make your life miserable just because you're at a party?*

The Explorer rolls to a stop in front of the vast green lawn encircling the stately brick clubhouse. My nose twitches from the smell of fresh-cut grass as I crane my head out the window to scan the grounds for the Ice Queen and her Things.

"Honey!" my mom shouts. "I've asked you twice what time you want to be picked up and you keep ignoring me."

I stop chipping at my pink rose nail polish and glance up. "Uh...sorry Mom. Didn't hear you."

"You never seem to hear me. I'm going to meet your father at his office and go out to dinner. Should we get you on the way back?"

"I don't know yet. I'll text you." I slide out of the SUV, brushing the tiny pink flakes off my lap. My eyes dart around the perimeter to see if anyone is watching.

Small clusters of people are scattered here and there,

some near the road, some by the clubhouse entrance, but no one seems to be paying any attention to me.

My fingertips cling to the edge of the car door as I make my final decision. *Should I really do this? What if Kayla's right?*

I push out a deep breath, then swing the door closed.

"Just make sure it's before midnight," my mom yells through the open window. "Your father's been working around the clock all week on this huge case and he's exhausted. He doesn't want another late night."

"Okay Mom," I call over my shoulder, adjusting the straps of my new bikini top that slipped out from under my turquoise cami.

At the sound of a high-pitched beep emanating from the bottom of my beach bag, I dig my fingers around until I find my phone. It's a Snapchat from Rachel, my other best friend: "Good luck!"

I immediately send a message back: "Going in now. Am I really stupid?"

"Yes, don't go."

"Need to," I reply.

"You really think Hunter Hartman will be there?"

"Hope so."

"Leave if things get bad."

"Okay."

I slip the phone back into my bag and continue up the long path. If I get to talk to Hunter Hartman this will all be worth it. We're in the same psychology class and he always says hello, but we've never actually had a conversation. He sits with his people on the far side of the room by the windows, and I spend every class trying not to stare at those incredible light green eyes and muscular arms.

The knots in my stomach tighten and travel up to my

throat as I near the front gate. I stop before I cross through, my legs feeling like heavy tree stumps, the tips of the knives in my gut growing sharper.

I give myself a pep talk: *I can fit in here, just like everybody else. There's nothing wrong with me. No matter what happens don't cry...not in front of them.*

As I take a baby step toward the main entrance, an animated voice bellows. "Blair! I'm so glad you came. It's great to see you!"

Mrs. Levine rushes over and plants a warm, welcoming kiss on my cheek, her dark ponytail grazing my bare shoulder. I know I got invited to this party because of her, and unlike her saccharine-sweet daughter Alyssa—who my friends and I call Splenda—she's genuinely excited whenever she sees me.

"Great to see you too," I say.

"Are you all ready for finals next week?" she asks. "I told Alyssa that after tonight she has to study every minute. She has physics and pre-calculus on Monday and English on Tuesday. What about you?"

"I have only one on Monday, but the rest of the week is going to be horrible."

Mrs. Levine pats my upper arm, her cherry-red lips extending into a smile. "Oh, you don't have to worry, you're such a good student. I always see your name on the honor roll. Alyssa, on the other hand—"

"Well, one more week and we're all free," I break in, trying to change topics.

Thankfully, she follows my lead. "Your mother said you're lifeguarding again this summer."

I nod, discreetly looking past her to see who's already there. She keeps talking, gesticulating with her hands, waving them back and forth in front of my face.

"That's wonderful that you're making some money. Alyssa's going to that performing arts camp in Upstate New York again—the one that costs a small fortune. I wish she'd get a job too."

"I hope you don't tell her that. She really loves that camp," I say.

"I always tell her she should be more like you...."

Uh-oh. You're only causing me problems.

I force a polite smile and nod some more as Mrs. Levine drones on, regaling me with stories of her own teenage jobs. I've completely stopped listening and am desperately trying to figure out how to escape when another mother interrupts looking for the paper cups.

"Mind if I borrow her?" the petite woman asks me as she places a hand on Mrs. Levine's forearm. "We need to set up the drinks area."

Please take her!

"No problem," I say.

Once I'm free, I practically dive through the main gates. But I have no luck. As soon as I step inside, I find myself blockaded by Splenda and her greeting committee—Molly Mullet and BM. These girls are not, and will never be, my friends.

The Mullet is really Molly DiFrancesco, one of the leads in the spring musical. She prances around with her nose tilted upward, like she's a Broadway star who's too good to associate with the common folk. Back in sixth-grade science when we learned there was a tropical molly fish, everyone started calling her Molly Mullet. My friends and I shortened it to just Mullet in high school when we got tired of her holier-than-thou attitude. We could've called her Bosc since her bottom half has a striking resemblance to a pear, but we went with the fish.

And BM doesn't actually stand for the gross body function. The initials represent the two words that best describe Erin O'Donnell: Big Mouth. The whole school calls her BM. It's because Erin makes herself into a caricature by accentuating her giant lips with deep burgundy lipstick and dark liner. At first glance all you see is this larger-than-life mouth popping out at you like in a 3-D horror flick. And it doesn't help that she's one of the biggest gossipers in the school.

"Oh...you decided to come," Splenda remarks in a cold tone, her embarrassment at seeing me dangling off each word. Of course, if our moms were watching, Splenda would be masquerading as my adoring friend. But there's no need for pretense now.

"You know you don't belong here," BM chimes in.

"You invited me," I retort, smiling as pleasantly as possible at Splenda.

"You weren't supposed to come though. You *know* my mother made me invite you." Splenda turns toward her friends and assumes a defensive air. "It wasn't my fault."

The last thing I want is a confrontation, but what am I supposed to do? I've had it with Splenda's saccharine-sweetness. Now that she's showing off for her friends, the artificial façade is gone and the real Splenda—the nasty, spiteful one—is fully exposed. She may think she's great, but I know everything about this girl, like she wore Pull-ups through fourth grade and was always such a spaz growing up no one ever wanted her on their team in gym class.

I'm not going to let her keep me from this party—I have to say something. The best I can come up with is: "Your mother is so nice. What happened to you?"

"She doesn't know you're such a freak!" Splenda fires back.

There's that "f" word that I hate more than anything. If I could, I'd remove it from the dictionary. My entire body stiffens, and my cheeks start to burn. I can't stop my long-suppressed anger and frustration from bubbling to the surface and spilling out.

"Yeah? You didn't think so when you hid in my house after your nose job," I say. Even though Splenda didn't want anyone to know the real reason for her Christmas-time operation, Mrs. Levine had been straight up with my mom.

Splenda gasps, as if shocked by my accusation. She places her right hand over her heart, like she's saying the Pledge of Allegiance, and loudly announces, "I had a deviated septum. *Everyone* knows that!"

The gloves are off. Why pretend there's anything left to salvage of our fake friendship? "The only thing deviated is your ability to tell the truth!" I retort.

"Are you calling her a liar?" Molly Mullet asks, hands on her wide hips.

I glare at the Mullet. "Was I talking to *you*?"

"I think you should leave now," BM declares with an authoritative edge, folding her thick arms over her humongous chest.

Is she really telling me to leave before I even walk in?

I'm speechless at first and don't know how to react. If I let them chase me away, I'll never get to the good people at the party. I hate doing it, but I have to match their rudeness or they'll think I'm weak and afraid and they can just squash me.

I finally recover enough to stammer, "I...I didn't know you could think. I thought your big mouth just moves by itself!"

The Mullet's awful fish face looks like it's about to start spouting out steam instead of water. "Blair, you don't belong at this party." She thrusts her right index finger between my eyes as she enunciates each word in a harsh staccato, "There-Is-No-Room-For-Losers-Like-You-Here!"

Now the "L" word?

It's three against one and they're relentless. I have to stop their attack. Fight fire with fire. "You're right. There's no room for me or anybody else here because of your big butt!" I extend out my arms, simulating the immense size of the Mullet's pear-shaped rear end.

This is obviously not the first time she's heard a butt joke and she comes right back at me. "At least I have a body and I'm not a pre-pubescent little twig like you!"

I happen to be rather self-conscious about my skinny freckled body, but I try to think of a clever response, spitting something else out that I'd never normally say. "Hey, this little twig broke the school record this year for the fifty-meter backstroke. What have you broken lately? Your kitchen chairs?"

"You're such a bitch, Blair!" Splenda spews, her face hot crimson.

I know from one look at my former friend that I've won this battle and need to get out of here fast. With my head held high I throw Splenda the widest, phoniest grin I can muster and brush past the nasty trio, flicking my wrist in a triumphant wave.

"Well, thanks so much for the invite," I call over my shoulder.

As I distance myself from the rotten threesome, I can practically feel the icy shards their eyes fire into my back. I don't need to hear their exact words to know they're cursing me out big time.

I walk about twenty more yards, stop, breathe deeply, and squeeze my eyes closed. Here I am so worried about the

Ice Queen and her Things when just getting through the front gate was a disaster. Maybe I should skip out back and head to Betty Boo's for Double Fudge Cinnamon Graham Cracker ice cream with my real friends before things get any worse.

CHAPTER 2

The Party

I stand on the edge of the expansive stone patio behind the brick clubhouse searching for someone—anyone—I can hang out with, but there are hardly any people here yet. Behind the large rectangular swimming pool the grounds are completely deserted. The clay tennis and basketball courts adjacent to the pool are also empty. I've arrived way too early.

Now what?

I feel my pulse accelerate and the stomach knots claw back up. Standing here alone, like I'm on display, only highlights that I'm an unwelcome intruder. I'm fair game for another encounter with Splenda, or worse, the Queen and her Things. I need to do something...fast.

I spot a small group who've started a pick-up game on the sandy volleyball court to the left side of the concrete pool deck. I can't make out any of their faces, but at the moment they seem to be my best bet.

As I approach the net I call out, "Hey, can I play?"

A boy from my Spanish class dressed in orange Hawaiian-flowered swim trunks glances over his shoulder and says, "Sure, go on that side. They can use some help." My eyes follow his pointer finger across the net.

"We really don't need any help," a short girl with glasses on the other side objects. "But if you want, you can play over here."

"Thanks," I say with a smile, grateful to be out of the spotlight.

The players all wait for me to move to an open spot in front of the net before resuming their game. I recognize most of them from school, but to my delight, no one questions my presence at this Class A event. They all just hit the ball over the net and move through their rotation, making me part of the lineup.

After about half an hour of playing, a loud rap song bursts from the clubhouse speakers and it begins to feel more like a party. With Eminem's lyrics hammering the air, we play through the deepening twilight. Several more kids join the game until there are nine players on my side and ten on the other.

Some of my teammates joke around and a few side conversations pop up, but the first time anyone talks to me is when I score four points in a row on my serve. Then a tall girl in the center cheers, "Woo-hoo!" and another in the back row gives me a high five. Other than that, I'm left alone, which is totally fine with me.

When it's too dark to see the ball and we're smacking at shadows, we call it quits. I'm both nervous and excited to re-join the rest of the party. The volleyball games have given me new confidence that I can fit in here, and the once empty grounds are now bustling with partygoers. Maybe Hunter Hartman is here too.

As I follow my teammates back to the main area, I notice that the strong halogen beams radiating off the clubhouse roof illuminate most of the patio and pool but leave the grassy section behind the deep end in total darkness. I derive some comfort in knowing that I can slip away to the back field if I need quick camouflage.

The hip-hop beats pound more intensely as I make my way toward the food and beverage tables lined up under the rear awning of the clubhouse. I'm happy, kind of dance walking along, almost forgetting where I am, until I have to instantly sober up: The Shape Shifters are on a collision course right for me. There's no way to avoid them.

The Shape Shifters are two awful girls, Meryl and Christina, who transform themselves into whatever will make them popular or look good for college. Starting in middle school, if a girl was having a bat mitzvah, they'd be her new best friends to get invited. When yearbook volunteers were needed, they were suddenly photography buffs so they could buddy up with the cool kids by taking their pictures. They became avid environmentalists when a high school science teacher was looking to start an ecology club, and they were diehard soccer fans when the boys' varsity soccer coach needed stat girls to operate the scoreboard. They just finished a stint as the backstage managers for the spring musical so they could get invites to all the cast parties. *Sickening!*

"Blair!" one of the Shape Shifters says to me, her eyes round with surprise. "Didn't expect to see you here."

I try to match her level of astonishment. "Didn't expect to see you here either!"

The other Shape Shifter jumps in. "Well...we were invited."

"So was I!" I exclaim.

"Uh, who invited you?" the first Shape Shifter has the nerve to ask.

"Sple...Alyssa. Who invited *you*?"

"Same."

I nod. "What a coincidence."

The first Shape Shifter eyeballs the second, then says, "We've gotta go. See ya."

I force my lips into a smile. "Yeah, see ya."

That was so awkward!

When I reach the food tables I'm thrilled that they have

two six-foot heroes and some large bowls of macaroni salad, otherwise I'd be eating potato chips and Cheez Doodles for dinner. The amazing smells of the fresh bread, deli meats, and onions practically make me drool.

After I help myself to a healthy wedge of an Italian hero, I slide over to the drinks. As I pour a raspberry iced tea, I glance around to see who else I know and whether I have to watch out for more trouble. Although I haven't spotted Hunter yet, I'm happy that the people around me are busy in their own little groups and no one is paying attention to me.

No one except Thing 2. "Is that a new purse Blair? I didn't know Walmart was having a sale this week," she mocks as she comes from behind, delivering a sharp elbow into my side as she reaches for a diet soda from an ice-filled plastic tub.

I whirl around, relieved that there are no other Things in the immediate vicinity. Thing 2 is alone. I'm very tempted to dump my iced tea over the rotten girl's head as payback for the nasty jab, but I decide not to waste my drink.

She and her group of Things have gotten increasingly meaner over the years and whenever they see me they take aim and fire. The nicest comment a Thing ever made to me was on one winter morning when there was no humidity and my hair actually looked good. The Thing said, "Where's the rat's nest Blair? You must not have had time to put your finger in the socket today."

I never respond to any of their taunts, but at the moment my ribs hurt from the elbow strike and I'm in hyper-defensive mode from the other ugly encounters. My mind is blank at first and I can't think of a fitting comeback, but then I catch a glimpse of her fluorescent lime-green eyeshadow.

"I thought you always knew when Walmart's sales are since that's where you get all your makeup. Maybe you should hurry over there right now and get some more flattering shades."

"You're such a bitch Blair!" Thing 2 wails. "I'm going to call the exterminator to get rid of all the rats!" She storms away, no doubt in search of backup.

Part of me is proud for standing up for myself, but another part regrets sinking to her level. I should've just ignored her like always, and not let her see she got to me. My friends and I decided long ago that our best approach to dealing with all the rotten girls was to brush them off, pretending we just didn't care what they said and they weren't even worth responding to. Tonight, I'd broken our golden rule, plunging into their meanness right alongside them, and I'm mad at myself for it.

But no time to self-reflect. I need to get out of here fast before the whole swarm of Things comes looking for me.

I slip away to the farthest picnic tables, wandering around for several minutes, struggling to eat while balancing my cup and plate. I don't dare sit down. If Splenda, the Ice Queen, or Things find me sitting alone in the dark, I'll be instantly dropped to Class D— the only level worse than mine, reserved for derelicts and drop-outs.

Once I get rid of my plate and can hold the second half of my hero sandwich with one hand, I make a wide circle around the pool deck looking for a friendly face. I come up empty. My phone rings in my bag, and since I have nothing better to do, I answer it.

"Are you there yet?" Kayla shrieks in my ear, her voice brimming with excitement.

"I'm here," I say, trying to sound more enthusiastic than I feel.

"Tell me everything! Who's there? Have you talked to anyone? Did you see Hunter?"

"Not yet, but the party's just picking up now." I'll fill her in later on Splenda, Thing 2, and the Shape Shifters.

"So, are the Queen and Things there? Who are you looking at right now?"

It would be so much easier to just FaceTime her so she could see the party for herself, but that would be social suicide. Instead, I report, "Arty the Ass Grabber is chatting with Brad Wallington near the pool steps, and—"

"Is Brad still as inflated as ever?"

"Yup."

"I guess there's a reason people call him HGH. He's either on human growth hormones or he sticks an air pump in his mouth every day and switches it on high."

I giggle. "He really does look that way."

"Who else do you see?"

"Bonnie Landau. She's on a lounge chair stabbing at her phone like she's in the middle of a fight."

"Ugh, she's so annoying. Rachel started calling her Enema this year because she's in all her classes and she says she sucks up to her teachers so badly she might as well live up their butts."

That makes me laugh out loud. I've seen Enema in action myself.

"Is there anybody good there? You haven't named one person I'd want to talk to," Kayla remarks.

I do a three-sixty, but there's no one I want to talk to either.

What am I doing here?

I can't help asking myself the same old questions that have plagued me on innumerable occasions: What makes these kids think they're better than me? How did they get to be popular? Do you have to make yourself popular, or do other people make you that way? Can a nice person be popular, or is being mean a prerequisite?

"Hi, Blair," a male voice beckons from behind. "I'm surprised to see you here."

"Kayla, I've gotta go," I say, whirling around to see who's actually talking to me.

It's Lucky Lenny Krazinsky, wearing his usual lopsided grin.

"Why are you surprised?" I ask.

Is everyone going to give me a hard time tonight?

"I thought you of all people would be studying every minute this weekend."

He thinks *I* study all the time? *He's* the one who's tied with Rachel for class valedictorian. "What do you mean by *me* of all people?"

"I just meant that you're one of the few people I know who has as many AP classes and finals as I do next week."

I roll my eyes and blow out a loud breath. "I'm going to be catatonic by Friday."

Lucky Lenny chuckles. "Sometimes I wonder how some of the teachers can be so idiotic. Like in physics, how does he expect us to know such an obscene amount of material in such a short time?"

"Or US history," I add. "There's going to be three new chapters on the final."

He adjusts his wiry glasses and slants his neck. "Have you found *anyone* who understands those calc problems in Chapter Twenty?"

I shake my head.

Although Lucky Lenny isn't very appealing to look at—with his stringy hair and pointy features—he's non-judgmental and easy to talk to. Basically, a welcome relief from the earlier hostility I've encountered.

Still, Lenny is about as uncool as you can get. My friends

and I know without a doubt that he would never be allowed anywhere near a Class A party if he didn't let the Things cheat off him in school. That's one of the reasons we call him Lucky. The other is that the scrawny little guy is a natural-born long-distance runner. In the fall he won the state championship in boys' cross-country track.

We chat it up for about fifteen minutes—long enough for me to finish my sandwich and check out the action in the pool. The Ice Queen and her Things are all flitting around the shallow end, surrounded by oodles of adoring guys, everyone giggling and flirting like mad. The girls all sport skimpy bikini tops with their long hair swept back in matching ponytails.

Nauseating.

Why would I even think the abominable group might not be here? It would be like Brie Larson or Jennifer Lawrence missing the Oscars.

The boys are splashing the girls relentlessly now, lunging for their waists, hoisting them in the air then tossing them into the water. High-pitched squeals and girly cries for help pierce my eardrums. Splenda and the Mullet jump into the Queen's cauldron to aid the "helpless" females and immediately begin flailing their arms and screeching the same sickening way. The Shape Shifters are in there too, of course, but what really turns my stomach is seeing Shape Shifter Meryl try to climb onto Hunter Hartman's shoulders.

I was hoping this party would give me the chance to hang out with Hunter outside of school, but clearly that's not going to happen. He seems pretty content with this annoying girl latched onto his back like a bloodsucking leech.

If I stay here any longer my hero sandwich is going to come back up the wrong way. My girlfriends asked me to take pictures, but not of this...

"Excuse me Lenny," I cough out. "I've gotta go."

Then I head as far away from the pool as possible.

CHAPTER 3

Davey & Frankie

The massive grass field behind the deep end is shrouded in darkness. Although a sliver of moon slices through the jet-black sky, it does little to illuminate the murky ground. Outside the glow of the clubhouse lights, it's almost impossible to see. I inch along the damp grass as my eyes try to adjust to the inky blackness, the only light source the miniscule flashes of orange from fireflies.

When my night vision finally kicks in, I set out for the far-left side of the field. There seems to be a lot of activity over there, and since the top people on my Avoid-At-All-Cost list are back in the viper pit splashing and screeching, this seems like my best bet.

I'm really not up for any more unpleasant exchanges, so if anyone else is nasty to me, I'm out of here. I'll have to tell Kayla and Rachel they were right—I shouldn't have come, and I'm forever destined to be a Class C.

As I draw closer to the commotion, the smell of pot hits my nostrils and I veer away, like I've ricocheted off a wall. If people want to fry their brains right before finals, that's their business.

Off to the right I spot a couple of dark figures near a bank of large evergreens. Over a symphony of crickets, I hear male voices and the unmistakable yapping of a small dog.

"Who goes there?" a deep voice calls out. I detect the hint of an accent, but can't quite place it.

I'm hesitant to say my name after the lovely greetings

I've gotten this evening, so I whisper, "Blair," hoping he won't be able to hear me well.

I brace myself for the worst, but the guy doesn't say anything bad. To my surprise, he drawls, "Hi Blair. I'm Frank and this is Davey."

"How ya doin'?" Davey asks with a playful lilt.

Wow! They know who I am and they're still being friendly?

"I'm good, thanks," I say. "Is this a puppy?" I can hardly make out the outline of the perky dog, but I crouch down to pet its super soft head.

"Yep, she's mine," Davey replies. "She's a black Lab. Kinda hard to see her out here tonight."

The puppy is going nuts, twirling around, jumping on my legs. "She's so cute. How old is she?"

"Ten weeks yesterday. We got her a few days ago," he says.

"She's *really* a baby," I remark. "What's her name?"

"Lady Gaga. My little sister Danielle is obsessed with Lady Gaga, and my mom made the mistake of letting her name the dog."

"It could be worse," I say. "My neighbors named their dogs Buttsniffer and Kissieface."

Davey and Frank both laugh.

"Hey, you're pretty funny," Frank says. "Do you have a boyfriend?"

"Frankie," Davey cautions. "She doesn't want to get involved with someone from Richmond."

Richmond? That catches me by surprise. "What are you doing up here?"

"I'm just up for the weekend. I used to be Davey's neighbor here in Cedar Woods, but we had to move four years ago when my dad took a job down in Richmond. We came back up this weekend for a big anniversary party my aunt and uncle are having tomorrow night."

"That's great that you guys are still friends," I say.

"Best friends," Davey corrects. The two boys click their beer cans in a toast to their long-standing friendship. It's such a black night I can't make out their faces, but I can tell that Frankie is way taller than Davey.

"Would you like one?" Frankie asks as he plunges his hand into a bag on the ground.

My parents would kill me if they found out, but after wrestling with my conscience for a few seconds, I give in to the moment. This is a party, I'm not driving—not until I get my license in the fall, anyway—and a few swigs of beer won't hurt.

"I'd love one, thanks." I stop petting Lady Gaga and reach for the beer. The puppy keeps leaping, trying to climb up my body with her claws.

"She really likes you," Davey observes. "But she does get over-excited." He moves closer to gently pat the frisky pup on the rear. "Sit," he commands.

Lady Gaga ignores him and continues barking, stretching her short furry paws up my legs.

"Sit," I order the puppy.

She instantly drops to the ground and sits.

"Hey! How did you do that?" Davey asks.

Frankie answers before I can utter a word. "She's a chick's dog, that's how. She only listens to chicks. I bet your sister is training her that way."

Frankie's pretty funny himself. Too bad he lives in Virginia.

"Actually," I say, "I volunteer at the animal shelter and spend a lot of time training dogs. We would've gotten a Lab ourselves, but my dad is allergic, so we got a Portuguese water dog instead. They have hair instead of fur."

Davey nods. "Yeah, my girlfriend is allergic too. Even to this tiny thing." He scoops up the black fur ball and pulls her to his chest.

Of course, he has a girlfriend. It's the same story every time I meet someone nice. At this rate I'll be twenty-five before I have my first boyfriend.

"I'll be right back," Frankie announces. "I had a really long drive up here and a killer history final today, so I'm going to go over there for a few hits."

After he leaves Davey says, "He needs to relax. He's so wound up he's making me crazy."

"Well, I think we're all going to be like him by the end of next week. I'm probably going to need electroshock therapy."

Davey chuckles. "Frankie's right—you really are funny. But I don't think I've ever met you before. You go to Westberry?"

"Unfortunately, yes. But I don't want to talk about school anymore. I came here to forget about finals. Next week's going to be bad enough."

"I hear you. I'd rather talk about *anything* else. Hey, are you cold? You look like you're shivering."

The little cami and cutoff shorts I've got on over my bathing suit are doing nothing to keep me warm, and the chilly ground has seeped right through my paper-thin flip flops. Add to that the icy beer, and I'm coated in goose bumps, my arms pulled tight into my chest.

"Yeah, I'm freezing," I say through chattering teeth. "I didn't realize it was going to be this cold tonight and my feet got wet from the grass."

"Why don't you take my sweatshirt?" Davey offers. "I don't need it." He reaches behind him and pulls a dark garment off the top of the fence.

"You sure?"

"Yeah, I'm not cold at all. You might as well use it."

"Thanks." I gratefully slip the shirt over my head. It's soft and thick, with that wonderful fresh, out-of-the-dryer scent.

"Hey, have you been to that new virtual reality center in the mall?" he asks.

I'd just spent five hours there the past weekend with Rachel, Kayla, and our other close friend Carrie, and none of us had wanted to leave. "That place is awesome!" I say.

"I wasn't sure if girls would like it."

"Are you kidding? I'm going to enter an eSports tournament there as soon as finals are over."

There's excitement in his voice as he says, "I want to do that too."

We spend the next twenty minutes discovering that we have tons in common. There's a giant overlap in our favorite sports teams, foods, music, and movies.

When Lady Gaga starts pouncing on me again, we both drop to the grass to play with her. We're rolling around, laughing, getting to know each other, when it hits me that maybe I do belong here after all. I just need to stay away from the nasty girls.

I watch as David props the puppy up on her hind legs and tries to dance with her. "She's such a great dog," he says. "But I've got to give her a better name."

Chuckling, I take another sip of beer. It's still super cold, but I like it. "You know, your sister may be on to something. At the shelter we had this poor dog Peasley that was there for over three years. We posted cute pictures of him online and taught him tricks, but he was a mongrel with odd coloring and no one ever picked him. One Saturday morning I decided to do an experiment. I changed the name on his cage to Bon Jovi—BJ for short, since it kind of sounds like Peasley—

and underneath put: Favorite song: *Who Says You Can't Go Home?* We played it over the speakers during visiting hours and that afternoon he was the first one out the door. This couple loved Bon Jovi and had to have him."

I could see him nodding in the dark. "That's a nice story, but what are the odds of it happening again?"

"Pretty good," I say. "There were two cats, a brother and sister, that were there for four years and after Bon Jovi worked, we renamed them Beyoncé and JayZ and they were also adopted within a day. People love rock stars."

David releases Lady Gaga and she dives into my arms, wriggling over my shoulder and down my back, her sharp claws leaving a trail of puncture wounds. She races around us in fast circles until David catches her and pulls her onto his lap. "Okay, you've convinced me. Maybe I'll just call her LG."

Frankie lumbers back over and is totally wasted. He's no longer the charming Southern gentleman I'd liked only minutes earlier. Instead, he's a complete jerk, singing loudly and cackling at his own cringey jokes.

The marvelous time I've been having with Davey comes to a screeching halt. Even in the pitch black, I can tell from Davey's tone that he's not too pleased with his buddy either.

"Listen guys, this was really fun," I say, springing to my feet, "but I must have a hundred bug bites from being out here and I need to find the ladies' room. I'll catch up with you later." I edge away in the direction of the pool, and yell back, "Thanks again for the beer!"

Although I hate to bail on Davey, I have to get away from Frankie. And I'm not kidding about the bug bites or the ladies' room. My legs are itching like crazy, especially around the ankles, and I really do need a bathroom.

Darn!

As I get to the patio area, I realize I'm a total idiot. I left so hastily I never found out Davey's last name or grade.

God, I hope he's not a freshman.

I wouldn't mind going out with someone a grade lower, but definitely not two.

But it doesn't matter anyway, I tell myself. He already has a girlfriend. And why would he want *me*?

CHAPTER 4

The Ice Queen

As I return from the dark field and step back onto the concrete pool deck, I see that there are even more people in the water than before. The music is also much louder now, the thunderous beats drowning out the roar of the partiers. I retrieve my beach bag from under a lounge chair and skim along the exterior of the clubhouse until I find the ladies' room.

I shove open the swinging door, whip around the inside corner, and sprint across the ivory tile into the first of three stalls. The floor is wet and dirty, and it reeks of mildew and chlorine, but when you're desperate you can't be choosy.

The restroom was empty when I first came in, but now that I'm exiting the stall, my luck can't be worse. In march my favorite people.

As I turn toward the bank of sinks and mirrors, I come face-to-face with the Ice Queen and all four of her Things. They're dripping wet, with towels wrapped low on their hips like sexy sarongs. Each of them flaunts a pierced belly button and small, colorful tattoos over their ribs and shoulders. They're all hyped up, laughing loudly, until the Ice Queen sees me. She stops dead in her tracks, her eyes flying wide open, and she emits an eerie guttural scream, as though she's just stumbled upon a corpse.

I freeze, afraid to move. The Ice Queen's feral cry has stunned me, and I have no idea what the evil girl will do next. Clearly, the great Krystal Cooper did not expect to find the lowly Blair Evans at an exclusive Class A bash, and she's taken aback. The Things remain frozen too, not knowing what to do for their master.

After a period of breathless silence, the Ice Queen's initial shock turns to rage. She wags a long vampy red fingernail at my chest and seethes, "Where...where did you get that?" All five of my enemies stare at the front of my sweatshirt in horror, as though it's an alien being that's just sprouted to life.

I'm gripped by fear, too terrified to budge. I have no idea what's triggered the Ice Queen's wrath, and I'm way too scared to find out. Several more frightful seconds pass before I muster up the courage to sidestep toward the sink mirror. When I finally see what's freaking them out, I, too, become wide-eyed with shock.

There, in the mirror, over my left breast, is the name *Woods* embroidered in cursive white letters underneath the title *Captain*. The embroidery embellishes a deep maroon hooded sweatshirt that I now know, without having to look at the crisscrossed sticks on the back, belongs to the Westberry High School ice hockey captain, David Woods— the Ice Queen's illustrious boyfriend.

Oh my God! That nice boy Davey was actually David Woods! How could I have known? Frankie kept calling him Davey and he was so friendly. It was so unbelievably black out there I couldn't really see him. We've never had any of the same classes and I never even heard his voice before tonight. And there's no way I ever could have known that Davey's girlfriend who's allergic to dogs is the Ice Queen. I literally have to have the worst luck in the entire world!

"You stole that, didn't you, you ugly rat!" the Ice Queen blares. She's still aiming her accusatory finger at my chest, her dark eyes fixated on the sweatshirt's lettering, her teeth clenched so tight her jaw quivers. She's assumed a precarious stance, like a vicious attack dog low on its haunches, ready to strike.

I can't help but think back to the delightful welcome I received earlier in the evening from Splenda and company. I guess BM was right—I don't belong here. And Kayla was right too—I should have gone to Betty Boo's. Now how do I get out of this mess?

I decide to tell the truth. "I didn't *steal* the sweatshirt. Davey gave it to me."

Oops!

Right after I spit out his name I realize I probably shouldn't be calling the Ice Queen's boyfriend *Davey*. But she's too singularly focused on the sweatshirt to notice my little flub.

"You're lying, you stupid bitch!" she howls, her entire frame shaking. Her chest is so enormous it's hard not to watch it move in and out to the rapid tempo of her frenetic breathing.

I force myself to act calm, digging my palms into my thighs. "It's true."

Even though my pulse is jackhammering in my ears and there's a tightening in my airway, I need to keep a poker face. Every instinct is screaming at me to get out of here, but how? I'm outnumbered, the Ice Queen is ready to lunge at my throat, and her four Things are blocking the exit. I need to think fast but can't. My brain is flooded with panic knowing that I'm trapped.

"Take it off now, you Class C piece of shit!" the wretched Queen commands, her manic voice echoing off the ecru-tiled walls.

"He gave it to me!" I shout back, trying to swallow my fear. Even though I'm acting tough, the truth is, I'm shuddering down to my freshly polished pink toenails. With the Queen unhinged, I'm a sitting duck. My mind races, desperately trying to formulate an escape plan, but I don't see a way out. All I can do is stall with a few more details.

"He gave it to me when I was playing with his new puppy and talking to his friend Frankie from Richmond," I say. "Why don't you go ask him?"

The irate Ice Queen seemed only seconds away from going for my jugular, but now stops dead, slack-jawed, and confused, like I've just slapped her. She obviously realizes that if I hadn't really been with her boyfriend, I wouldn't have known about Frankie and the puppy.

I stare back at her, wondering for the trillionth time what makes this girl such an idol to so many. There's really nothing extraordinary about her looks—she isn't exactly a sizzling supermodel. In fact, Krystal Cooper is pretty plain. She's average height with shoulder-length dark brown hair, plain brown eyes, and a round face. Most people outside of Westberry High probably wouldn't give her a second glance. They'd probably describe her as chunky and okay-looking.

The fact is, there isn't an athletic bone in this girl's body. Her jeans are always too tight, and she has very noticeable muffin tops. How come no one ever comments on those? My girlfriends and I know the answer. It's because everyone— even the teachers—is too busy staring at her two most potent attributes. In school there's always at least a hint of them protruding from a low-cut shirt. At the moment they're shaking up and down, barely held in by her skimpy wet bikini top.

Would I like to be a bit chestier? Sure. Am I a little jealous? Maybe. But it's a hard lesson to have crammed down your throat at the ripe old age of sixteen: Having a brain and being a good person mean absolutely nothing to the vast majority of people. All you need to light the world on fire is a large pair of boobs. And being a bad girl who likes to party is a huge plus. Or maybe that's just the way it is in my screwed-up high school.

"Excuse me, can I get through here?" an irritated voice asks from behind the wall of Things.

One of the Things pivots sideways to allow a large girl with a high, dirty-blonde ponytail to squeeze through. It's Annie Russo, and her annoyed expression shows that she's not at all happy about having the bathroom entrance blocked.

As soon as I lay eyes on my old friend Annie, relief courses through me. She easily towers over the Queen and Things and is probably bigger and broader than most of the boys in school. She could probably tackle all of them too.

Annie is the quintessential jock with no tolerance for the catty games girls play or their obsessions with clothes and boys. She concentrates on school and sports, and nothing else. She works hard at everything she does, her natural size and innate strength helping her to be a standout in track and field, girls' basketball, and even the varsity ice hockey team. Annie doesn't care that she's the only female on the ice, and once opposing teams meet up with her, they learn very quickly not to underestimate the player with the long ponytail stretching down the back of her jersey.

I got to know Annie really well during my freshman year when we were lab partners in biology. We seriously bonded during the dissection of dead mice and frogs, trying not to gag on the noxious formaldehyde fumes.

There's nothing bad that my friends and I could ever say about Annie. We love her because she's a straight shooter who treats everyone fairly and with respect—a foreign concept at our high school. Of course, we hear the nasty rumors that she's a lesbian, but we ignore them. Whether she is or isn't, who cares? It seems people can't just live and let live—not at Westberry, anyway. Girls like the Ice Queen thrive off of putting others down, especially those who are different.

"What's going on?" Annie asks the Queen, her eyes bouncing back and forth between us.

Her Highness, accustomed to her lofty status, is not used to having to answer to her peers, but Annie is intimidating, and she seems to realize that under the circumstances it would be wise to play along. "This geeky bitch stole my boyfriend's hockey shirt!" she cries out.

Annie raises her eyebrows at the Queen's accusation and turns toward me. It's pretty clear I'm in a bad predicament.

"Blair, where did you get that shirt?" she asks, folding her arms and shifting her weight to her heels. My guess is she's trying to appear neutral to diffuse the situation.

"David Woods gave it to me," I say. "We were hanging out on the grass together with his best friend and new puppy, and I was cold, so he let me wear it." Even though I have no idea why they were back there, I add, "They had to go out to the grass because Krystal hates dogs."

"I do not *hate* dogs, you retard!" Her Majesty shoots back. "I'm allergic!"

Having Annie there empowers me to stand up to the Queen and say something I normally would never have the nerve to: "That's too bad, because David and I had such a great time playing with her."

Before I can blink, the Ice Queen flies into orbit, swooping down on me like a giant raptor. Annie instinctively dives between us, blocking the Queen with her own body.

"Krystal!" Annie shouts, struggling to pin down the Queen's flailing arms. "Stop it!"

"I'm gonna kill her!"

"You're insane, Krystal! It's just a shirt. She was cold.

She'll give it back!" Annie tries to talk rationally to the crazed girl. The Things just stand there idle, not wanting to mess with Westberry's shot put champion.

"Get off me you ugly dyke!" Krystal roars, slapping at Annie's biceps and shoulders, frantically trying to break free.

"Get out of here now!" Annie yells to me.

My feet are moving before I can think. I shimmy around Annie, whose face is reddening with the strain of holding back the writhing Queen. Even with her large build, Annie is struggling to contain the frenzied girl.

"Thanks, Annie!" I call out as I maneuver past the Things. With their leader "tied up," they're directionless, letting me pass without so much as a word.

"Just give back the shirt, Blair!" Annie commands.

"Of course," I murmur, slipping out the exit to safety.

Out on the stone patio I heave in the crisp night air, my heart pounding a million miles an hour, my hands sticky with sweat. The tip of my ear that I burned with a flat iron while I was getting ready for the party feels like it's on fire and my legs are so itchy I want to scream, but there's no way I can dive into the pool. I'm immediately envious of all the other guests in the cool blue water—at least a hundred of them now—carefree and happy. Of course, they have no clue about the grisly scene that just occurred in the bathroom.

I scurry toward the main gate, stopping around the corner of the snack bar to catch my breath and consider my options.

First, I silently thank Annie. If it weren't for her, I would've ended up in a horrible fight with five wild vultures trying to rip my shirt off. Well...David's shirt. There's probably no other girl in the school who would've had the nerve to take on the Ice Queen. Other kids are afraid of her. They obey her. They revere her.

I know I need to return the sweatshirt right away to avoid further trouble, but it could take a while to find David Woods—especially if he's still out on that ridiculously dark field. And how much longer can Annie hold back the Queen? With Her Highness on the warpath, another confrontation is a certainty. My only real option is to escape before the lunatic is unleashed.

Fortunately, no one is hanging out by the clubhouse entrance anymore, so I don't have to make excuses for my early departure. Once I hit the sidewalk, I trek a safe distance before pulling out my phone. It's only 10:22 p.m. but looks and feels more like midnight. I decide to hike another ten blocks to a nearby friend's house where I'll have my parents pick me up.

So much for my first Class A party, mingling with the "elite," trying to fit in. I should've known better.

CHAPTER 5

The Debriefing

"No way!" Kayla says in disbelief. "You hung out with Yak!"

"Get out!" Rachel screeches.

We're on a FaceTime call, so I can fill them in on the evening's events. Carrie must've fallen asleep early so she's not with us, but I know she'll be just as shocked when she hears how the night played out.

"I didn't know it was Yak," I repeat for the third time. "Like I said, it was totally dark, and I couldn't even see what he or Frankie looked like. And since Frankie called him Davey, I never made the connection that he was David Woods."

"Wait, wait…slow down a minute! You talked to him for *how* long and he didn't know who *you* were?" Kayla asks, her words punctuated with surprise. "Didn't you tell him your name?"

"Of course I told him my name, but he didn't know me either. And we talked for like half an hour. I played with his puppy. We both like the same bands—"

"Hold on. Can you back up a minute?" Kayla interrupts again. "I don't think there's another Blair in the school. How could Yak be the Ice Queen's boyfriend and not know who you are?"

"I don't know," I answer honestly. "I was wondering the same thing. But he really didn't. We've never been in any of the same classes and I didn't even know what his voice sounded like. And don't forget, there are like two thousand kids in the school."

"Hmmm," says Rachel, brushing some clumps of blonde flyaway curls out of her eyes. "Maybe David Woods is just a nice guy who minds his own business? I mean, didn't we give him his nickname 'Yak' because it's a large, harmless ox? We assumed he's a jerk because he's Her Highness's boyfriend, but we don't really know anything else about him."

Kayla can't get the details fast enough, her wide, almond-shaped eyes prodding me through the computer screen. "So where was the Ice Queen when you were with her boyfriend?"

"You never had a clue you were talking to Yak?" Rachel asks at the same time.

"Can you both just let me tell you what happened?" I start from the very beginning, recounting everything from Splenda's loathsome theater crew to the snarky Shape Shifters to Annie's heroic rescue. I stress again how unbelievably dark it was on the back field where I'd met Yak and his puppy.

Now that I'm finished, there's dead silence. I scratch at the zillions of red bumps that have erupted over my ankles and calves as I wait for a response.

"You guys going to say anything?"

Rachel is the first to speak. "She's gonna kill you."

"Yeah, you're lucky it's summer; otherwise, you'd have to transfer schools like Chloe Esposito," Kayla adds.

This is news to me. "Chloe's transferring?"

Rachel's eyebrows hike up. "Didn't you hear what happened?"

I shake my head.

"Apparently her boyfriend taped them having sex together and she didn't know it. When they broke up last week he showed his friends the videos and they sent them to their friends...and now she won't even leave her house."

"Are you kidding?" I say. "That's horrible!"

Kayla nods. "Beyond horrible."

I can't wrap my brain around her boyfriend doing this to her. "Didn't they want to get married?"

Kayla nods again. "Yup. And then look what he went and did. I heard she's so upset she's not even going to take her finals."

Rachel's mouth inverts into a hard scowl. "We have such lovely people in our high school, don't we? And somehow we're the ones who are relegated to Class C."

Kayla catches my eye as she says, "I don't think we'd ever be popular enough to make the A-list, but we'd definitely be in B with the majority of the grade if we weren't friends with you."

I know she's right, but I hate hearing it. I'm super defensive as I say, "There shouldn't be a Class System in the first place. None of my lifeguard friends who go to other schools have ever heard of anything so stupid."

"It may be stupid," Kayla agrees, "but we're stuck with it. Kids treat the Queen's ratings list like it's the Bible."

I press my lips into a tight line. "The problem is most people are followers. If she said we had green extraterrestrial blood they'd believe her."

Kayla grimaces. "After tonight she's going to be saying far worse things than that."

"Yeah, Kayla's right," Rachel says. "This is really, really bad."

Their tone is startlingly serious. "What's with you two? I didn't do anything wrong. It's just a stupid sweatshirt, for Chrissake!"

"Blair, she already hates you," Kayla says in a voice so sullen it sounds like an apocalypse is about to hit. "Wearing her boyfriend's shirt is like walking up to her and spitting in her face. Now she's really gonna go after you."

"But I didn't even know it was his!" I protest. "I told her that. I'm sure David will tell her that he didn't know who I was either. Then this whole stupid thing will blow over and she'll forget all about it."

Rachel releases a long breath and purses her lips, which are still coated in her favorite lilac-colored lip gloss even though it's almost midnight. "There's no way she's going to forget about this. This is way worse than the Red Eyes fiasco. Just be happy Annie was there to save your butt. Give back the sweatshirt as fast as you can and stay away from her during finals."

I'm already on edge, but my friends' gloom-and-doom attitudes are even more disconcerting. "You think this is worse than what happened with Red Eyes?"

"Way worse," Rachel repeats.

"I agree," Kayla chimes in. "Red Eyes was just her friend. This is her boyfriend."

"But I didn't do anything to either of them!" I screech. "You both know that I was falsely accused with Red Eyes. I'm not the one who ratted her out."

"We know that," Rachel says. "But the rest of the school doesn't."

Every time this topic comes up I get aggravated all over again, like I'm at the start of freshman year. Back then I had no idea that the greasy girl with the red spider web eyes whose locker was near mine was a drug dealer. It was only after the principal and school D.A.R.E. officer cut off Red Eyes' lock on the sixth day of school and discovered that she was selling weed, cocaine, and amphetamines from her locker that my fate was sealed. I'd apparently been spotted at my locker an hour earlier sparking a rumor that it was me who'd ratted out the school drug supplier. And, as if my luck couldn't have been any worse, it turned out the Ice Queen was a good friend and customer of Red Eyes.

"I...I can't believe this is happening again," I sputter. "For three years I've tried to stay far away from that rotten witch and now she's got another reason to hate me."

"You really don't have any luck," Kayla remarks, slicking tufts of black silky hair behind her ears. "I mean, out of all the people at that party you end up with the Queen's boyfriend and he gives you his sweatshirt. That's just crazy."

Rachel nods. "It really is."

I give out a long sigh. "And you want to know what the worst part of the whole night was?"

Neither girl responds.

"It's when I realized that we've been right all along. Whenever we say things would be so different if we just had a clean start without the Ice Queen and her pathetic Class list, we're right. This just proved it tonight. Her very own boyfriend liked me when he didn't know who I was."

"Well, I'm sure he knows who you are now," Rachel says with a snide tone. "I'll bet she's not very happy with him, either, for loaning you that shirt."

No doubt Rachel is correct. I wouldn't want to be him tonight. "I left right after I escaped from the bathroom, so I have no idea what happened. Let me know if either of you hear anything."

"Of course," both girls chorus.

"And just for the record," Kayla adds. "I also think it's crazy that two of the meanest girls in the grade called *you* a bitch."

Rachel bobs her head. "Seriously, if you ever get invited to a Class A party again, please don't go."

"Don't worry," I assure them. "This one cured me for life."

When we end our call, I slather my legs with a topical anti-itch cream I find in the medicine cabinet, pull back my covers, and collapse face-down on my bed, still in my prized maroon sweatshirt. I wonder if Rachel's right and tonight's events will end up being worse for me than the Red Eyes debacle. If that's true, then Kayla's right and I should probably transfer schools.

D A V I D

◆

CHAPTER 6

Krystal

D avid Woods sank against the back of his hard plastic
deck chair, contemplating the ups and downs of the
evening. Instead of swimming and having fun like all
the other kids, he was stuck hiding in a dark corner, shielding
Lady Gaga with his beach towel. The puppy was curled up in
a loose ball on his lap after knocking herself out on the grass.

"You know," he said to his best friend, stretched out in
the chair to his right. "I should've just stayed home tonight
when my mom said I had to watch the dog."

Frankie kept his eyes on the action in the pool. "Why
didn't you just tell her you had this party, and she needed to
get somebody else?"

"Of course I told her that, but she didn't care. She was
going out, and my little sister was invited to a sleepover
party...so that left me."

"But it's not your dog. Didn't your mother get the puppy
to help Danielle deal with the divorce?"

"Yeah," David nodded, his lips curling downward. "But
she got really mad when I told her how unfair it was to dump
Lady Gaga on me. She said I had the opportunity to grow
up with a dog, so now it's Danielle's turn, and I have to do
my part to take care of her. And since she wanted me home

studying anyway, she had no sympathy for me. Bottom line, she went out and I got the dog."

"Well…at least she let you take her to the party."

David grunted. "Believe me, she didn't want to. I had to promise not to let the puppy out of my sight and to keep her away from the pool. And I had to swear I'd study really hard all weekend so I don't jeopardize my sports scholarships. If I don't do well on my finals, I'm never going to hear the end of it."

Frankie took in David's dour expression and socked him in the shoulder. "And you told me *I'm* uptight. Look at you!"

David whacked him back. "You didn't exactly help things tonight—starting with making me late for the party."

"Hey, it's not my fault I got stuck in traffic. And I'm not the one who yelled at you for bringing a dog to *her* party. That was Krystal."

"Don't remind me," David groaned. "She thinks every party is *her* party. And it really sucks that she runs off with her friends at parties and ignores me. She could totally care less that I'm here."

"She may have a hot bod, but I wouldn't put up with her mouthing off like that. She's got a bad attitude."

"Not as bad as that bitchy chaperone who kicked us out to the grass."

Frankie inclined his chin and mimicked in a pretentious soprano voice, "No dogs allowed in the pool area! The Club has rules prohibiting animals in and around the water. You must escort your canine off the premises at once! The only place you can go is back there on that field…and clean up after him or you *will* be fined!"

His imitation was so spot-on David couldn't help but laugh. "You're lucky you're so funny because I'm still mad you chased Blair away."

"What? I didn't chase her away! She had to go to the bathroom."

"She was being nice because you were acting like such an asshole."

Frankie crossed his arms and sulked. "Gee thanks, pal."

"Well, it's true. And how am I supposed to find her now? It was so dark back there, I'm not even sure what she looks like."

"Yeah, I've been searching around for her too, but I can't tell if she's one of the girls in the pool or in one of those groups over there by the food."

"I really liked hanging out with her. I wanted to talk to her more."

Frankie slowly turned to face his old friend. "Uh, I thought you told me Krystal doesn't want you having any friends who are girls."

"She doesn't, but I don't care anymore. I let her chase away all my girlfriends all year, and I'm tired of it. I miss my friends. I would've broken up with her a thousand times, but you've just gotta know how it is in my school. All my buddies keep telling me I'm the luckiest guy in the school to be going out with the most popular girl, and I'd be out of my mind to dump her."

Frankie burst out with a hoarse laugh. "I think you're out of your mind *not* to dump her. She can't tell you who to be friends with."

"Actually, she goes ballistic if I even talk to another girl. What really pisses me off, though, is that she has plenty of friends who are guys."

"Ah! The old double standard!"

"Yup, and I'm so done with that. I told her straight up that I'm going to be friends with whoever I want again, and now we fight all the time."

"So why are you still going out with her? End it."

David ran his thumb up and down one of the puppy's soft, floppy ears and pushed out a heavy sigh. "It's not so easy. Her dad is my hockey coach, so I'm worried about how he'll act toward me if we break up. And, since Krystal is the class president and I'm captain of the hockey team, everyone says we're at the top of the school and the perfect match."

Frankie snorted. "But you're not."

"Not anymore, but at first things were great."

David's thoughts wandered back to the very first night he'd met Krystal—*really* met Krystal, not just passed her in the hall. It was at a mutual friend's house back in the fall when a large group of kids had been invited over to watch movies and share some beer and wine. Krystal's friends kept steering him toward her spot on the couch. He knew who she was because everyone knew who she was, but he'd been a bit intimidated. When he ultimately sat next to her, she acted like the movie was really scaring her and buried her face against his shoulder. He liked the flowery way her hair smelled and the feel of her large chest pressing against his upper arm. The beer had loosened him up and he'd stopped paying attention to the horror film. His hands found their way all over his new couchmate.

He wasn't alone. Soon, the intoxicating effects of the chardonnay and Budweiser transformed the innocent movie gathering into a wild make-out session. He was nearly out of his mind as Krystal rubbed her enormous breasts against him and caressed his inner thighs. Her moist lips traveled down his neck and shoulder, then back up to his mouth. When he tried to take off her bra, she reached for his hand and pulled him off the couch. She swiftly guided him to an uninhabited den off the living room, where they found their own private recliner. It was an unforgettable evening.

No doubt, Krystal was fun. In fact, she was the ultimate party girl. Sex, booze, drugs, she did it all. He liked to have a good time too, but she was extreme.

Frankie slugged him in the arm again. "What are you thinking about, man? You stopped talking."

David reflexively delivered a back hammerfist to Frankie's left bicep. "Nothing much. Just that we've got some major problems."

"Shoot."

David sighed again, not sure where to begin. Stroking the silky fur along Lady Gaga's neck, he kept his eyes cast downward and confided, "Well, for one thing, we have nothing to talk about. Krystal is only interested in superficial things like shopping and gossip. I tune her out and she gets really mad."

"Oh, come on, you're telling me she really expects you to listen to all that girl crap?"

He nodded.

"Why don't you try talking to her about this year's top NFL draft picks and see how interested she is?"

David managed a weak smile. "If that was our only problem maybe I could deal with it, but she's really paranoid too. A couple of months ago she changed the greeting on my cell phone to say, 'Hi, this is Krystal, David's girlfriend, please leave a message.' I let her have her way for a few days, but then I changed it back to my own voice. When she found out I switched it, she flipped out and accused me of cheating on her."

Frankie whistled, shaking his head. "Amigo, you've gotta get rid of this one. I don't care how big her boobs are or what your buddies up here say."

Lady Gaga's head jerked up at the sharp whistle. David tried to coax her back to sleep, stroking her face and rubbing her paws. "I know you're right—I just have to do it. My mother doesn't like her either. She says I can do better."

When the puppy wouldn't stop squirming, he passed her to Frankie. "Here, you take her. You woke her up."

David angled his head back against the wide plastic slats thinking about how his earlier conversation with Blair had highlighted the void he'd been experiencing with Krystal. Blair had been so easy to talk to and had an awesome sense of humor. He could definitely see himself hanging out with her at a baseball game or enjoying a nice dinner—as long as she wasn't a total bow-wow. But something in him really wanted to find out. The only problem was, what was he going to do about Krystal?

DAVID

◆

CHAPTER 7

The Meltdown

David's thoughts were jarred by Frankie's elbow jabbing him in the ribs.

"Bro, this is amazing. The dog's a chick magnet!"

Lady Gaga sat perched on Frankie's lap as a steady stream of girls flocked over to pet the adorable pup. Frankie was in heaven, blabbering, "I'm gonna get me a dog. Yup, that's what I'm gonna do. As soon as I get back. I can't believe I never thought of this before!"

David rolled his eyes. A few more minutes of Frankie's elbow jabs and mutterings and they were out of there. He truly cared about his childhood friend, but at the moment he just couldn't stand him.

There had been no sign of Krystal since his puppy had been banished from the pool area, but now no one could miss her. She and her girlfriends were running at warp speed around the pool's perimeter, Krystal's jumbo-sized breasts bouncing so high it seemed like they were going to smack her in the face. He had no idea what had happened, but all the girls looked frantic.

"David!" Krystal screamed from the other side of the deep end. "David, I have to talk to you right now!"

By the time she got around to his side of the pool she

was breathless, and the triangles of her gold crocheted bikini top had shifted, partially exposing both breasts. They were jiggling all over the place, making quite a spectacle. The strings on one side of her matching bikini bottom had also loosened, and it looked like they were about to unravel. The only person who didn't seem to notice she was in the midst of a complete wardrobe malfunction was Krystal.

"David, how did that stupid bitch get your hockey shirt?" she roared, her hands planted on her hips.

He wasn't paying attention to her words—he was mesmerized by her nearly naked body shimmering and shaking. When the realization struck him that everyone else was watching the same thing, he sprang out of his chair to stand in front of her and block the exhibition with his own frame.

"Krystal, your bathing suit is falling off," he whispered. He was trying to do the right thing, be considerate and protective, but she wanted no part of it. Her right hand shot out and shoved him back.

"David!" she repeated in a shrill cry. "I asked you how that stupid bitch got your shirt. Answer me!"

"You need to fix your bathing suit!" He reached out to slide the bikini top's triangles back into place, but she knocked his hand away. She seemed to neither notice nor care that a sizeable crowd had gathered around.

To his right he eyed a navy blue-and-white striped towel wrapped around the hips of one of Krystal's best friends. "Morgan, can I borrow your towel, please?"

Without hesitation, she slipped it off and handed it to him.

"Thank you," he murmured, and tried to drape it over his crazed girlfriend.

"David!" she bellowed, her face glowing red hot. "I don't

care about the friggin' towel! I want to know how that dumb bitch got your shirt!" She whipped Morgan's towel out of his hands and hurled it onto the concrete decking. Part of it landed on Frankie's feet, but he was too busy gawking at the live entertainment to notice.

"What the hell are you talking about, Krystal? What shirt?"

"Your hockey shirt! For the tenth time, how did that Class C loser get your shirt?" Her dark brown eyes were dilated and wild, her nearly nude body shuddering with rage. He had never seen anyone have a nervous breakdown before, but he'd bet this is how it looked.

"Would you mind telling me *who* you're talking about?"

"You know damn well who I'm talking about! Don't play fucking games with me! She had on your shirt. She said you gave it to her!"

A light bulb went off. He hadn't been thinking clearly under the circumstances. "Oh, you mean Blair."

"Yes, Buhlllaaairrr," she repeated, stretching out Blair's name like a taunting pre-schooler.

He shrugged. "What's wrong with Blair?"

Krystal's snarl—with her lips pulled back and long, pointy canine teeth ready to chomp—gave him the impression she would've bitten his head off if her mouth had been big enough. "What's wrong with her?" she hollered, her saliva spraying him in the face. "The question is, what *isn't* wrong with her? How could you go out with me and not know how much I hate that disgusting rat?"

"Hey, Krystal," Frankie interjected from his deck chair. "Why do you have such a hard-on for Blair?"

The wild girl whipped her head to the right, turning her full wrath on him. "What are you, a retard? Look at me! I'm a girl! I can't have a hard-on, you moron!" She poked herself in the breastbone to make her point, but she needn't have worried. Everyone watching her would've agreed she was a girl. And now there were dozens of spectators.

"Krystal," David explained, "It's just an expression. He wants to know why you hate her so much."

"Oh my God! How could you *not* hate her? She's gross. She's scum. She's disgusting. *Everybody* hates her!" Her words were laced with such venom, white froth collected at the corners of her mouth.

Frankie was persistent. "She seemed all right to me. I still don't understand why you have such a boner for her."

Krystal couldn't contain her exasperation with Frankie. "*All right?*" she aped, trembling with outrage. "You think she's all right? Someone who's all right wouldn't send a gigantic dyke into the bathroom to kill me!"

Frankie shot David a what-the-hell-is-she-talking-about glance and circled his index finger in a loony motion.

Krystal switched her fiery gaze back to David and launched another verbal assault. Gesturing toward Frankie, she quaked, "How the hell can you be friends with such a fucking retard?" Then she directed her quivering finger at poor Lady Gaga. "And how the hell could you bring that filthy mutt to my party? And how the hell could you give that Class C piece of shit *my* sweatshirt? If anyone wears it, it's *me*! Are you out of your fucking mind?"

She worked herself into such a funk that she neither seemed to care what she said nor who heard it. And even worse, when she put her hands back on her waist, her left pinky finger dislodged the last string that had been keeping her bikini bottom in place. The gold crocheted triangle that covered her front privates slid sideways, revealing way too much.

This time her friend Kelly stepped up with another

towel, but Krystal ripped that one out of Kelly's hands too, shrieking, "Get the fuck away from me!"

That was the final straw for David. This girl was insane. Whether she was drunk or stoned or just plain crazy, he didn't care. He and his oldest friend, and even the innocent puppy, had borne enough insults. He spun toward Frankie and cocked his head in the direction of the exit. Needing no further prodding, Frankie sprang to his feet.

Flames spewed from Krystal like a volcano in mideruption. "Where the hell do you think you're going? You still haven't told me why you had to ruin my life! How could you do this to me?"

David couldn't look anymore and pressed forward, positioning his body sideways to blade through the thick mass of gawkers, Frankie at his heels.

"I was attacked by a giant lesbian! Don't you care?" she yelled after him. "We are through! You don't belong in Class A anymore! I hate you! Do you hear me? We are so through!"

In their haste to get to the front gate, David and Frankie knocked into a sea of heads, chests, and limbs, doing their best not to fully trample anyone. The two hung their heads low and stayed silent, like celebrities weaving through a dense throng of paparazzi. When they finally reached the car, Frankie held Lady Gaga tight as David gunned the engine, barreling out of the parking lot before some crazy naked girl could sprint after them.

As they cleared the clubhouse, Frankie flung his head back against the seat and released a whoosh of air. "Well, thanks for a fun evening, amigo."

CHAPTER 8

The Morning After

*B*zzzz. *Bzzzz. Bzzzz.*

David Woods dragged himself out of bed, the endless buzzing of his cell phone and the incessant ringing of the house phone destroying any chance of sleep. He snatched his Android off his dresser: only 9:30 a.m. and eleven missed calls.

What the hell is going on? He stumbled to the bathroom. *Someone must have died or something.*

Saturday mornings were normally quiet. He'd planned to sleep until at least noon then study for finals late into the night. In the off-season—when he had no games or practices—weekends were for catching up on sleep. If he was going to be up this early, there'd better be a good reason.

"Mom," he called out as he bounded down the stairs. "What's going on? I keep trying to go back to sleep, but the phone keeps ringing."

His mother lowered her newspaper and pushed a note pad with two columns of names across the kitchen table. Her wavy dark hair was uncombed, still matted on one side from her pillow, and her yellow-and-blue paisley sleepshirt peeked out from under her white terry robe. "Your cell phone must be off because all your friends have been calling the house phone." Her tired brown eyes flickered with concern, her pale lips pressed into a thin flat line. "What exactly happened at that party last night? Does this have anything to do with Lady Gaga?"

David shook his head. "No, she was fine. Krystal and I just had a fight, that's all." On his way to the fridge, he almost stepped on the excited puppy who'd scampered under his feet. Her silky tail thumped against his calves as she waited to be picked up or petted.

"What did you fight about?" his mom asked.

The prior evening's events came tumbling back into focus as he poured himself a tall glass of chocolate milk. He hesitated, not sure how much he should tell his mother. "Well, Krystal acted like a total idiot. That's gotta be why people are calling."

"It must've been pretty bad. Look at this." She grabbed the pad and read down the list. "Tommy, Mike, J.D., Dallas, Ricky, Morgan, Kelly, Tommy again, Ann Marie, Brian, Pam, and Francesca." When she was done, she didn't say another word, just angled her head to the side, crinkled her brow, and waited for an explanation.

David hated that look. The critical, probing one with the squinted eyes that made him squirm. Krystal's behavior had been so bizarre he didn't even know where to begin. But thankfully his cell phone rang again. *Saved!* He waved goodbye to his mother as he spun toward the stairs.

It was Morgan, one of Krystal's closest friends. He knew she would never call him on her own. Krystal must've put her up to it. "What's up, Morgan?"

"I wanted to talk to you about last night. You know, Krystal is really hurt. You totally humiliated her. Everybody's talking about it."

He blinked hard, trying to keep his cool. When he

reached the top of the stairs, he said, "Actually, the way I remember it, Krystal totally humiliated *herself* last night. I was just hanging out, playing with my dog."

As he made his way to his room, Lady Gaga zipped past him and waited in his doorway with a what's-taking-you-so-long look. He pushed the door closed behind her and squatted down to play with her floppy ears.

"You backstabbed her at the biggest party of the year—in front of everyone she knew. How could you do that to her?" Morgan's tone was pained, like she was recounting a traumatic, life-altering event.

David was positive Krystal was sitting right next to Morgan, listening to the whole thing—which she undoubtedly scripted herself.

His phone beeped with an incoming call from his soccer buddy Mike.

"Morgan, can you hold on a minute, I have another call." Without waiting for a response, he switched over to his friend. "Hey, Mike. What's up?"

"I heard that you cheated on Krystal last night. Is that true?"

David sucked in a sharp breath. "No, you saw me at the party. I spent the entire night with Frankie and my dog."

"That's not what I heard. I heard you went onto the back field and got it on with that Class C girl Blair Evans, then gave her your sweatshirt."

"Well, you heard wrong!" David snapped. "Gotta go Mike."

He switched back to Morgan. "Sorry about that. Now what were you saying?"

Morgan continued with the same pained speech. "I asked you how you could backstab Krystal like that in front of everyone?"

David hadn't fully woken up yet, and the twisted

accounts of what had happened at the party were getting under his skin. "I didn't do anything to Krystal. She made an ass out of herself."

Morgan gasped. "How can you say that? You gave your shirt—the same one you'd given to Krystal—to the biggest loser in the school. And everyone saw it!"

"Hold on, Morgan, I have another call."

This time it was Tommy. "What's up, bro?"

"Did you really ignore Krystal last night so she had to dance around naked to get your attention?"

Oh my God! This is out of control!

"No," he said in a testy voice. "Don't know where you heard that."

"From everybody. They say you went off with this Class C chick, and Krystal tried to talk to you, but you totally ignored her."

David hurled himself backward onto his bed and squeezed his phone in a death grip. "Tommy, that's bullshit. I'm on the other line so I'll catch up with you later."

He didn't want to get back to Morgan, but knew he had to. "Sorry Morgan. Busy morning."

She didn't miss a beat. "You still haven't answered how you could humiliate Krystal like that. Have you even thought about how *she* felt, having her boyfriend go off with the biggest freak in the school? And then you gave her your captain's shirt so everybody would know about it!"

This was way too much way too early. His brain whirled around like a carnival teacup ride. "Gotta go Morgan, my mom needs me. Catch ya later."

He tossed his phone onto his covers and kicked out his legs. Lady Gaga crawled onto his chest, painting his face with her rough little tongue.

At least somebody's being nice to me this morning.

CHAPTER 9

Finals Week

Over the weekend I hear the outlandish rumors about how I stole the Ice Queen's boyfriend. I don't really understand how borrowing a shirt is stealing a boyfriend, but I do my best to ignore the absurd stories so I can study for an awful week of finals.

I'm afraid of running into trouble with the Queen and her Things getting to and from my exams. Just thinking about another encounter with them in the parking lot or hallway makes my stomach flip over into a tangle of knots. When Annie volunteers to walk me to my classrooms, I readily accept.

Summer is almost here, I keep telling myself. *Just get through this week.*

Monday morning comes all too soon. I'm bleary-eyed from staying up most of the night studying for physics. I already took the AP test a month ago, so I'm pissed that my teacher is making us take a final too. When Annie honks in my driveway at 6:50 a.m., I stagger out my front door and collapse half-dead into her passenger seat.

Once inside the school, my first order of business is to get rid of the damn sweatshirt. Since Annie knows where a bunch of the hockey players congregate in the morning, we make our way to the east wing. Sure enough, a large group of jocks, including David Woods, is hanging out by the science hall lockers.

Wasting no time, I fish the hockey sweatshirt from my

bookbag and march up to the boy I knew as Davey out on the dark field. He needs to shave and his hair is a bit messy, but he still looks super cute. And I love the hazelnut aroma of the coffee he's sipping.

"Thank you," I mumble as I hold out the thick, crumpled maroon ball.

He glances over at me, then the shirt, and curtly nods as he lifts it from my hand. And that's it. He takes another sip of coffee and goes right back to his friends as if I don't exist.

A hurt that I couldn't have anticipated spreads through me, landing in my gut. I didn't know what to expect if we met again after the party, but after the fun time we had together I thought he'd be a whole lot nicer. Not so cold...so indifferent. I know I have no right to expect more—not from the Ice Queen's boyfriend—but we'd made a connection that night, and it stings to be so completely blown off.

I must have stood there looking like a colossal idiot, because the next thing I know Annie's got a fistful of my jacket and is leading me away. She doesn't say a word about my humiliation, just waits dutifully by my locker. As I shove my bookbag and white hoodie inside, I hear a loud group of girls clattering down the hall. When I glance up, I'm overcome with dread. The Ice Queen and her Things are aimed right for me.

I can smell them before they get close. Each one is bathed in such strong perfume it's like they jumped into big vats of it on their way to school. I pick up musk, fruit, rose, lavender, and vanilla. Together, the jumble of scents is so overpowering I want to vomit.

Although it's finals week and barely 7:00 a.m., the evil gaggle is dressed to kill in full makeup, platform heels, black shimmering spandex leggings, and tight magenta T-shirts with suggestive sayings. The Queen in the middle is *Too Hot*, and the Things surrounding her are *Too Good*, *Too Much*, *Too Sexy*, and *Too Bad*.

The rest of the school may be preoccupied with finals, but not these girls. Somehow, they've had the time to go shopping and coordinate outfits, down to their long dangling earrings and multi-colored bangle bracelets. I feel wholly inadequate in their presence, shrinking a little in my faded swim team T-shirt, baggy sweatpants, and sneakers. I've got no make-up on, and my unruly red curls are gathered in a sloppy ponytail. My focus is on finals, not fashion.

As much as I pray the Ice Squad will suddenly veer away and pass me by, they don't. Annie shuffles to my side and rests a protective hand on the top of my locker as the loathsome five skid to a stop in front of me.

"Oh, look! It's Blair the Mare! What an awful glare!" They chant in unison, each shielding their eyes, then slipping on dark sunglasses.

They are so stupid and cheesy I want to gag.

"So, you've got a personal bodyguard now?" Thing 2 mocks.

"You're gonna need one!" Thing 1 adds, obnoxiously smacking her gum.

Annie leans forward, her broad muscular frame towering over Thing 1. "That's not a threat now, is it?"

"No one's making any threats," the Ice Queen breaks in, distancing herself from Annie. "We just want to deliver a message." Even through the dark indigo tint of her lenses, I can see the fire in her eyes.

"What message?" Annie asks, eyeing the Queen closely.

I hold my breath, waiting for the ax to fall.

"The message that there's a price to pay for messing with somebody's boyfriend."

Annie smirks. "That sounds like a threat to me."

"You can take it any way you want to," says Thing 4. "But that's our message."

Their voices are so chilling, I get goosebumps. The truth is I'd be shaken to the bone if Annie weren't here. She takes a step toward them. "Well I've got a message for *you*. If you go near her," she says, pointing at my head, "you'll have to deal with *me*."

"She's not the only one you'll have to deal with," someone says from farther down the hall. The Queen and her Things swivel around to see my friend Carrie coming up behind them. Carrie is nowhere near the size of Annie, but she's a field hockey player with a tough attitude. I wish I had a fraction of her fearlessness.

"Oh, how cute," says Thing 3, her hands on the waist of her *Too Bad* T-shirt. "It's Half-and-Half to the rescue!"

I see Carrie's coffee-colored eyes instantly grow dark. Her mom is black and her dad is white and she absolutely despises being called Half-and-Half. It's a good thing she doesn't have her field hockey stick with her or she'd probably take them all out.

The Queen angles her sunglasses at me. "Aww, the Mare's motley friends need to protect her. That's what happens when you're a Class C rat!"

"Yeah," Thing 1 adds in between gum smacks. "Why don't you take all your ratty friends with you back to Boca!"

Ever since we learned the English translation of American cities with Spanish names in Spanish class sophomore year, the taunts about Boca Raton—*Rat's Mouth*—have never stopped. They seem to derive endless amusement from their Boca insults, even though I automatically tune them out.

Annie places her hands on her hips. "You all need to get lost." She deepens her voice until it has a gravelly edge. "We have finals to worry about, not stupid threats from a bunch of pampered pinheads. Now scram!"

She stomps her mammoth high-top Nike sneaker, propelling the mean mob back about four feet. They quickly retreat down the hall, flocking together like a mass of buzzing hornets, their shimmering spandex backsides wiggling as they strut along in their outrageously high heels. They leave behind a nauseating cloud of mingled rose, musk, and vanilla.

"Thank you so much," I say, giving each of my friends a heartfelt hug. "You guys are the best!"

"Any time," says Carrie.

Annie chuckles. "That was actually kind of fun."

Fun? I have a different version of the word but no time to get into that now. We wish each other luck and head off for a horrific morning of exams.

CHAPTER 10

The Club

I remain on high alert every second of finals week, having Annie—and sometimes Carrie—accompany me to my classrooms, but thankfully the nasty quintet stays away.

When exams are finally over, my best friends and I decide to do something really big to celebrate the end of our junior year—something Class C losers certainly would never do. We convince Rachel's older sister, Renee, to help us sneak into a dance club in New York City.

We're sitting in the back of Renee's Corolla on the way to Bon Vie, the hottest new club in Manhattan, when I start to get jittery. I tuck my hands under my thighs to stop myself from chipping away at the high-gloss, fire-engine red nail polish I've just applied.

"What happened to Carrie and Annie?" Renee asks. "I thought they were coming too."

"No," Rachel says. "They both didn't think we'd get in, so they figured it would be a wasted trip."

I lean in toward the driver's seat, holding out the fake ID Renee had given me earlier. "You sure this will work? I mean, what if we can't get in? Then what are we going to do?"

Renee glances at me in her rearview mirror. "You'll be fine. That ID works for all my friends."

"But your friends are older."

Kayla, in the middle seat to my right, shines her phone flashlight on the laminated ID. "I think it looks *so* much like you! You just need to remember your name is Grace Palmer, you live at 405 North Century Way, your birthday is March 12th, and you're twenty-one years old."

I study the photo on the fake license. "I don't think it looks like me at all, and I don't look anywhere close to twenty-one. I hope I don't ruin this for everyone."

"Relax, Blair," Renee says over her shoulder. "It's Kayla who I'm worried about. She looks nothing like her picture."

"Yeah," Kayla nods. "That's why I'm wearing my hair like this and I have on all this makeup." Her long silky hair is parted to the side and styled so it hangs over most of her face like a black curtain. "But if they look closely they'll see that the girl in the photo isn't Asian like me, so if anyone will ruin it, it'll be me."

"Listen girls," Renee interrupts. "I know the pictures aren't perfect. That's why when we get there we need to go to the stocky bouncer with the blond crew cut. He's my roommate's sister's boyfriend, and I've met him a bunch of times. He said he'd let you in. You just can't drink when you're in there or else he'll get in a ton of trouble."

"If he changes his mind and doesn't let us in, we can always go for pizza and find an ice cream place," Rachel suggests.

Kayla glares at her. "No, we're getting in. I didn't get all dressed up like this to go have ice cream."

I take in Kayla's outfit. She sports an off-the-shoulder metallic silver top and a stretchy black satin skirt, giant silver mesh earrings, and six-inch platform pumps that glitter like her shirt. She looks like a hooker.

But then again, so do Rachel and I. In our efforts to look older, we're all decked out in skimpy, clingy, shiny, Halloween-like get-ups that Rachel refers to as slut attire.

I feel a little ridiculous in my flaming-red lace top, matching slingback sandals, and black snakeskin-print micro-mini skirt, but I've never been to a nightclub before and I'm determined to get in. Like my friends, I've got on gobs of makeup and flashy jewelry.

In another forty-five minutes we're parked and making our way to the front entrance of Bon Vie. The club is located on a narrow side street in between an old brick warehouse and a shuttered apartment building. It's not at all what I expected. There are no huge signs or bright lights like on Broadway or in Times Square. There's no grand, glitzy entranceway. Truth be told, the place looks like a forgotten dump.

A few dozen people cordoned by plush velvet maroon ropes are waiting out front, but Renee whizzes right past them to the two bouncers standing guard. We follow in a straight line like little ducklings behind their mother. She gives the short, beefy blond bouncer a quick hug and peck on the cheek. Then, after a perfunctory glance at our fake IDs, our group of provocatively dressed high school girls is shepherded inside.

It turns out that the drab exterior of Bon Vie doesn't even hint at what we find behind the cavernous doorway. Once we step through the dark, tunnel-like entry corridor into the club's grand atrium, Kayla, Rachel, and I stand bug-eyed at the incredible sight before us. Four levels of dimly lit dance floors, bars, and lounges pulse with loud music, bright flashing lights, and sexy dancers. Sinewy acrobats swing from trapezes high over the main floor and pairs of female dancers in barely-there black underthings gyrate to the hypnotic beats from tiered balconies scattered around the perimeter.

Some of the guests are so scantily clad it's hard not to stare. One in particular makes me grab Kayla's arm and point. All the woman has on are two flesh-colored tube tops, one across her chest and one across her bottom. The lower one is so skimpy it doesn't fully cover her butt cheeks.

Other women are in thigh-high leather boots and satin shorts, or fishnet stockings and tiny slip dresses. And, to make their own fashion statements, plenty of men parade around in spandex and leather too. If I had to describe the dress code, I'd use two words: *Anything goes.*

We're not there five minutes when a bunch of twenty-something-year-old guys edge up to our underage party and hand each of us cocktails in swanky blue glasses. The one who picks me is a cute preppy type in a classic pink Polo shirt with crisply pressed khakis. He's got neatly combed caramel-colored hair and adorable dimples.

I want to take a second to pinch myself. An older guy just bought me a drink!

"Thank you," I say with an appreciative smile. "What is it?"

"A G&T."

I think that means gin and tonic, but I don't want to ask and sound stupid. Although Renee's warning rings in my ears, I can't stop myself and take an obligatory sip. After all, I'm in a real club for the first time in my life, and it would be rude not to accept the drink. Besides, Renee and her girlfriend have already disappeared, and Rachel and Kayla are sipping their cocktails too.

"So, what's your name?" Preppy Boy shouts over the heavy rap music.

"Blair. You?" I shout back.

"Tim."

I hold up my drink for a moment. "Well, this is so nice of you, Tim."

"My friends and I saw you and your friends walk in, and we thought it would be a good way to meet you."

"It is." I glance over at Rachel and Kayla again. Rachel's

new companion is sliding his palm up and down the back of her tight cheetah-print dress and playing with her springy blonde curls. Kayla is bobbing her head and giggling at whatever her guy is saying.

"So, where are you from?" he asks.

"Westberry. You?"

"Queens."

I nod. "First time here?"

"Nah, we've been coming since it opened last month. You?"

"First time."

"Then let me show you around."

He drapes his arm across my shoulder blades and steers me toward the back of the club. We climb this unbelievably ornate staircase that winds around six times before we reach the topmost level. There's hardly anyone else up here, and it's a nice break from the packed main floor. We peer over the upper balcony, taking in the aerial view. I'm mesmerized as I stare at a nighttime circus of exotic performers, colorful lights, and gyrating guests.

He points to an arched doorway to our right. "That's the Chill Out Room over there. Come on."

We peek in, and I see a long, narrow room lined with plush red velour couches and large-screen TVs. At the moment it's empty.

"People start crashing in there after two, when they're done partying," Tim explains. "A couple of weeks ago there were so many bodies on the floor you couldn't walk."

"That must be a sight," I say.

He laughs and guides me back to the balcony. There's a fast, catchy Latin beat blaring from the speakers that makes my shoulders start to sway on their own. I say, "Great music."

He smiles. "Want to dance?"

"Sure."

We move down to the third-level dance floor, and Tim immediately launches into some snappy salsa moves. I, on the other hand, stand there like a fool, holding my full glass of gin and tonic. I don't even like it, but it would be really rude to dump it or leave it somewhere when he just bought it for me.

I glance around and see several other people managing to dance with their drinks, so I decide to do the same. But as soon as I move my left arm, half the liquid splashes over the sides. He doesn't seem to notice, so I keep going, kind of happy that I won't have to drink it all. We spend only about ten minutes dancing together before Tim announces, "I hate this song," and leads me off the floor.

"So, what do you do?" he asks as he tucks his shirt back into place. "You work? Go to school?"

"School," I reply, afraid of where this conversation is going.

"Where?"

I know Westberry High is the wrong answer, so I say, "University of Connecticut." At least I was on the campus once when my older brother Brett was looking at colleges.

"Grad program?"

Shoot! He thinks I'm over twenty-one because I'm in this club, but there's no way I can pull off being a grad student who's six years older.

"No," I lie. "I'm still in the regular college."

His caramel eyebrows crunch together and his head tilts slightly to one side as he asks, "How old are you?"

I'm pretty sure I can get away with pretending I'm three years older—with my slutty outfit and all—so I say, "Nineteen."

He reacts as though I've just revealed I'm twelve.

"Uh...I thought you were much older," he stammers, his eyebrows shooting up and his pale preppy face deepening to a tomato red. "See ya around." Then he scurries toward the exit, leaving me standing alone by the balcony.

Okay, lesson learned. From now on I'll be twenty-one.

I head back down the stairs to see if Rachel and Kayla had any better luck with their men.

CHAPTER 11

Surprise Guest

I only make it down to Bon Vie's second floor when I'm stopped by a tanned surfer-type dude with long, tousled, sun-bleached hair. He does an about-face after he passes me on the stairs, his right arm shooting out, maneuvering me off to the side.

"Hey, I haven't seen you yet tonight. You just get here?" he asks, his light eyes unapologetically checking me out.

"No," I grin. "I've been upstairs."

"Want to dance?"

"Sure," I say for the second time that evening. I follow him onto the packed floor, ready to burst from the excitement of having two older guys ask me to dance at this amazing club where I don't belong.

This is so much fun!

I'm far more at ease this time around, letting my body sway freely to the new-wave rock blasting from the mega-sized speakers. Surfer Dude is a much better dancer than Preppy Boy, moving fluidly to the heavy beats. He doesn't even attempt to talk. He just smiles and dances, which is fine with me. The rapid rhythmic flashing of the white and blue bulbs gives off the spellbinding effect of dancing in slow motion, and it isn't too long before I'm hypnotized by the combination of the pulsating music and the incessant blinking of the lights.

After about half an hour of immersing ourselves in the sea of rippling bodies, Surfer Dude takes my hand and escorts me off the dance floor. "Mind waiting while I use the men's room?" he asks with a polite smile.

It's been great dancing for so long, but I have no idea where Rachel and Kayla are, and I'm kind of skittish about losing them in this massive club, so I say, "You know what, I'm going to find my friends, then I'll meet back up with you."

I peer over the edge of the second floor balcony to see if I can spot them on the vast dance floor below, but it's impossible to find anyone in the dark ocean of bobbing heads. I give up and make my way down to the main level to search for them.

As soon as I step out onto the bottom floor, someone taps me on the shoulder. I wheel around expecting to see Renee or one of my girlfriends, but instead find myself face-to-face with David Woods.

I'm so shocked, I stand there speechless and immobile. He's probably the last person in the world I could ever imagine tapping me on the shoulder at this club. All I can do is stare as a thousand different questions roll through my head, starting with, *where is the Ice Queen?*

I wish he didn't look so damn good, but he's absolutely delectable. His tall, buff body is clad in a tight black T-shirt and perfectly faded jeans, his dark brown hair gelled up in the front. There's some sexy five-o'clock shadow going on too.

"Would you like to dance?" he asks.

"No thank you," I reply, super proud of myself for standing up to him. The truth is, no matter how good he looks, I want nothing to do with the Evil One's boyfriend— even if we're far away from Westberry. Not to mention it's been less than a week since he blew me off at school in front of his hockey friends.

I start to walk away, but he gently grabs my arm. "Why not?"

My, a bit conceited, aren't we?

"Because I don't want to dance," I blurt out.

"But I saw you dancing with someone else. Why not me?"

Super conceited is more like it.

"Why don't you go dance with your girlfriend?"

"I don't have a girlfriend."

I can't help but snicker. "Why don't you play your games with someone else?"

"I'm not playing any games. I don't have a girlfriend. We broke up."

Sure you did, buddy.

I sigh and back away. "Well, that's too bad. I've gotta go. Bye."

Not three steps later, a raven-haired, jaw-droppingly handsome guy in a green silk shirt reaches his hand out for mine. He's got one of those chiseled, beautiful faces that makes you do a double take and stare. This guy could be on the cover of GQ.

I place my palm in his, and he whisks me onto the dance floor, spinning me around in a fancy pirouette, then drawing me in close. Within seconds his hands settle on my waist, and he sways his hips against mine. I could kiss this gorgeous creature knowing that David Woods is right behind me watching the whole glorious thing. If only the Ice Queen and Things could see this too. And BM—then the whole school would know!

After dirty dancing with Mr. GQ for a few songs, I finally spot Rachel. It's easy to find her since her wild sandy-blonde mane is flying all over the place. She shimmies up next to me with a heavyset dude about half her height. Granted, she's in obscenely high heels, but it looks like she's dancing with a fifth grader.

Rachel takes one look at my dance partner and mouths,

"OMG!"

I shout, "Kayla?"

She shrugs and holds her palms out.

As much as I like hip smacking with Mr. GQ, his moves are getting raunchier with every song. At first I think it's my imagination, but when he keeps rubbing himself against me and pressing into me like he's trying to have sex through his clothes, I have to push him away and make a break for the ladies' room.

Rachel follows, and we excitedly share our adventures while we wait on the long bathroom line. As we near the entrance, Kayla comes out the exit door and stops to exchange stories.

"I've been with the same guy who bought that first drink when we came in," she says. "His name is Lance, and he's from Queens. I really like him."

"Well, I've been dancing with two guys, and I don't like either of them," Rachel admits.

It seems I've got the most to tell, and I fill them in on Preppy Boy, Surfer Dude, Yak, and GQ. I get huge high fives when I disclose how I refused to dance with Yak.

"Yeah," Kayla says. "Yak walked past me earlier, and he did *not* look happy."

When we finish in the ladies' room, I take my friends to the top level to show them the eye-popping view. It's far less crowded than the main level, so we decide to stay up here and blow up the small dance floor together.

I'm super relaxed, soaking up the beats, thoroughly enjoying my time with my girlfriends, when there's another tap on my shoulder. I twirl around to see Yak—David Woods. Again.

"Can I talk to you?" he asks.

Bolstered by my popularity at the club, I smile and reply,

"No, I'm busy now."

"Just for a minute?" he pleads.

Wow, Yak pleading with me?

He does look kind of hurt. I glance over at my friends and they motion for me to go. I hesitate, shrug, then ultimately relent.

It's impossible to hear anything over the blaring music, so I lead him into the Chill Out Room.

Inside, he says, "You know, I thought we got along really well at the pool party. I don't understand why you won't dance with me."

"Are you kidding?" I cry. "You didn't care whether I was dead or alive when I brought back your shirt. You completely ignored me, and now you want to dance?"

His eyebrows arch way up. "I didn't know who you were that morning when you showed up at my locker. Remember how dark it was that night? I didn't even know what you looked like. In school that day I was talking to my friends, thinking about my Spanish final, and the next thing I know I'm being handed a shirt. It took me a minute to figure out who you were, and before I could say anything, you were gone."

It's a plausible story. It could explain the impassive look on his face that morning. But he might also be full of baloney.

He must be able to tell I'm contemplating whether he's lying because he adds, "Why would you think I'd ignore you after we hung out together for so long?"

Well, that's an easy one.

I fold my arms and say, "Maybe because your girlfriend hates me and says horrible things about me."

He shakes his head. "She's *not* my girlfriend anymore. I thought the whole school knew that."

"But she did say horrible things about me, didn't she?"

Surprisingly, he doesn't cover for his ex. In fact, he sighs, digs his fingers into his front jeans pockets, and says, "I'm not going to lie. She does hate you, and she did go off about you. But what I don't understand is, why? What happened between you two?"

I purse my lips. "Good question—one I've never been able to figure out. But she flipped out when she saw I had on your shirt and threatened me. I really don't think it's a good idea for me to even talk to you."

He peers intently into my eyes. "I don't care what her problem is, and I can talk to whoever I want. She's out of my life."

"Well, unfortunately she's not out of mine," I say, reaching for the handle to the Chill Out Room door. "So let's just forget we ever met."

I step through the doorway, but turn back for one last lingering look. "Goodbye Davey," I whisper.

He stays away from me for the rest of the night.

CHAPTER 12

A Second Chance

I'm genuinely excited to start my second summer as a lifeguard and swimming instructor at the Birchville Municipal Pool. Between volunteering at the animal shelter and working at the pool, I know the next ten weeks are going to be great.

How can I be certain? Because no one from Westberry goes to Birchville. And it's only a short drive from my side of town, it pays really well, and I get free food from the snack bar. Best of all, I love hanging out with the other guards—Nikki, Angela, Zac, and Rob.

Somehow, they're all really nice, even though they're popular in their own schools. I have a hard time understanding how their popularity hasn't corrupted them since Westberry has conditioned me to think that popularity and niceness are mutually exclusive. But they're normal and nice, and none of them have ever heard of any type of "Class System."

The first time I unloaded my high school horror stories on them, all four looked at me with utter amazement, like I should get an Emmy for my incredible storytelling.

"Are you kidding?" Nikki asked. "There's one girl who controls the entire school and everybody follows her? That's insane!"

Nikki's become a close friend of mine. She's a super tall, pencil-thin volleyball player with an awesome sense of humor. When I'm around her, I find myself laughing all the time and feeling really good. She's so much fun to hang out with—I just love her.

It took longer to convince Angela—my college-bound friend—that my Westberry tales were true. "This doesn't sound real," she said. "I mean, we have cliques at my school, and there are all different types of kids—jocks, nerds, sluts, brains, whatever—but nothing anywhere close to what you've described."

Nikki scrunched up her eyes and nose. "Yeah, your high school sounds like it's out of a sick movie."

"I only wish I invented the Ice Queen and her Class System, or even exaggerated a little, but every word is true. And believe me, it's as bad as it sounds."

"Why do people go along with what this Krystal says?" my tennis buddy Zac asked. "Don't they have minds of their own?" All summer long I had to put up with his tasteless Ice Queen and Thing wisecracks while he and I volleyed on long breaks. Of course, he was trying to make me laugh, but what was comical to him was all too real to me.

"How could they not see how cool you are?" asked Rob, the other swimming instructor. "Are they dumb and blind at your school?"

"All of the above," I replied, overjoyed that a hottie like Rob thought I was cool. I had a secret crush on Rob that nobody else knew about, so one compliment from him and I was smiling for a week. The previous summer he'd invited all the guards sailing and water skiing on his family's boat, and I hadn't stopped thinking about him since. He was a little on the short side, but with such a cute face I didn't really care.

It's great to know that my summer friends truly like me, because I developed serious self-esteem issues by the time I finished my sophomore year. I mean, how long can you be put down and not be affected by it? No matter how well I did in my classes or on the swim team, going to Westberry High was like stepping into a war zone. Every day I was ambushed and defeated, and I'd gotten to the point where I didn't want to get back up.

Thank God for my Birchville Pool buddies who don't care about my lowly status in school and aren't afraid to be seen with me. We hang out together after work, listen to music, go to dinners and movies, and invite each other to parties all year long. Both Zac and Rob have even offered to be my prom date if I don't have one—which is pretty much a given at this point. I'd be thrilled to go to the prom with Rob, of course, and he seems oblivious to the fact that I'm an outcast.

So, the real question is: Why am I an outcast? My lifeguard friends have convinced me that if I went to a different school or if there were no Ice Queen, I'd have a normal existence. Now that I'm back at work, surrounded by people who make my days enjoyable, it's easier to put the bad stuff aside and see a light at the end of the tunnel. With only one more year to go, I can practically taste the fresh start I'll have at college. I haven't decided whether I want a school in Boston or Washington, D.C., but it'll definitely be one of those.

As I sit in my lifeguard stand on the second day of work, my umbrella angled sharply to the left to block the late afternoon sun, I'm startled to hear my name shouted from the grassy area behind me. I glance over my right shoulder, stunned to see David Woods—Yak—waving at me from the other side of the silver chain-link fence. He must've come from soccer or dry-land hockey practice, because he has on a cut-off Westberry T-shirt with white-and-red sweatbands wrapped around his head and wrists.

"What are you doing here?" I call out, not trying to mask my surprise.

"I want to talk to you."

"How did you know where I work?"

"I asked around."

"Couldn't you have just texted?"

"And take the chance you'd ignore me again?"

There's that massive ego.

"Well, as you can see, I'm kind of busy." I gesture at my surroundings.

"That's okay," he says with a smile. "I'll wait until you're not."

If his ego got any bigger, it would push all the water out of the pool.

"Why don't you just talk now, and then you can leave?" I say, a bit snappier than I intended.

"I'd rather talk in private than shout across the pool. Don't worry, I don't mind waiting." I watch as he lays a towel on the grass, pops in ear buds, and taps his phone screen.

Angela, on the next stand, is practically falling off her chair trying to get my attention. She's waving wildly, pointing toward Yak. I don't feel like explaining everything at the moment, so I mouth, "Not now."

Fifteen minutes later, when I go on break, I leave the pool area and venture onto the grass toward my uninvited visitor. I feel four pairs of eyes on me.

"Who's that?" Nikki whispers through the fence as I pass by. "He's really hot!"

"Long story," I murmur. "Tell you later."

Then Zac yells, "Hey!" causing me to spin toward his lifeguard chair.

As I glance up, he lowers his sunglasses, hikes up his eyebrows, and chants, "No hanky-panky in the pool area!"

I roll my eyes at him and move faster. I'm grateful my "guest" is wearing ear buds.

Yak sits up when my body casts a shadow over his. My

toes are poised on the edge of his towel, my arms folded, as I ask, "So what is it you want to talk about?"

He pats his towel for me to sit, but I stand firm, shaking my head. I'm not going to make this easy for him. And, besides, the newly mowed grass makes my nose itch.

Tossing me an easy smile, he says, "It seems we've gotten off to a bad start. I was hoping we could start over."

Now it's my turn to smile, only mine is one hundred percent forced. "I think you need to go back to your girlfriend and forget we ever met."

I've already verified what he told me that night at Bon Vie—that he and Krystal have, in fact, broken up—but I still don't trust him. He's one of *them*.

He swings his head from side to side. "I don't have a girlfriend. And even if I did, it wouldn't stop us from being friends."

"Why would you want to be friends with *me*?" I blurt out. "I'm not exactly in your Class A crowd."

There. I said it.

But his face breaks into a huge grin. "You think I care about any of that? That's all Krystal."

I eye him closely. "And everyone else."

"Not me. I'm not like everyone else. That's all BS."

I raise my shoulders and let them drop. "Why should I believe you?"

"Well, I'm here, aren't I?"

"Why *are* you here?"

He springs to his feet and holds out his hand. "I told you, I'd like for us to start over. Friends?"

I glance down at his outstretched hand.

Should I believe him?

I guess a part of me does, because before I know it, my fingers are clasped in his shaking away. I find myself mesmerized by the honey-gold specks in the centers of his warm brown eyes. They glisten in the sun like brilliant kaleidoscopes.

He says, "Let's celebrate our new start. Let's go to the V-Zone tonight. How about it?"

As much as I love the new virtual reality gaming center, I don't know how to react. I mean, this *is* the Ice Queen's ex-boyfriend. And I've never been on a date before. I'm not even sure this would qualify as a date, but if it did, shouldn't I be clean and dressed nice? I'm all sweaty and disgusting, coated in oily sunblock. And I only have running shorts and a lifeguard T-shirt with me—not exactly date attire. "Uh...I can't. After work I need to go home, have dinner, take a shower—"

"Don't worry, we'll grab something to eat at the mall. What time do you get off work?"

I stammer some more, scrambling for the right words. I feel like an idiot, but this is happening way too fast. "Um... seven, but—"

"Great. I'll pick you up here at seven." He smiles, scoops up his towel, and pivots toward the parking lot.

"Are you sure?" I call after him. "I mean, we don't really—"

"See ya later!" he yells back, waving his hand.

There's a sharp whistle from one of the lifeguard stands.

Zac.

CHAPTER 13

The First Date

After Yak leaves the Birchville Pool, I update my lifeguard friends on the end-of-year pool party/sweatshirt/Ice Queen/Yak/Bon Vie saga.

Zac is the most concerned about the evening's plans. "I'm with Nikki. I don't think you should trust this dude. You shouldn't go with him alone."

Rob is far more laid back. "Aw, come on. The guy shows up in the bright sunlight, we all see him, he asks you out on a date. Seems on the up-and-up to me."

Nikki shakes her head, her expression so serious it scares me. "What if he has his friends corner you at the mall? You don't know what he's planning."

"Or what if you never make it to the mall?" Angela throws out.

"You're all crazy!" Rob exclaims. "He likes her and wants to hang out. Why is that such a problem?"

"Because he's the Ice Queen's boyfriend!" Nikki shoots back.

I can't help but smirk. "*Ex*-boyfriend, I've been told."

"Even so, you can't trust him," Nikki states with conviction, her face set, mouth pinched. "Either you shouldn't go, or we should go with you."

My eyes widen. "You want to come with me?"

Zac nods. "Great idea, Nik. We'll all go."

"Oh, that won't be too awkward," I giggle. "He shows up here to pick me up and all five of us get in his car."

"Four of you," Rob corrects, frowning at the other guards. "I think you're being ridiculous, and I'm not going to be a part of it. The poor guy just wants to take her out. *Alone*."

"Well, I guess it'll be the three of you," Angela apologizes. "I've got a dentist appointment after work."

I turn to Zac and Nikki. "How about you just meet us at the mall?"

Nikki eyes Zac and nods. "It's a plan. We'll watch you from a distance. But if he tries anything crazy—like he heads in the opposite direction from the mall—text us immediately."

I bob my head. "Of course."

My heart gallops for the rest of the afternoon as I try to decide whether I should be very worried or very excited.

◆ ◆ ◆

It turns out that I needn't have stressed. Yak drives straight to the mall, and there's no attempt to dump me onto the side of the road. He acts exactly the same way he did the night we met at the pool party when I knew him as Davey, the nice guy with the puppy. He's polite, friendly, and funny—the perfect gentleman. And he's a good driver too. He tells me he's had his license since March.

Of course, he doesn't know that I've got two different sets of friends spying on him to make sure he doesn't play any cruel tricks on me or let his Class A cronies do anything nasty. Zac and Nikki have dinner in the mall food court a few tables behind us, and Kayla, Rachel, and Carrie wander by repeatedly, making frequent trips for hot pretzels, ice cream, and Cinnabons.

Both sets secretly give me the thumbs-up signal as Yak and I head toward the V-Zone. I can't get it through my head that I'm really hanging out with the Ice Queen's ex-boyfriend.

To someone of my lowly status, a guy like Yak is so far out of my league, it's like I'm on a date with Prince Harry.

The fact is the Ice Queen and I are such complete opposites that it doesn't make any sense to me that Yak can like us both. It makes far more sense that he's playing some kind of dirty trick, setting me up to look like a fool. Frankly, I'm kind of expecting him to stop short and start singing his ex-girlfriend's "The Brainy Bunch" song in the middle of the mall.

I remain on high alert, unable to relax or let my guard down. The truth is, I've been treated so badly over the past three years by "his people" that I can't stop wondering why he wants to be with me. I'm almost certain this is a prank, because it seems impossible that one of the most popular boys in school would like *me* when he's been told for so long that I'm the biggest loser in the grade. No...the school.

At the V-Zone, I'm super surprised when he insists on paying for my admission pass. And I'm really impressed that he focuses all his attention on me. When his cell phone rings, he doesn't even glance at it. He just turns off the ringer.

Is this an act, or is he really a good guy? But how can he be a good guy if he went out with the Ice Queen? I can't help wondering what he's really up to.

As we head toward a row of virtual reality driving seats, Yak doesn't realize that he's surrounded by my friends. They're keeping a close eye on me in here, because none of us trust him. Once I strap on my clunky gaming headset, I won't be able to tell who's around—and I might need some help.

But after an hour of speeding around a European racetrack, killing zombies, and piloting a flight simulator, I slip off my headset and motion for my friends to go. It seems that Rob was right. No Queen or Things have popped out, and I feel comfortable staying here alone with Yak. Nikki and Zac leave right away, but Carrie, Rachel, and Kayla stick around—just in case.

When the lights blink at five to eleven, we leave. Even though he takes my hand, a part of me still expects him to ditch me in the empty parking lot and peel away laughing. I'm hoping my girlfriends are somewhere nearby.

To my immense relief, nothing out of the ordinary happens, and he graciously escorts me to the passenger side of his car and opens the door. As we approach my neighborhood, I figure I'm close enough to my house to safely ask him the questions that have been plaguing me all night. If he gets really pissed off, I can easily walk home.

"David, there's something I need to ask you."

"Sure."

Might as well get it over with.

I clear my throat and let the words tumble out. "I heard that you and Krystal got into a big fight the night of the pool party—because of me—and she broke up with you because of it, so I was just wondering if...well...if you're going out with me to get even with her."

He turns his head to glare at me while he's driving. "I can't believe you just asked me that."

"Well...look at the timing. Right after she dumps you, you go out with me—the same person who you had that fight over."

He gets so mad so fast, I instantly regret saying anything. Before I know it, he jerks the car to the curb and rams the gearshift into park.

"It seems you heard wrong," he says through a clenched jaw, a hard edge to his voice. "We didn't have a fight over *you*. Krystal flipped out over a stupid shirt. I don't know whether she was stoned or drunk or both, but she was insane, screaming like a psycho in front of everyone. Her bathing suit was falling off, she was completely irrational, and she kept putting me and my best friend down—and even my puppy. I tried over and over to stop her from making an ass out of herself, but she didn't care. She kept going on with her crazy accusations until we got fed up and left. Then she cursed me out and broke up with me. And for the record, our relationship was over anyway. She just announced it first."

After his long-winded speech he throws himself against his seatback and breathes heavily. I must admit, I hadn't expected such a visceral reaction from him. The rumor mill hadn't exactly delivered his account of the now-famous break up. The versions I'd heard were all about how he'd ignored poor Krystal for a Class C loser he'd fooled around with on the grass.

Still, I feel the need to defend myself. "I didn't see what happened that night, because I had to leave fast. Krystal saw me wearing your sweatshirt in the ladies' room and freaked out. She tried to attack me, so I ran out of there."

He spins back to face me, his eyes snapping all the way open. "She tried to attack *you* in the ladies' room? She kept screaming that *she* was attacked by a giant lesbian!"

I burst out laughing before I can stop myself. And it grows—a pure, spontaneous belly laugh that erupts from my core and envelops me. I laugh so hard my eyes start to tear and my sides ache. It's contagious, and David starts laughing too. It takes several minutes before we catch our breaths.

"I'm sorry, but that was really funny," I murmur, wiping my eyes with the side of my sleeve. "Maybe it's the way you said it."

"I couldn't make that one up if I tried. And if you want to know everything else she said, she also accused you of sending a gigantic dyke into the bathroom to kill her."

I become hysterical again, to the point where I'm doubled over, clutching my middle. He joins me, and we both laugh until the windows turn to foggy sheets that we can't see through at all.

"This is the first time I've talked about everything since it happened. I guess I was still angry about the breakup," he admits. "Thanks for helping me put it in perspective."

I dry my cheeks with the hem of my shirt, then stretch it back into place. "I don't think I've ever laughed so hard."

"Me neither," he says, hitting the defroster button. Then he takes my hand. "See, isn't it good we met each other?"

I half smile. "But somehow I feel responsible for what happened between you two that night."

"I told you, it had nothing to do with you. If anything, you did me a favor. Going out with her got to be like having a chokehold around my neck. I'd been wanting to break up with her for a while, but I didn't know how to do it. Every time I mentioned it to my friends, they told me I was crazy. They said, 'You don't break up with the most popular girl in school. Where do you go from there?'"

Straight to the bottom.

I peer directly into his eyes as I say, "It's hard to believe things weren't good with you two. Everyone always talked about how you were the perfect couple."

He scowls. "That's what Krystal *wanted* everyone to think, but believe me, we were fighting *a lot*—like all the time. I know she's had a different boyfriend every year since seventh grade, so I guess at the end of our junior year my useful life was up."

Interesting theory.

I hesitate, then say, "Can I ask you something else?"

"You might as well. Let's get everything out on the table."

"Okay, I was wondering how you could go out with

someone like Krystal and then someone like me—I'm *nothing* like her."

"Exactly!" he exclaims. "I knew you were smart. Now can I ask *you* a question?"

"Sure."

"Krystal says you're a rat—that you told the school her friend Julie was dealing drugs out of her locker freshman year. Is that true?"

I shake my head so hard the tips of my hair whip him in the face. "No! I had no idea who that girl was or what she was doing. My locker was near hers, but I just thought she had a lot of friends hanging out there all the time. I was a naive thirteen-year-old back then, just starting high school, and it never even occurred to me that she was selling drugs. I thought her bloodshot eyes were from sleep problems or something."

He squeezes my hand. "I believe you. Unfortunately, Krystal has her own take on it."

Even though he says he believes me, I feel like I need to give him more information. "My friend Rachel sat next to the school D.A.R.E officer at a football game and asked him how he would know if someone had drugs in their locker. He told her that there are cameras in the hallways that he monitors, and teachers report suspicious activity. They also have drug-sniffing dogs that they take through the school periodically, and if someone fails a drug test, they always check their locker and car."

His eyes expand slightly. "So, it could've been any of those things?"

"Yeah, but Krystal and everyone else would rather blame me. It's so unfair."

"It was like three years ago anyway. I think they need to get over it."

I sigh. "They're never going to get over it. It's practically etched into the brick on the front of the school. And now, add to it the fact that she thinks you cheated on her with me. I'm permanently on her Most Hated list."

He chuckles. "I've learned not to lose sleep worrying about what Krystal thinks. And you shouldn't either."

Then he leans in close until our lips almost touch. He has on really nice cologne, a light spicy one that makes me close my eyes and breathe in deeper. He kisses me sweetly on the cheek and ends what was astoundingly, but undeniably, our very first date.

CHAPTER 14

Best Summer Ever

Over the next few weeks, without consciously intending it, David—formerly known as Yak—creeps into all facets of my life. At first I'm extremely guarded, happy that he's interested in me, but still not allowing myself to fully trust him. After all, our relationship seems too good to be true, and my mom instilled in me at a young age that when something seems too good to be true, it usually is.

My close friends keep warning me to watch myself. Rachel repeatedly says, "Be careful—you can get really hurt by someone like David." And Kayla says, "I know you really like him, but don't ever forget who he is and where he comes from."

I know they're right, so I call Annie, who's been on the same ice hockey team as David for three years. "Tell me the truth," I implore. "Is he a jerk, or is he a nice guy? I want to know what he's really like before I go any further."

Annie's response: "He's a good guy—fair, hardworking, nice."

She's not a big talker and I can't get anything else out of her, so I go to Carrie. "Do you think I can trust him?" I ask.

Carrie doesn't mince words. "Let me put it this way. He can have any girl in the school he wants, so no offense, but why would he pick one of the least popular ones?"

Of course, I know she's right, which makes me wonder the same thing: How can *I* be with someone like *him*? How can *he* be with someone like *me*? I'm the exact opposite of the

Ice Queen in every respect. She's dark and big-boned with gigantic boobs. I'm super fair and skinny and hoping one day to get out of an A cup. She's into partying and bragging about everything she does on social media. I keep a low profile and mostly worry about grades and getting into a good college.

Because I'm so different and have been branded as Class C, I'm ridiculously insecure. During the first half of the summer I call my friends every single day and ask, "Is this real, or am I setting myself up for a big fall?"

Their answers are always lukewarm. Kayla likes to say, "You can go for the ride, but be ready to slam down the emergency brake if you have to." And Rachel cautions, "Don't let yourself get in too deep. You can get really hurt."

I hear them, but continue to see David anyway. And even though I try to stop myself, I like him more and more.

As cynical as I am, I find my doubts ebbing away as he showers me with attention. By the end of July he's met my lifeguard friends, my swim team friends, and my best friends. He's also met my parents, older brother, grandparents, and a smattering of other relatives. He's always ultra-polite, and everybody likes him.

Carrie remains skeptical. I tell her, "If he has a hidden agenda, it hasn't poked through yet."

She presses her lips into a hard line and shakes her head. "I'm still not convinced."

I argue, "Why would he invite me to a family barbeque and introduce me as his girlfriend? And he's brought me to restaurants, movies, and parties as his date...and included me in get-togethers with his closest friends. Why would he do all that if this wasn't real?"

Carrie shrugs but has no answer, so I continue.

"You know how upset I've been since my grandparents' dog died a couple of weeks ago? They got Vonnegut right before

I was born and we grew up together...he's in all my baby pictures. I've been having a really hard time and David's been there for me every second."

She can't really say anything to that either, and it takes her until August to finally back down. By then David's completely won me over. I wake up and he's the first thing I think about. I go to sleep and can't wait until I get to see him again. Excitement rushes through me every time he so much as sends me a text. I've fallen head over heels, and there is no emergency brake.

The good news is that David seems just as crazy about me as I am about him. When we're together, we hold hands, giggle, and talk about everything. And when we kiss, the world seems to melt away. His kisses are so soft and slow and sweet, I want them to go on forever.

I have a lot of fun when I go to his house too. An added bonus of seeing David is that his younger sister Danielle and I get along really well. One day, she confides in me, "I'm so happy that David is with you now. I hated his last girlfriend. She was so mean."

"Really?" I ask. "What did she do?"

Danielle rolls her eyes and replies, "She and my brother went out for almost a year, but she still couldn't remember my name. And whenever she came over, she pointed her finger at another room and told me to get lost."

"That's terrible," I say. I'm not going to tell Danielle everything I know about the Ice Queen, but I certainly sympathize with her.

"Will you help me paint my room?" she asks at the beginning of August. "I want to paint these funky geometric designs on my walls, but my mom says she doesn't have time to help me now that she's gone back to work after the divorce."

"Of course," I say, delighted to assist her. She's such a sweet girl.

David is elated that I pay so much attention to Danielle, but other than that, our new relationship is much harder on him than me. He's actually lost friends because I'm his new girlfriend.

The previous Saturday night we're strolling down the sidewalk from the movie theater to a dessert café when we pass a broad-shouldered guy with a buzz cut in a Westberry ice hockey T-shirt. David says hello, but the guy gives me the once-over and turns away.

"Wow," I say. "That was so rude. Isn't he on your team?"

David mumbles, "Yeah, he's one of the goalies."

From the guy's disapproving expression—his turned-up nose and raised upper lip—it's pretty clear he's a casualty of my relationship with David. I can't help prying a bit. "Were you friends with him before we started going out?"

David nods and shrugs so big his shoulders almost touch his ears. "Look, if who I date matters so much to people that they won't talk to me, then they're not my friends anyway."

"I feel bad, though," I say.

He loops an arm around my waist. "Don't. Some of my 'friends' stopped talking to me when I broke up with Krystal—even before you came along. So I've come to realize that they don't really care about me, and I'm better off without them."

I smile. "Thank you for saying that."

He draws me closer. "It's true."

We continue on to the café and end up in another uncomfortable situation. An older couple is walking out as we enter. I recognize the man immediately: George Cooper, the Ice Queen's father.

Mr. Cooper isn't a big, strapping guy like one might expect of the Queen's father. In fact, he barely reaches average height and isn't very attractive at all. His balding head, black rectangular glasses, and wide girth make him look extra dumpy, but at our school he gets a free pass on appearance because he's a deity. Not only is he the Queen's dad, he has an amazing win record as the school's varsity ice hockey coach, and hockey rules at Westberry.

"Hi Coach," David says, letting his arm slide off my waist.

Coach Cooper nods at him, and the woman steps forward to kiss him on the cheek. "It's always so nice to see you, David," she gushes, her smile warm and friendly. "I hope you're having a nice summer."

I assume this is the Queen's mother even though I can't see any similarities to Krystal. Her features are small and delicate, and she has much lighter hair and skin coloring than her daughter—who is clearly the female image of her father.

"Yeah, my summer's been great," David replies, his face reddening. Now I feel *really* bad for him—this is beyond awkward.

"I'm so glad," says the woman, clasping one of his hands in both of hers, and broadening her smile. "I miss seeing you. You know, you're always welcome at our house."

"Uh, thank you," David says, stiffening his spine and pulling his lips into a smile too.

Coach Cooper plants a palm on the woman's shoulder blade to nudge her along. "See you at practice on Monday," he says to David, throwing me the tiniest nod of acknowledgement before moving toward the street.

Inside the café I brush my fingertips along David's bicep. "You okay?"

He blows out a lungful of air. "I guess. Mrs. Cooper has always been so nice to me, but I didn't know what it would be like seeing her again now that Krystal and I broke up. I'm glad she still likes me."

"You really think she still likes you and this wasn't just an act for her husband?" I ask.

David shakes his head. "No, you saw her. You saw how nice she was to me."

I scrunch my nose and mouth. "If you ask me, she seemed super phony. And you probably didn't notice, but she didn't even look in my direction. She pretty much turned her back to me."

"No, I didn't see that," he admits.

I spend almost our entire time in the café trying to convince him that there's no way the Ice Queen's mother could be a nice person and raise a daughter like Krystal, but he doesn't get it. He keeps saying, "No, she really is nice. And think about how hard it had to be for her to see me with someone else."

I ultimately let it drop because the reality is, it doesn't really matter to me. David is the one who has to deal with the Queen's family, and it's definitely better for him if they're nice to him, even if it's an act.

And although I do feel terrible he's lost friends because of me, my girlfriends and I have been experiencing the exact opposite because of him. Kayla, Rachel, and Carrie readily admit that there's been a seismic increase in their popularity since David became my boyfriend.

Rachel says, "You know I was on the fence about him, but it's so cool that we're getting to meet all his Class A friends who never knew we existed before." I know she's making a direct reference to David's soccer teammate Tommy who hit it off with her the instant they met. I'm so happy for Rachel because she's always been so self-conscious about her weight, and it's the first time any boy has paid attention to her.

Of course, being "the smartest one in curls" in the Brainy Bunch song hasn't exactly helped her social status either. Even though she's as pretty as she is smart and has wild blonde hair and the most expressive blue eyes you've ever seen, kids have been almost as brutal to her as they've been to me, making fun of the "gluttonous geek" and mooing when they walk by.

And now that Carrie has fallen madly in love with David's ice hockey friend Dallas, she concedes that she's a total hypocrite. "I know what I said all summer about David, but I get it now. He and his friends are just really nice guys who don't care about this whole Class thing. They just like us for who we are."

Kayla isn't interested in anyone in particular, but really enjoys hanging out with a whole new crop of people who don't call her Kimchi Kayla, slant their eyes, and ask her for chop sticks and eggrolls. And she finds it absolutely hilarious that both HGH and Arty the Ass Grabber have asked her out. Being part of the Brainy Bunch has segregated us from so many of the "cool" kids for so long, Kayla keeps saying, "It's so weird that all of David's friends are like total strangers. It's like we went to different schools and are now meeting for the first time."

She's right. Because Rachel's dating Tommy and I'm seeing David, we're getting invitations to parties from kids who've ignored us since freshman year. "Would you believe that BM asked me to roast marshmallows and make s'mores at her fire pit?" Rachel discloses to us one night in early August. "And the Shape Shifters want me to go with them to the movies."

"Just stay away from Enema," I joke.

But the truth is, I've risen meteorically on the popularity scale too. It's a little late now that I'm seeing David, but

Hunter Hartman added me on Snapchat and followed me on Instagram. And wherever I go, Westberry kids are a whole lot nicer to me. No more snickering as I go by.

With the Ice Queen out of the equation, my close friends and I are having the amazing high school experience we've been robbed of for three years.

CHAPTER 15

Beach Day

The seven weeks since my first date with David have flown by, and it's taken me this long to get it through my head that he's sincere and our relationship is real. I'd rather not admit to anyone—not even to myself—that buried deep, deep down, there's still the teensiest part of me that's paranoid, but I won't allow it to reach the surface. If I even sense a whisper of it flare up, I stomp it back down.

When we finally coordinate our calendars for a day trip—which has been next to impossible with David's intensive summer practice schedule—we take off for the shore. Between his soccer and hockey dry-land training, he's had some kind of practice every single day, so it takes us until mid-August to sneak away. We luck out with a top ten beach day—cloudless blue sky, pure sunshine, high of ninety-five.

I love every minute I spend with him. Even the long drive doesn't bother me as long as he's in the next seat. Everything we do together is fun—singing at the top of our lungs through the open sun roof, stopping for brownie ice cream sundaes for breakfast, even figuring out how to work the parking meter.

When we finally kick off our flipflops and sink our feet into the soft white sand, I'm ecstatic. The beach is my happy place. I can't get enough of the salty ocean air, the squawking of the gulls, the steady rhythm of the breaking waves. Add in David and I might as well be in heaven.

We pick a spot near the waterline that's far from other

people, but close enough to hear the bubbling of the foamy white swash as it rushes to the shore. I lie down on an oversized beach towel, slip off my lacey black cover-up, and pull out a bottle of coconut-scented suntan lotion. I already have a base tan from my job, but my skin is still so fair that I always have to use a high SPF sunblock. And I definitely don't need any more freckles.

David sets up his portable Bluetooth speaker, drops next to me, and asks, "Want me to do your back?"

I nod. "That would be great, thanks."

I roll onto my stomach and hand him the palm tree-decorated bottle. He doesn't just slather on the lotion like I expect. He takes his time working it in, branching out from my lower back to my arms, smoothing the creamy liquid over my warm skin, dipping lower to my legs. Other than light kissing and hand holding, it's the first time he's touching my body, and I can't believe the sensations that are traveling through me. His fingertips are strong, yet gentle, and they seem to know the exact spots to linger, the perfect amount of pressure to apply.

When he reaches my upper thighs he uses long, easy strokes that extend from my bikini line down to my knees. I suck in air and clutch the corners of the towel. He doesn't seem to notice the effect he has on me and keeps going, kneading the lotion into the backs of my thighs, slicking it along the edges of my royal blue bikini bottom. He stays there, on the exposed fleshy part of my backside, using small, intimate circles to rub in the remaining lotion. My heart is beating off the charts, and I've got fistfuls of the towel now.

"You've got such a great body," he says. "You're all muscle. There's no fat on you."

All I can do is grunt. I couldn't formulate a coherent sentence if you paid me a million dollars. My breathing is heavy and loud, the rush of heat pulsing through my veins overwhelming. My skin is on fire too, sparking against the hot pads of his fingers. I don't want him to stop.

He's onto my shoulders now, massaging and pressing, stroking and caressing. Every part of me is tingling, wanting more.

His phone rings. He takes his hands away and wipes his fingertips on the front of his shirt before swiping the screen. It must be his mother, because he says, "Yeah, no problem. We got here a few minutes ago."

He stretches out next to me and finishes his call. I'm in a whole other dimension, my mind and body someplace else, but I catch a couple of phrases like "plenty of gas" and "probably after dinner."

The sensual massage is over, but we're lying close on the same towel and I'm still supercharged. I can hear my heart pounding in my ears, my breaths coming far too fast. I angle my face away from him in time to catch a beautiful white seagull as it swoops down and snatches some kind of crab out of the sand. Other seagulls follow, and I watch as a whole swarm dives to the same spot, scampering for more treasures.

David hangs up with his mom and taps the top of my hand. "Can I tell you something?"

I eek out, "Sure."

"This is the best summer I've ever had."

That gets my attention. "Really?"

"Yeah, really. Last summer my parents announced they were getting divorced and my father moved out, the summer before that my grandmother died, the one before that I broke my arm playing football. And the ones before that really aren't memorable. This is definitely the best one."

I interlace my fingers with his and squeeze. "For me too."

Neither of us says anything after that. We just lie there, soaking up the intense rays, listening to Spotify. It takes a while, but I finally calm down and relax, my body molded to the sand under my towel. After about twenty minutes, he props himself up on his elbows and announces, "I'm getting hot."

I'm broiling, so I say, "Me too. Let me know when you want to go in."

He cranes his neck toward the sky at a noisy propeller plane flying low overhead. It's dragging a banner advertisement for all-you-can-eat lobster at a local seafood restaurant, a thin streak of white puffballs trailing in its wake.

"I'm going to learn how to fly one day," he says. "It's something I've always wanted to do."

I smile. "Well, you can fly the plane and I'll jump out of it."

He gazes at me with wide eyes. "You want to go skydiving?"

I nod. "And I also want to go helicopter skiing in the British Columbian Cariboos and scuba diving in the Great Barrier Reef."

"What about hot air ballooning?"

"Yes!" I exclaim, thrilled that he hit on something else I've dreamed about. "That too!"

"I can't believe you want to do all that!" His exquisite chocolate brown eyes beam at me.

"Why not?"

"Because those aren't the types of things I usually hear girls say they want to do."

I poke him playfully in the ribs. "You think all the fun things are for guys?"

"No, of course not," he chuckles. "It's just that you're the first girl I've met who wants to jump out of a plane."

"Well, how many have you asked? I bet if you took a poll, you'd be surprised."

"I'll have to remember to do that."

"Good. Then let me know the results."

"Are you ready? I've got to go in and cool off."

I sit up. "Yeah, I'm burning. Let's go!"

I spring to my feet and dash to the shoreline, David at my heels. We dive right into a bank of cresting waves, laughing and screeching as the powerful tide bounces us around. He seems to love the ocean as much as I do, and we body surf for hours, both of us riding the waves endlessly, reveling in the cool, shimmering water. Then, hand in hand, we take a long walk down the beach, squishing our toes in the wet sand, searching for odd-shaped seashells.

The late afternoon clouds have rolled in by the time we collapse back on our towel, salty, sandy, and spent. He covers my hand with his. It's close enough to my face to pick up a hint of tropical coconut that lingers on his skin. "Did I tell you that this is the best summer ever?"

"No," I tease. "You'll have to tell me again."

"How about I tell you over dinner? Want to try that pancake house near where we parked?"

"Sure," I giggle. "If we can have dessert for breakfast, then we can have breakfast for dinner."

"See what you would've missed if you didn't go with me to the V-Zone that night?"

In response I throw an arm over his wet, muscular body. This might be my best day ever.

CHAPTER 16

Senior Year

After three horrendous years wallowing in Westberry High School's social abyss, I never would have dreamed I'd be entering my senior year with the most popular boy at my side. Things like that only happen on TV or in the movies.

I try hard to cast aside the doubts that keep creeping into my head. Is it too good to be true? Will he abandon me at the last minute?

On the morning of the first day I give myself a pep talk: *He's my boyfriend. He told me he loves me. He's not going to desert me.*

But I also know the unmistakable truth: Hanging out with me during the summer was one thing; marching into school with a Class C reject on his arm is another. I want so badly to believe that he really meant all the wonderful things he said to me the past few weeks and he won't drop me like a searing rock when other Class A kids mock him for hooking up with a bottom-dwelling loser.

Will he really face the Ice Queen and tell her that I, the object of her hatred, the target of her animosity, am her replacement? That certainly won't sit well. She went nuts just because I wore his sweatshirt. What will she do now that we really *are* together? My stomach churns just thinking about it.

Since I live on the other side of town from David, I told him not to go out of his way to pick me up—that I'd hitch a ride from a neighbor. Seniors don't take the bus at our school, and I'm less than two weeks away from my seventeenth birthday, so I plan to catch rides until I get my license. At the moment, though, I'm wondering if it was a huge mistake not having David get me. By being so considerate, I may have given him the out he's been waiting for.

Dumb, Blair. Really dumb!

My anxiety heightens as my neighbor Flora inches along the local roads, driving slower than my grandmother can jog. It seems like hours have passed by the time we pull into the school's student parking area. I'm so tense and nervous I'm about to have a panic attack, but to my incredible relief, I spot David waiting for me on the far right side of the lot, just as we'd planned.

He didn't ditch me!

I'm so excited I practically fly out of Flora's car before the wheels come to a full stop. I yell "thank you" over my shoulder as I rush toward David. He greets me with a huge smile, treats me to a delicious kiss, then slips his hand in mine.

So far, so good.

"I can't believe we're seniors," he says as we cross the pavement. "I remember my first day of freshman year like it was yesterday."

I nod. "Me too. Only this is sooo much better."

As we approach the double glass doors leading to the school's senior wing, a bolt of fear hits me and I pull back.

Can I really do this?

David tilts his head to the side, his eyes probing.

"What about Krystal?" I whisper, clamping down on his hand. Isn't he worried about an encounter with his ex too?

He turns to face me, the warmth in his sweet brown eyes dispelling my anxiety. "What about her?"

I toss him a weak smile. "She's not going to be happy about this."

He brushes my cheek with his fingertips. "You don't need to worry about her anymore. You're with me now." Then he presses his lips against mine. "It's no secret that you and I are together. Our pictures are all over social media, my friends have met you, and we've been all over town together. Believe me, she knows."

"That's what I'm afraid of. What she'll do to me."

David chuckles. "She's not going to do anything to you. You're with me." He gathers me in his arms and holds me in a reassuring embrace. "Ready?"

I love the way it feels to be so close to him. The rhythm of his heart beating against mine, the smell of his spicy cologne, the warmth of his strong chest. I could stay here forever, happy and content, wrapped in the safety of his arms.

A jumble of loud voices moving toward us brings me back to reality. I snap my head up and release a long, slow breath. I'm not ready—not at all—but what choice do I have? "Okay. Let's do it."

Winding through the halls together, I quickly realize that David is right. We're apparently old news, and in the excitement of the first day of school, nobody gives us a second glance. That is, nobody except Splenda.

I know that at her exclusive performing arts camp in Upstate New York the campers aren't allowed to bring cell phones or computers, and clearly no one has updated her on the latest gossip. Her face is frozen in shock as she watches me find my new locker with David's arm draped over my shoulders.

I drop in some new notebooks, slap on my lock, and spin around, but Splenda hasn't moved. Not a millimeter. Her lips are so still they may as well be sculpted in stone.

A moment like this will probably never come again, so I can't resist playing it. In my most syrupy sweet voice I say, "Hey, Alyssa. How was your summer?"

The stunned girl still doesn't move; only her eyes dart back and forth between David and me. Evidently, her acting training didn't prepare her for a situation like this. Her mom might want to a get a refund from that camp.

"Guess you'll fill me in later," I add with a sunny smile, relishing every second of Splenda's tongue-tied disbelief.

A couple of David's hockey buddies, J.D. and Dallas, pass by and high-five us. One of them even whistles at me and says, "Lookin' hot today, baby!"

I can't help stealing another glance at Splenda, who's blanched so white the blue veins under her skin are popping through. Clearly her brain isn't registering what her eyes are seeing.

I'd give anything to hear Splenda tell Mullet what she's just witnessed, so I linger a bit, but David curls his fingers around my waist to steer me toward our homerooms.

"We need to get to our classes before the bell," he whispers. "Don't want to be late on the very first day of our last year."

I'm grateful that our homerooms are diagonally across from each other so my time alone in the halls is limited. Even though it was extraordinarily fun to see Splenda's reaction to David and me, it wouldn't be so fun if I ran into the Ice Queen or Things by myself. I'll never forget the venomous rage in the Queen's eyes in the clubhouse bathroom when she saw me in her boyfriend's sweatshirt. Now that I'm actually with her boyfriend, I can't even imagine the animosity she'll harbor.

I know that if I'm with David or a group of friends I'll be fine, but I truly dread a confrontation by myself. It's something that's been gnawing at me since David and I got together, but really, what am I supposed to do? I have to go to school, and I'm kind of hoping for the best.

The good news is that Kayla has the same homeroom as me and Rachel is only a few doors down. The bad news is that they've already texted me they're going to be late because Rachel can't find her school parking permit.

Strolling down the hall with David, I feel like a modern-day Cinderella. I want to twirl around and shout out loud how great life is right at this moment. Things have been so bad for so long that now I want time to just stand still. We reach my homeroom way too fast.

"I don't want to let you go," I say, tightening my grip on David's hand.

He squeezes back and smiles. "Me neither, but in four periods you're meeting me for lunch, right?"

I smile too, anticipating our special first-day-of-senior-year lunch together at a new Greek restaurant that opened nearby. "I can't wait."

He leans in to give me a quick kiss but stops short when he hears his name called by a familiar voice. A deep, authoritative one.

We both look up to see our principal, Mr. Scott, approaching with two large armed police officers. They wear suits, not uniforms, but they make sure their guns are visible as they hold up their badges. One of them is a head shorter than the other, but they both look really menacing. I notice that our school D.A.R.E. officer is trailing the principal and two officers by about five yards, allowing the trio to take the lead in whatever is about to happen. David and I exchange troubled glances, then face Mr. Scott.

"What's this about?" David asks, his expression a mixture of fear and confusion.

Our principal scowls, rakes his fingers through his combed-over graying hair, and states, "I'm very sorry to tell you this, but these detectives are here to arrest you."

David's eyes bug out. "Why...what did I do?"

"It's what you both did," the taller, wider detective announces.

Did I just hear right?

I step forward, aiming my index finger at my chest. "*I* did something?"

"You both need to come with us," commands the shorter detective. Now that I'm up close, I see that he's got a ruddy face and receding hairline, and silver handcuffs dangling from his fingers.

My eyes plead with Mr. Scott for help, but he shrugs, shakes his head, and utters, "We've already called your parents. David, they'll meet you at the police station. Blair, we couldn't reach yours."

"But what did we do?" David repeats in a panicked whine, his lower lip trembling.

The lines on Mr. Scott's forehead twitch, but he says nothing else. Then he steps aside as the tall detective pulls out a sheet of paper and reads the list of charges: "Creation of child pornography; possession of child pornography; distribution of child pornography; exhibition of child pornography; endangering the welfare of minors...."

A significant crowd has formed around us, everyone intrigued by the police presence. They all watch in sheer astonishment as the captain of the ice hockey team and his new redheaded girlfriend are handcuffed, read their rights, and led away before the first period of the new school year.

CHAPTER 17

Arrested

"I didn't do anything!" I scream as the metal cuffs lock around my wrists. "You have the wrong person! This is a mistake!" But no one listens to my frantic cries of innocence. Not the principal. Not the police. Not the D.A.R.E. officer.

Instead they gawk at me like somehow I deserve this... to have my purse and bookbag confiscated, my combination lock cut off my new locker, my life ripped apart. I want to believe this is a nightmare...that I'll wake up and it'll be a regular day again, but the numbing fear and heavy dread pumping through me hammer home that this is real.

And as if being escorted out of the school by armed detectives isn't traumatic enough, I have to endure the unsettling, accusatory stares of my teachers and classmates. It's undeniably the worst moment of my entire sixteen-year existence.

When I pass by BM and Mullet, I see that they're positively gloating. They're smirking as though all the nasty things they've ever called me were completely justified and their wicked wishes have finally come true. And the Things look pretty pleased with themselves too, like they should skip the first day of classes and break out the champagne. At least when I catch Hunter Hartman's expression it's not one of joy—it's more an odd mixture of curiosity and concern. And shock.

Truth be told, no one is more shocked than me.

I keep my face forward and my chin tucked low as I'm ushered away. I can't stand to see anyone else glaring at or pitying me. Some kids are holding out their phones to permanently capture my descent into hell. I avert my eyes and tilt my head in the opposite direction, but my cheeks burn like they're being torched.

Endless questions whirl through my head amidst blinding panic. *Who made up these charges? What do they mean? Why did they accuse me?* Clearly somebody has screwed up.

When we reach the main entrance of the school, I shudder at the sight of the two police cars waiting out front. The first one is apparently mine, and every inch of my body trembles as I'm pushed into the back and the door slams behind me. The air is thick and hot, but I don't see any window controls or door handles. I feel trapped, like a caged animal.

Through the glass partition separating the front and rear seats, I watch the taller, beefier detective climb into the vehicle with a smug, triumphant expression. He seems oblivious to the fact he's irreparably destroying a young honor student's life, carting her away like a dirty, common criminal. To the contrary, he seems proud he's hauling his prize back to the station.

Out the window to my right, through the black steel bars covering the glass, I see David being hustled along by the stout, ruddy-faced detective. In the slanted rays of the early morning sun, David's eyes show everything I'm feeling: panic, confusion, disbelief.

And terror.

Before our eyes can meet, my car surges ahead, the force throwing me backward against the seat. The detective drives like he's trying to win the Grand Prix, banking hard to the right as he exits the school parking lot. The fast, sharp turn hurls me against the door, my head banging off one of the steel bars. The blow sends a fiery pain shooting through the right side of my skull, but the detective neither seems to notice nor care.

I pull myself away from the window, fighting back an intense wave of nausea. Up close, the bars and glass reek of cheap cologne and stale liquor. My insides twist from the sickening jumble of foul smells.

Before long, the oppressive heat sends streams of sweat oozing from my pores. I try to reposition myself and smooth out my new back-to-school outfit, now damp and wrinkled, but the heavy metal bracelets dig into my wrists. I can't even rub the side of my head, which stings and burns like someone's holding a flame to it. I've never felt more helpless.

Shifting in my seat, I make an awkward attempt to slide toward the driver's side. "Hello!" I holler through the glass partition. "Can you turn on the air, please?" The detective doesn't respond, but mercifully stretches his hand out toward the center console and pushes a button. As grateful as I am for the cool breeze that brushes against my legs, it still smells like a drunken homeless person died back here. I try hard not to wretch from the overpowering stench.

In the rearview mirror I catch the first glimpse of myself since the arrest. Now I understand why mug shots are so unflattering. My face is flushed, my jaw tight with pain, my eyes wild with panic and fear. The side bangs that I'd so painstakingly flat ironed only an hour earlier are now moist and frizzy, crinkled into miserable red coils against my forehead. I look like somebody from *America's Most Wanted*.

As the cruiser speeds up a hill, I see the reflection of the blue and red flashing lights from the patrol car behind us. That one, of course, is David's. We weren't allowed to talk to each other before they hauled us away like dangerous criminals, but I know from the bewildered expression on his face that he's wondering the same thing as me: *Why?*

The charges that had been read are completely insane. I try to remember them all, but it's a terrifying blur—the detectives, their badges, arrest warrants—it's all hazy and surreal. I feel so stupid that I can't recall everything I've been accused of. From the whole list, all I can remember are two charges: endangerment of minors and child pornography distribution.

What are they talking about?

I squeeze my eyes closed, trying to figure out how a mistake like this could have happened. I don't baby-sit. I don't have younger siblings. The last time I was near children was during the summer when I gave swimming lessons, but nothing I'd ever done could possibly have been construed as child endangerment—unless I was arrested for making kids dive into the deep end.

I heard one of the officers mention a search warrant for my house. Certainly the police would never find anything on my computer even remotely related to pornography. Really, I'm not the type. They could just ask the Ice Queen and her Things, who constantly berate me for being the ultimate goody two-shoes. Maybe there's some truth to that. I've never even looked at a dirty magazine, let alone seen a porn DVD or X-rated movie. How could they accuse me of distributing them?

I lick the salty sweat off my upper lip as I think about the YouTube videos I've recently watched. Some of them used bad language and many were in poor taste, but child pornography? No way.

My mind races back to the emails I've sent and received over the last few weeks. Dirty jokes? Yes. Some crude and possibly offensive? Yes, but nothing pornographic.

Then a terrifying thought seizes me. David was arrested

too. Maybe this was about something he's done, and they think I'm in on it. What if he downloaded or emailed kiddie porn, and somehow I'm being accused of it too? After all, I did use his computer several times over the past month. But would that link me to anything illegal that he did?

My eyes spring open wider as an even more alarming realization hits. I *have* distributed a nude photo from my own computer. Not of children, but of a nude man. I'd recently received an email that I forwarded to friends because it seemed so funny at the time.

It contained a picture of a dining room table and chairs for sale with a caption that said, "How can you tell this dining room set is being sold by a male?" From the photo and description of items it was impossible to tell, until you scrolled down to the very bottom where you saw the reflection of a naked man in the mirror holding a camera. Someone must have turned me in.

Was forwarding that photo to my friends pornography distribution? If so, then wouldn't everyone on my list be arrested too?

This is way too much for me...I'm only sixteen! And I can't even think this early—my brain doesn't fully wake up until about fifth period. All I know for certain right now is that it's barely 7:30 a.m. on the first day of my senior year, and I'm on the way to jail for reasons I can't comprehend.

As the cruiser slows, I glance out the window and see we've entered the municipal complex that houses the police headquarters. I pray hard that Rachel or Kayla got through to my parents. They passed me in the main hallway when they came in late, just as I was being led away on my humiliating perp walk. I yelled out instructions for them to call my mom and dad.

The last thing I can imagine doing is making a jail-house

phone call to my parents: "Hi, Mom. Hi, Dad. No, nothing's wrong. It's just that I've been arrested for child pornography, handcuffed, thrown in the back of a police car, and raced off to jail like a serial killer. How's your morning going?"

I draw a long, deep breath as the vehicle crawls to a stop, and swallow the bile that's crept up my throat.

This is it. Time to be fingerprinted, photographed, and searched like the seedy prisoners on TV. Only this is real.

I choke back tears, trying to stay strong.

"Anything you say can and will be used against you," keeps reverberating in my head. What I need is a lawyer— someone who can get me out of this fast.

Ironically, my father *is* a lawyer, but he won't be able to help me. He handles personal injury cases, like automobile accidents, slip and falls, and dog bites. Under-age daughter hauled off to prison for sex crimes? Not exactly his specialty.

As I emerge from the rear of the police cruiser onto a pair of wobbly legs, I see David's vehicle turning into the lot. I desperately need to talk to him, so I try to stall for time.

Planting my shaky feet, I say to the detective, "Can you please give me a minute before we go in there?"

He shakes his head, grasps my upper arm, and surges me forward. I'm already inside by the time David's car rolls up to the door.

In the beige brick lobby of the police station, a uniformed female officer with a short dirty-blonde pageboy is talking to the front desk sergeant. As soon as I spot her, I erupt with rapid-fire questions.

"Do you know if anyone got through to my parents? Can I go to the bathroom? I think my head is bleeding. Can I get ice? Do I get a lawyer?" I'm scared out of my mind, spewing out my sentences in a single breath.

At first the blonde officer appears startled by my barrage

of questions, squinting at both me and the tall detective, but when she takes in my frightened face, bloody hair, and handcuffs, she assumes a more compassionate air.

"Yes," she says. "You can definitely call your parents, and I'll be happy to take you to the bathroom. Then we'll have one of the officers check your head."

I don't know if it's purposeful or not, but she fails to address my lawyer question.

CHAPTER 18

The Precinct

Sitting in a stark interrogation room, I tap my feet and fidget in my seat while I wait for my mother or father or lawyer. Whoever comes first.

Somebody, please!

My gaze is fastened on the door as I press an ice pack to the side of my head and try not to do any more damage to my pitiful fingernails. They'd looked so pretty for the first day of school, all shapely and smooth, coated with my favorite dusty mauve polish, but now I've gnawed most of them down to their nail beds, and they're red and raw and ugly.

A different detective—not one of the ones who'd arrested me—sits across the table, and I shift my body so I don't have to face him. He doesn't seem very interested in me anyway, his shaved head bent over his lap as his thick fingers tap away at his cell phone.

They did allow me to call my parents, and thankfully, Rachel had already gotten through and broken the "news." I was surprised that my dad didn't scream and curse at me as I'd expected, since he's not known for handling family crises very well. Instead, he was calm and composed: "Don't say anything until Uncle Marv and I get there."

My mom is the first to arrive, bursting into the small interrogation room in a frenzy of high-pitched shrieks. "Oh my God, are you okay? What's going on here?" She envelopes me in a protective bear hug, her arms squeezing me like a nutcracker.

The detective barely glances up, but I guess he must realize this woman is my mother from the way she looks. We have similar facial features and the same pale blue eyes. The only major differences are that my strawberry blonde hair is a few shades lighter, and my skin is much fairer.

She releases her wrestling hold and points at the ice pack I'm holding above my right ear. "What happened to your head? Did the police do that? And what's this Rachel told me about child pornography? I couldn't believe what I was hearing!"

I look her straight in the eyes. "I don't know what these charges are about. They must've confused me with somebody else."

My mom eyes the stern-faced detective across the table, flashes me a warning look, and drops into a chair. "Let's just wait for Daddy and Uncle Marv to get here."

We sit in silence for several minutes, the detective completely ignoring us. He's so focused on typing his message, he probably wouldn't notice if we danced on the table.

It feels like an eternity before my dad enters the room, my criminal defense attorney, Marv Sherman, at his side. Whenever they stand together, I'm always struck by how opposite they appear even though they're the same age. My dad is a very handsome man, his dark wavy hair still full and rich in color, his body in pretty decent shape. Uncle Marv, on the other hand, has a shock of white hair that matches a curly mustache and long beard, and an ultra-wide midsection. He's also rosy-faced with twinkling brown eyes, making it hard not to look at him and think of Santa Claus.

Uncle Marv is my dad's best friend from law school, and my older brother Brett and I have always known him as our jolly, fun, wise-cracking honorary uncle, so it's super weird that he's here now as my lawyer. He wastes no time, setting his briefcase on the table and sliding up a chair. He directs his focus at me and gets right down to business. "I just learned why you were arrested. It seems the charges against you stem from a relatively new crime known as sexting."

"*Sexting*," my mom repeats in a shrill voice. "What's *that*?"

My brand-new defense attorney clears his throat and raises his eyebrows. "Sexting is when people, typically teenage girls, send sexually explicit material over their cell phones, tablets, or computers. Usually, they send nude or partially nude photos of themselves, and since they're minors, it's considered by law enforcement to be child pornography. More charges get tacked on when they transmit the sexual material to other minors."

I almost fall off my chair. "Nude photos? I've never taken any nude photos!"

With that declaration, Uncle Marv spins toward the detective. "I need a few minutes alone with my client now, please."

Once the detective steps out, Uncle Marv grows more serious, his normal congenial demeanor turning dour. "Blair, tell me the truth. There's an attorney-client privilege that now exists between us, which means that anything you tell me is confidential. If I'm going to represent you, I need to know that you're telling me the absolute truth. You have to tell me everything you've done on your cell phone, Snapchat, Instagram, Facebook, Twitter, and any other social networking sites you've been on. I need to know about emails, instant and direct messaging—everything."

I hinge forward, knowing my face must reflect the frustration I feel, hoping he can see my sincerity. "But I haven't done anything, so I have nothing to tell you."

Uncle Marv narrows his gaze at my statement of innocence.

"You have no idea how much trouble you're in, sweetie. I don't think you realize how serious this is. If you get convicted on all of the felony counts against you—creation, distribution, exhibition, and possession of child pornography, contributing to the delinquency of a minor—you could go to jail for the next thirty years and be registered as a sex offender for the rest of your life. You'll be getting your GED and taking college courses from prison. You'll be getting out when your friends are having grandchildren."

Stunned into silence, I stare at him as though he's just announced the end of the world. In fact, he's just announced the end of *my* world. All I can do is shake my head.

My mother's complexion has drained to a pasty white. She grasps Uncle Marv's forearm and says, "Are you telling us that if she posted a nude picture of herself on the Internet, then she's going to be prosecuted the same way as a rapist?"

"I didn't post any nude pictures!" I wail.

"Let Uncle Marv answer," she chides.

He continues. "Unfortunately, this is a nationwide problem that state legislators across the country are grappling with—"

"So the answer is yes!" my mom shrieks. "She's going to be prosecuted like a rapist!"

Uncle Marv covers her hand with his and speaks with a slow, confident tone. "No, she's not being accused of rape. The charges are for child pornography crimes. Yes, they are sex crimes, but they don't rise to the level of rape. And the good news is that there are pending bills in the Assembly and Senate to decriminalize sexting done by teens so they can avoid prosecution."

This time my dad breaks in. "But you just said *pending* bills. How does that help Blair?"

"This is ridiculous!" I holler, jumping to me feet. "I am

not a child pornographer! Why am I being accused of this?"

"Let Uncle Marv talk!" my mother snaps. "And sit back down."

Uncle Marv rubs his fleshy temples and adjusts his glasses. "The good news is that most legislators are recognizing that these teens aren't really child pornographers—they're just kids who need some education and counseling about what they're doing and why they're doing it. The bad news is that right now these teens are still being charged with criminal offenses. Some under federal law."

My mom turns to Uncle Marv, her face crinkled in bewilderment. "How can this happen in our country? Teenagers who don't fully understand what they're doing— acting like typical adolescents—being prosecuted for adult sex crimes? Why isn't there a huge outcry about this?"

"Because it's still under the public radar. Most people don't know this is happening. School administrators want to keep it quiet, parents quickly cut deals to make it go away, policymakers are working hard to change it...and by the way, it's not just a problem in our country. Now that technology has exploded, every country has to deal with it."

My dad takes this all in, leans back in his chair, and speaks in a low whisper. "Marv, what exactly is it that they have on her? I know my daughter, and she's telling the truth."

Thank you, Dad!

Slowly, without another word, Uncle Marv fishes a manila folder from his briefcase, slides it across the table, and fastens his gaze on me.

Fingers trembling, I flip up the cover. There are sharp gasps from my parents and me as we view the large color photo.

CHAPTER 19

The Photo

My father is the first to find his voice. With his eyes glued to the eight by ten color photo of me standing in my bedroom in a hot pink bra and panties set, he asks, "Who took this? David?"

I nod, not comprehending how this private picture ended up in the hands of the police. "But he was supposed to delete it. He promised me he would!"

My dad sighs, his voice heavy with disappointment. "Why were you parading around in your underwear in front of him?"

Anger rumbles through me and my cheeks flood with heat. "I wasn't parading around! I was getting dressed when he walked in!"

My dad looks incredulous. "So you let him take your picture?"

I can't stop my teeth from clenching. "I didn't *let* him. He just took it while he was waiting for me to get dressed. We were going to a party, and I couldn't figure out which outfit I wanted to wear. When I came out of my closet he held up his phone. I asked him, 'Did you just take a picture?' and he admitted that he did. He said I looked really cute. I told him to get rid of it—erase it right now—but he begged me to keep it. I said, 'No, delete it,' and he finally said, 'All right.' I thought that was the end of it."

Before my father even opens his mouth, I can tell by the harsh way he's squinting at me that he's not happy with my response. "Well, obviously that wasn't the end of it, or you wouldn't be here. You shouldn't be parading around with no clothes on in front of him!"

"Oh, Sam," my mother intervenes. "She spent all summer long in bikinis in front of him. What's the difference?"

I glance appreciatively at my mom. At least one of my parents is reasonable.

"I'll tell you what the difference is," my dad argues. "Bathing suit tops aren't see-through. You can see her nipples here! And if this was a picture of her in a bikini, she wouldn't have been arrested!"

I take a closer look and see that he's right. You *can* see my nipples. I want to crawl into a crack in the floor and die.

Uncle Marv puts an end to the family squabbling. "That's enough! She can't go back and change what she did, so we need to move on and figure out our strategy going forward."

"What do you mean, 'what *I* did?'" I cry, enraged at his insinuation. "I didn't *do* anything. I told him to delete it, and he didn't. How is that *my* fault?"

"Well, unfortunately, he didn't listen, and since this is a photo of you in your see-through lingerie that can be considered sexually explicit, and since it was transmitted via cell phone to other underage kids, it doesn't matter whether it's your fault or not, you have to deal with the consequences."

"That's so unfair!" I blurt out, shoving my chair back. "And it's not lingerie—it's underwear! I was getting dressed, not posing for a nude picture. Look at the skirt I'm holding in my right hand. I was putting clothes *on*, not taking them off!"

My mom places a warm, comforting hand on my shoulder and squeezes. "Please try to calm down, honey. This whole thing is really out of hand, and Uncle Marv is going to fix it for us. Right, Marv?"

I can't calm down. I'm consumed with such overwhelming rage that I grind the soles of my feet into the floor and curl my hands into tight balls to keep from exploding.

Uncle Marv nods at my mom. "I'll do everything I can, you know that. It's just a crying shame our laws haven't caught up to the present times. Before the Internet and cell phones, a policeman would've looked at a photo like this and said, 'So?' Now you get arrested for it."

My dad rubs his chin, visibly distraught. "We need to make sure she doesn't get a record over this. If any of these charges stick, they'll stay with her for life. She'll never get into college or find a job if she's a sex offender."

The burning flame in my chest flares all the way up my neck, scorching my skin. I bounce to my feet and bolt for the door. "I am *not* a sex offender! This is so ridiculous, I can't even stand it!"

Uncle Marv shoots an arm out to block my path. "Sweetie, you can't leave. The police won't let you. You need to have an arraignment and post bail."

I stop dead. "What's an arraignment?"

"It's when you plead guilty or not guilty before a judge."

"Well that's easy," I declare. "I'm not guilty. If I explain all this to a judge, I'm sure he'll get rid of the charges, right?"

"I wish it was that simple, but it's not. Unfortunately, you've got to go through a long process now. The good news is that I made some phone calls on the way here, and we'll get you arraigned right away—as soon as the courthouse opens—so you won't have to spend any time in a jail cell. The judge will read you your rights and explain the penalties for the charges against you, then you'll be on your way."

Relief washes over my parents' faces, but I'm still just as tense. "What about David? Will he have to go to jail?"

Uncle Marv snaps his briefcase closed and stands. "If I were you, sweetie, I'd be worried about myself right now. That boy's already gotten you into enough trouble."

CHAPTER 20

Betrayed

I lie on the family room couch scrolling through dozens of channels, but there isn't a single thing that holds my interest. Soaps, talk shows, cooking programs, B movies, ancient reruns...nothing worthwhile. I toss the remote onto the glass coffee table and stare out the window.

It's a beautiful September afternoon. Rays of warm sunlight spill through the treetops and shimmer off the velvety purple and red-plum petals of the petunias and geraniums lining the back patio. But I could care less about the weather or scenery. I've had some bad days over the past few years, but this is the mother of them all. And getting arrested, booked, and arraigned isn't the worst of it. I think what bothers me the most is what my lawyer told the prosecutor and the judge.

Uncle Marv stood before them and said, "This boy David Woods took a seminude photo of my client against her will, broke his promise to delete it, lied about deleting it, then betrayed her yet again by sending it to other people. She was victimized by someone who lacked good character and judgment and acted solely for his own personal pleasure at the expense of her feelings and well-being."

I was numb by this point, but he went on. "Let me be very clear: Ms. Evans did nothing wrong. She is the innocent victim of her boyfriend's errant behavior. David Woods won her trust, then violated it."

A slow burn ripples through me just thinking about Uncle

Marv's speech, because the gut-wrenching truth is that he was right about everything he said. The pain and humiliation of his words cut right through me, leaving me bleeding inside. Was this the same David who'd been so caring and sweet? The one who'd told me repeatedly how much I meant to him? The one who'd said he loved me only the week before? It certainly didn't sound like it.

By the time my father posted bail, I was so distressed I could barely function. All I could think about as I left the courthouse was that this amazing boyfriend of mine was really a double-crossing, backstabbing lowlife. I'd been ambushed, sucker punched, blind-sided—whatever you call the least popular girl in the school thinking she's landed a Class A star athlete, when in reality she's been set up for public disgrace. And here I'd thought I'd been so lucky. It turns out my mom's pearly words of wisdom were spot-on: *When something seems too good to be true, it usually is.*

How could I have been so duped?

I'm probably the laughingstock of the entire school. My tears are unstoppable as I realize how badly I've been played. David never really broke up with the Ice Queen—he's been a double agent the whole time.

It all makes sense now—how he came on so strong, how he didn't care that I was a lowly Class C, how he kept telling me not to worry about Krystal. All the while they were playing the ultimate cruel joke on me.

As hot streams rush down my face, my Portuguese water dog Snowy is immediately at my side, resting his large, black head on my lap, gazing up at me with his soulful dark eyes. He always knows when I'm upset and is always there for me. If only I could find a boyfriend as loyal and sensitive as my dog.

I flip myself over and bury my face in a tufted sofa cushion.

David isn't any different from all the other horrible people at Westberry High who've made my life so miserable. Not only is he one of them, he's the worst.

My body shakes with endless, racking sobs at the realization that I was used in the most despicable way. All the attention he showered on me, the time we spent together—all part of the plan. The dreamy way he looked in my eyes, the loving way he touched me—pure lies. The sweet things he said, the deep feelings he claimed he had—total garbage. He's nothing more than one of the Ice Queen's pathetic Things.

I pummel the mosaic design in the center of one of the throw pillows. It's either that, or hammer strike myself for being so stupid and gullible. How could I have been so dumb? The captain of the hockey team—the boyfriend of the most popular girl in school—interested in *me*? I smash my forehead into the sofa cushion over and over.

The real question is, whom do I hate more right now? Him for doing this to me, or me for letting it happen? One thing is for certain: I'm never stepping foot in that godforsaken school again. I never want to see any of them as long I live.

I spring off the couch and race to my room. My mom must hear my footsteps slapping against the wood floor, because she yells from the kitchen, "Honey, are you all right?"

"Yeah," I shout back, even though I'm not.

I know I should do something productive like go to the animal shelter or practice the piano or start my college essays, but I have so much negative energy flowing through me I need to diffuse it before I explode. I throw on running shorts and a tank top and bolt out the back door. For the next two hours I dash through my neighborhood and surrounding streets until my legs give out. I try to force them to walk back toward my house, but after a couple of miles I collapse on the base of a paver driveway.

The hurt and humiliation haven't abated, but at least I've exhausted myself enough to stop wanting to punch things. Somehow, I'm going to have to learn to live with the fact that I've been such a fool.

Assuming I can stay out of jail, I'm never going to trust another male for the rest of my life.

"Blair!" someone shouts from a passing car. "There you are!"

It's Rachel, in her old tan Accord, skidding to a stop alongside me, Carrie in her passenger seat. She tears off her Ray-Bans and scolds me with her bright blue eyes. "Where have you been? Your mom's been looking for you everywhere! She asked us to help find you. Kayla's riding around with her—she's ready to call the police."

From my sanctuary on the driveway apron, I groan, "That's all I need. More police."

"Well, she hasn't called yet, but she's about to. She's really panicked—you've been gone for hours. You didn't say where you were going, when you'd be back...and you didn't take your phone."

"I don't *have* my phone anymore," I remind her, bitterness coating my words. "The police took it."

"Well, your mom's giving us another ten minutes to find you before she calls them. And what are you doing all the way out here?" Without giving me the chance to respond, Rachel snatches her leopard-cased cell phone and dials my mother.

I prop myself up on an elbow to listen.

"We've got her! She's totally fine!" A short pause. "On Farmingdale Road—about twelve miles away. We'll meet you back at the house."

I hear the click as Rachel unlocks the doors, then climb into the backseat. As I wriggle across the faded taupe upholstery, I'm hit with the familiar scent of her apple cinnamon air freshener.

"How could you not tell your mom where you were going?" Carrie chastises. "She's been thinking these really terrible things, like you got kidnapped or jumped in front of a bus. You can't just disappear like that!"

"I didn't just disappear—I told her I was going jogging. Only problem is I went too far, so I've been walking home. It's just taking a while."

"Well, you should've at least borrowed her phone so something like this wouldn't happen!"

I'm too drained to answer.

My friends stay silent the rest of the way to my house, and I know it's because they don't know whether I'm ready to talk about everything yet. That much is true, but I'm also wiped out, sinking into the seat like a limp rag doll. It's tempting to stay back here forever.

When Rachel coasts onto my driveway, my mother and Kayla are waiting by the garage doors, ecstatic to see me. I swallow a heavy pang of guilt when I see the deep worry lines embedded in my mom's brow. Up close, her entire face is riddled with creases. The traumatic events of the day have clearly taken their toll on her, and it's all because of me.

Kayla and Carrie each grab an arm to help me out of the car and stabilize me on the blacktop. My legs are unsteady, jiggling like Jell-O as we cut through my house to the rear porch. I topple face-first into one of our cushioned patio chairs.

Snowy tumbles onto the patio and curls himself around the foot of my chair. After I flip over and straighten out, he rests his big hairy head on my feet. I reach down to pet him, and he immediately rolls over for me to rub his long belly. I love this dog more than I can put into words, and I don't know what I'd do without him. If only people were as genuine and caring as dogs, our world would be a far better place.

Right now, I'm so thirsty I could drink a swimming pool. When my mom brings out pitchers of fresh-squeezed lemonade and water, I gulp down two large glasses of each. Then it's time to share my double-agent theory with my friends.

"David was never really my boyfriend," I begin. "He and the Queen were setting me up the whole time."

I unload all the painful truths that have been tearing me up inside, the words rushing out as I piece my conspiracy theory together with supporting facts. "I know I'm right," I conclude, slumping all the way back in my chair. "He was just using me the whole time. It's the only thing that makes sense."

An awkward silence settles over the patio table until Kayla remarks, "No, that actually doesn't make sense at all."

We all turn to gaze at her, but she makes us wait for an explanation while she slurps up the dregs of her lemonade. When her lips release her straw, she flicks a long strand of dark silky hair behind her shoulder and asks, "Why would he take a picture of you with his own phone and then turn it in to the police? He had to know he'd get himself arrested."

"Because maybe Blair's right," Carrie says. "Maybe he's so under the Ice Queen's spell that he'd do anything for her, even if it means sacrificing himself?"

"No," Rachel breaks in. "I think Kayla's right that he wouldn't want to get himself arrested. Doesn't he already have two scholarship offers for hockey when he graduates? Why would he do something that would put those in jeopardy?"

"And he did get arrested...just like you," Kayla emphasizes. "So how could he be setting you up? He'd be setting himself up too."

I sink farther into my chair, disturbed that Rachel and Kayla aren't getting it. "Don't you see, he never intended to get himself arrested—that's why the photo of me was sent in anonymously."

Kayla whips her head back and forth. "But the photo originally came from *his* phone. Your mother told us someone anonymously forwarded it to the police *after* David sent it out. If he was part of the plan to get you in trouble, why would he leave a trail that led right back to him?"

I hate to admit that Kayla and Rachel each have some good points—ones that puncture gaping holes in my theory. *Damn.*

"And you know," Rachel adds. "Not for nothing, but I saw his face when you two were arrested this morning. He was totally shocked. You can't fake the look he had. If he was trying to set you up, then it backfired on him in a big way, because he didn't know this was coming."

My eyes widen. "Maybe he didn't know it was coming. Maybe he thought he was just setting *me* up, and the psycho-bitch threw *him* into the fire too?"

Kayla cocks her head to the side. "Oh, come on! Aren't you getting a bit carried away? You think he pretended to break up with her, but was really still her boyfriend pretending to be your boyfriend so he could set you up, and then unbeknownst to him, she set him up too? That's crazy. And why would she do that?"

Carrie had the answer. "She was jealous. Look, I was fooled by him too—we all were. I would've sworn that he was the real deal seeing him and Blair together. Maybe the bitch thought he crossed the line with Blair, and she didn't like it."

My mother slides open the glass door to the patio and holds out the cordless handset from the kitchen. It's ringing as it dangles from her hand. She locks eyes with me. "The caller ID says Woods."

"Don't answer it," I instruct.

Her features harden. "Believe me, after what he did to you, he's the last person I want to talk to."

I glance at each of my friends, but none of them offer an opinion as to what I should do. The loud, tinny ring fills the space between us as they stare at me with flat poker faces. "I'm not speaking to him ever again," I finally say.

My mom nods and shuts the door, the ringing handset clutched in her fist.

In less than a minute Rachel's cell phone vibrates against the glass tabletop. She hinges over the metal lip to glance at her new message. The corners of her mouth sink.

"What is it?" Kayla asks, craning her neck to read sideways.

"It's a text from David—he's sending it from Tommy's phone. He wants me to tell Blair that he's really, really sorry and he needs to talk to her." Rachel lifts her eyes till they meet mine. They're expectant...hopeful.

But I'm done with that rotten liar. "Tell him what I just told my mom. I never want to speak to him again!"

Kayla shakes her head, her eyes teeming with skepticism. "Why would he be sending you that if he didn't care about you? Think about it. If this was all a set up and he and the psycho-bitch got what they wanted, why would he be apologizing?"

"Maybe now he feels bad about what he did, and he wants to clear his conscience," Carrie suggests. "I mean, getting arrested is pretty traumatic."

"If he could do that to me, then he doesn't have a

conscience," I snap.

"But it doesn't make sense," Kayla presses. "Like I said before, why would he put his own future on the line?"

Carrie shrugs her shoulders. "To please his bitch."

Everyone laughs but me. They cut the giggles when they catch my dire expression.

Kayla taps my arm. "I really think you should talk to him. At least hear what he has to say."

"What do you think he's going to say?" I fire back. "He's sorry he ruined my life? There are no words for what he did!" A familiar rage wells up inside me, and I choke back the thick lump that's swelling my throat closed. If I hadn't just run a half marathon I'd be off again.

Rachel reaches out her hand and rests it on my shoulder. "Yes, taking that picture and sending it around was awful, but I don't think he meant to get you arrested—it doesn't make sense. And Tommy just sent me a text saying that he's never seen David so down. I think Kayla's right. You should talk to him."

Carrie shakes her head.

We're split, two against two. Time for a dinner break.

CHAPTER 21

The Instagram Account

As darkness descends over the worst day of my life, Kayla, Rachel, Carrie, and I sit on my backyard patio eating pizza, drinking lemonade, and debating whether or not David is really the two-timing, backstabbing, scum-sucking slimeball I think he is. My friend Stef from swim team drops by as we dig into our second pie. Eating is a great coping mechanism, and I'm about to start my third slice.

"You're all over Snapchat and Instagram," Stef blurts out, dropping into a chair.

I tear off a string of gooey mozzarella that's hanging off the edge of my plate and give her my best *no kidding* look. "I'm sure the entire world is talking about me right now."

"No," Stef corrects. "They're not *talking* about you, they're *looking* at you. Your picture—the one that got you arrested—is everywhere."

"*What?*"

"You're lucky you were wearing such a cute bra and panty set," she remarks. "How embarrassing would it be if you were caught in plain white granny briefs or something hideous?"

I didn't think there was a part of me left that was capable of being more shocked, but Stef just found it. "Are you kidding? That picture's on Instagram?"

Stef nods. "It's gone viral. I just never thought of you as the type to wear lacey see-through bras. Is that Victoria's

Secret?"

Oh my God! "Can you see my nipples?"

Stef nods again as she grabs a slice. "Plain as day. Is that part of their Secret Angels collection?"

Rachel holds up her iPhone, ready to investigate. "Where should I start?"

Stef shifts uncomfortably in her seat, her eyes darting between Rachel and me. "Someone also made up a finsta in Blair's name."

Rachel's fingertips dance across her screen until she brings up the fake Instagram. We know the moment she's found it because her jawline slacks and eyelids flutter. "*Oh boy,*" she murmurs.

I lunge across the table and snatch her phone. She, Kayla, and Carrie huddle over my shoulder as I survey the damage.

The name on the finsta is *Blair Evans—Freak of the Century.* The handle is *@BlairTheMare.* My profile photo is the infamous one David took, and beneath it the Bio reads: *Interested in: Boyfriend Snatching; Sex: Never—don't know how & would be terrible if I tried; Race: Rodent; Address: Cell Block 6; For Inquiries: ExtremeLoser@ClassC.net.* There are also several close-up shots of horse faces with reddish-tan and brown manes captioned *Blair the Mare,* along with photos of large gray rats captioned *From Boca Raton.*

And my comments are filled with vicious phrases and what appear to be porno links. I really don't want to read them, but can't seem to stop myself:

Change the Bio to: Interested in Anything Losers Do!

Favorite Activity is crashing parties where I don't belong.

Passions include picking my nose, twirling it in my frizzy mane, and stealing boyfriends.

I can't force myself to read anymore because the pizza

slices in my stomach have congealed into a solid, indigestible ball. How many knock down blows can I handle in one day? I feel so sick I want to vomit, and the overwhelming urge to run again overtakes me. I drop Rachel's phone on top of the pizza box and dash inside my house. My friends all race after me, but I lock myself in the bathroom with Snowy, who clings to my side.

Through the door I hear Rachel shout, "Mrs. Evans! We have an emergency!"

I listen as she and Stef explain what happened, and my mother makes a terrible gasping sound. I decide that I might as well do something useful while I'm in the bathroom, so I turn on the shower. I never had the chance to clean up after my fourteen-mile excursion.

As I peel back the shower curtain, there's pounding on the door and my mother yells, "Blair, honey, you need to come out and talk about this. We'll all help you get through this together. You're not alone. We all love you, and we'll help you deal with this. Please come out!"

I step under the hard spray and wish I could stay here forever. The powerful hot streams are tranquilizing, slicing the hard edges off my rage and humiliation. As they wash over me, they block out the entire world. I don't want to see anyone, talk to anyone, or listen to anyone. What is there to say? My life is over. Ruined beyond repair.

When the pounding on the bathroom door intensifies, I realize that my dad must've come home. I can feel the tub floor shake under my feet.

"Blair, you've got two seconds or I'm kicking in the door!" he hollers over the water. "One, t—"

I pull back the curtain and yell, "Can't I take a shower in peace?"

I keep my head out of the water so I don't miss his

response, but I hear my mom ask, "Do you really think she's taking a shower?"

My father answers, "I don't know, but if she doesn't come out in the next three minutes, I'm going in."

I finish in two. The last thing I need is my dad joining me in the shower.

As soon as the water stops my mother shouts, "Blair! Are you okay?"

"Yes, I'm wonderful!" I bellow, wrapping myself in an extra-large bath sheet in case my dad doesn't wait for minute three.

My sarcastic reply must have satisfied them that I'm okay because it grows quiet. I inch open the bathroom door and poke my head out to discover nobody's there. I tiptoe down the hall and sneak a peek around the corner into the dining room. My dad has his laptop set up on the long cherrywood table, and my mom and friends are crowded around him. By the way they're all grimacing, they must be viewing the malicious Instagram posts.

Anger flashes across my mother's eyes as she says, "Tell me how some sicko can put up all this vicious stuff and get away with it, and Blair gets arrested for doing nothing? It's not quite fair, is it?"

My father is seething too. I can tell by the way he's scrunching his face and gritting his teeth that he's barely holding it together. "Any idea who did this?" he asks.

My band of friends eye each other uneasily, but Rachel speaks up. "We all know. There's this one girl whose queen of the school—literally—and she hates Blair. David used to be her boyfriend. She's always been mean to Blair, and this is definitely something she would do...especially now."

My dad exhales deeply as he turns to face my friends. "Any way to prove that? I have no idea how this Instagram thing works."

Kayla, our computer guru, shakes her head. "I doubt it. Anyone can create an Instagram account anytime, anywhere." She pauses a moment, then adds, "Unless maybe you could somehow track their IP address."

My mom cuts in, "How would we do that?"

Kayla shrugs. "I don't know. I guess you'd ask the Instagram people or go to the police."

My dad rubs his temples and says, "I started and ended the day meeting with a prosecutor, but I guess I'm not done. Excuse me, ladies."

As he rises with his laptop, I scoot back down the hall to my bedroom to get dressed, Snowy tagging at my heels.

It doesn't take too long before my mother is banging on the door to my room. "Honey, are you all right?"

"Yeah!" I wail. "I'm having the best day ever!"

DAVID

◆

CHAPTER 22

Frankie

D avid camped out at his kitchen table, tethered to the wall-mounted Trimline phone—the last non-cellular telephone in the house. Without access to any other electronics, this had become his lifeline. Everybody he knew was calling except for the one person he needed to talk to most.

As she'd promised, his mom checked in at five-thirty on the dot. "Did you get in touch with Blair?"

"No, she still won't talk to me." It was the same conversation they'd already had twice that day. "I can't exactly blame her. Look at all the trouble I've gotten her into."

"You do realize that the more time that goes by, the worse she's going to think of you?"

"Believe me, I know. That's why I need to tell her the truth—that I didn't do this—but I can't tell her if she won't get on the phone."

His mother sighed. "I know you've tried her home phone, but did you try her friends?"

"Yeah, of course. And I've asked my friends to reach out to her too."

"Well, hopefully she'll come around soon."

He pushed out a long breath. "I doubt that—not if I can't talk to her. Why don't you just let me go over there and see her for myself? This is ridiculous—that I'm stuck here."

"Uh, excuse me, darling, but didn't I just hire an outrageously expensive lawyer for you this morning and post a whopping bail? You're not going anywhere today."

"Well, tell me what I'm supposed to do while I'm stuck at home? I've taken care of Lady Gaga, lifted weights, detailed my car—even replaced the bulbs that blew out near the garage door."

"You can do your college applications."

He snorted so loud the puppy's head shot up from her hard sleep under the kitchen table. "Gee, thanks Mom. Why didn't I think of that? I can write my essays on how I just got arrested, and put, 'Do you allow criminals at your university? I hope so, because I'm an excellent candidate. Won't you please overlook my prison record and take note of all my other accomplishments?' That'll go over big."

"Didn't you hear your lawyer this morning? He said that your arrest won't go on your high schoool transcripts. Colleges will only be notified if you get a conviction. So as of now, your hockey scholarships still stand, and you have to complete your applications just like everyone else."

"Yeah, just like everyone else," he mimicked, twisting his lips. "Has everyone else had their cell phones, tablets, and computers confiscated? What am I supposed to do, drag up your ancient typewriter from the basement?"

"David, I don't need your attitude. Believe me, this hasn't exactly been a good day for me either. Why don't you go out and take a walk?"

He squeezed his eyes closed. "Sure, a walk. Why not?"

Five minutes later he and Lady Gaga rounded the corner of his block, the puppy flapping her tail like a metronome, thrilled to be out on an adventure with new sights and smells. He, on the other hand, stumbled along with a vacant expression, lost in his thoughts.

His mind kept going back to the date the prosecutor had said the crime was committed: August 24th. There was only one person who had access to his phone that Saturday, and that was Frankie. His old friend had taken the train up from Virginia to hang out for a couple of days before school started, but he'd forgotten his phone charger and constantly needed to borrow David's cell phone. He had to have been the one who'd sent out Blair's picture.

But David didn't want to mention Frankie's involvement until he had a chance to speak to him. All he told the police and his mother was that he never transmitted Blair's photo. Yes, he did take it, and yes, it was on his phone, but it was a personal photo and he hadn't sent it to anyone. Of course, the prosecutor didn't believe him.

Since returning home from the arrest and arraignment, David had left at least a dozen messages for Frankie, but all had gone to voicemail. Whether Frankie was at football practice or out with friends, his elusiveness was getting frustrating.

It took until eleven-thirty that night for Frankie to return his calls. Despite David's frantic messages, Frankie sounded as calm and nonchalant as though they were planning a Sunday bike ride. "Hey bro, what's going on? You said you had an emergency?"

David craned his head around the kitchen wall to make sure no one was listening. "I do have an emergency!" he whispered, his tone desperate and strained. "But first you need to tell me something. Remember when you stayed here a couple of weeks ago and you kept using my phone?"

"Yeah, sure. So what?"

"Did you by any chance look at my photos?"

"I don't remember. Why?"

"Well, I had a picture in there of Blair when she was getting dressed—in her underwear. Did you see it?"

Frankie chuckled. "Oh yeah. *That* I remember! She was in this pink lacey thing. Great photo, man. You've got one sweet girlfriend."

"So you did see it?"

"What's the big deal if I saw it? She looked really hot."

David slipped into the pantry and pulled the door closed behind him. It was pitch black and cramped, but he needed the privacy. "Frankie, did you send that picture to anyone?"

Frankie barked out a laugh. "I may have. I really don't remember. I think I'd already polished off a six-pack by then."

David curled the phone cord around his wrist, trying to keep his cool. "Try and think back. If you sent it, who would you have sent it to?"

"Probably some random people in your contacts list. Why are you asking?"

"Because I got arrested!"

"*You what?*"

"You heard me. I got arrested! On the first morning back at school. Blair too. They put us in handcuffs, read us our rights, and took us down to the police station. My mother just spent the money she's been saving to fix our roof on a lawyer, and I'm facing five felony counts and thirty years in jail!"

"You're fucking kidding me bro, right?"

"I wish I was kidding! I've been charged with creation, possession, and distribution of child pornography, and endangering the welfare of minors."

"*Holy shit!*" Frankie screeched. "I can't believe it!"

"Well, believe it, because it happened and I need you to

fix it."

"*Me?*"

"Yes, *you!* You're the one who sent the picture, so you need to fess up."

"Whoa, you want me to get arrested too? What good would that do?"

"You won't get arrested if you say that it was an accident...that you meant to send another picture and you sent that one by mistake. Or you were trying to delete it and you hit "*send*" instead. I don't care what you say, you just need to tell them something!"

After a long, irritating silence, Frankie stated, "I can't do that."

David's breath hitched, panic surging up his spine. "What do you mean *you can't do that?* You're gonna let *me* take the heat for something *you* did? This will ruin my life!"

"Amigo, relax a minute. This won't ruin your life, you'll see. You're a hockey star. They won't let you to go to prison. You'll get out of this."

David yanked a box of rigatoni off the door rack, clamping the middle so hard the cardboard top popped open and sprayed dried pasta all over the tight space. He could feel a few ridged pieces land on the tops of his bare feet. "Are you saying you won't help me? You're gonna let me go down for this?"

"Hey," Frankie protested. "You're not exactly innocent here. You did take that picture." Then he paused for a moment and softened his voice. "Of course I want to help you. It's just that I can't get involved."

"*Involved?*" David repeated incredulously, struggling to keep his fists from going through the wall. "You're the one who sent it! How much more *involved* can you get?"

"Look," Frankie said in a hushed voice. "I'd help you out

if I could. You know I'm always there for you, bro, but I can't go anywhere near this thing." His voice dropped even lower. "Some shit happened that I never told you about, and if I get involved with this, I could go away for a long time."

David wanted to stretch his arms out to Virginia and strangle his friend. Instead he asked, "What kind of shit?"

Frankie blew out a loud breath. "I've been arrested four times and convicted twice. I can't get into any more trouble. I'm over eighteen now, and you know that whole three-strikes you're out thing. I could get life in prison."

David leaned against a waist-high stack of water bottles, raking his fingers through his short hair. He'd hoped talking to Frankie would straighten out his legal mess, but instead it was getting more complicated by the second. "What did you do?"

"If you really want to know...I shot out a couple of highway lights with an air gun, set off some firecrackers in school lockers, and had a DWI after midnight when I still had my provisional license. The locker thing was a harmless prank—to have a fire drill so we'd get out of a chem final—but some asshole called the bomb squad and turned it into a really big thing. It made the TV news that night. And I thought that one was bad until someone tipped them off that I grew my own pot and they searched my house and found my homegrown cannabis in the basement."

Frankie heaved a deep sigh. "I never wanted to tell you any of this, but I've spent most of the last year in juvie. I was kicked off the football team, and I'm in this special intervention program through the Richmond courts. When I'm not in school, I'm doing community service or chores at the juvie home. I only have one free weekend a month, which is when I came up to see you. My life totally sucks. *Now* do you understand why I can't get involved?"

David was speechless. If his parents had known about Frankie's delinquent history, they'd certainly kept quiet. His story sounded more like that of a poor inner-city street kid than a well-off suburban teen.

"Davey, you there?"

"Uh…yeah. I just can't believe you did all that. What the hell happened to you?"

"Swear to me you won't tell anyone I was the one who sent that picture," Frankie demanded. "I mean it! You'll destroy any chance I have of clearing my record and moving on. They told me the next time I did anything else, my ass would end up in jail—permanently."

David shook his head over and over, his despair multiplying ten-fold. "You can't put me in this spot. I don't know what to do now."

"Yes, you do. You take care of this one all by yourself. Look at everything I've been through and I survived. This is only one little thing, and it's really stupid, if you ask me. Clicking one little *send* key and they're treating you like a child pedophile? That's really dumb."

"It may be dumb to you, but they're accusing me and Blair of a whole bunch of felonies. This isn't fair, Frankie, and you know it! *You're* the one who hit that little *send* key, not me!"

"Don't do this to me, bro. Could you really live with yourself if you knew you put me in jail?"

David was so livid he braced his palms against a wooden shelf to keep from exploding. "So you're gonna put *me* in jail?"

"You're not going to jail—this is your first offense. You'll see—you'll get out of it. I won't."

"You think I'll get off just because it's my first offense? First time offenders convicted of producing child pornography can get a minimum of fifteen years!"

"But you didn't produce it."

"Taking the picture *is* producing it. And I found out it's illegal to even possess it. Just having it on my phone is a crime."

"Damn, those laws really suck."

"Ya think?"

David suddenly couldn't breathe, the walls of the tiny space closing in, lines of sweat streaking down the center of his back. "I gotta go," he said, shoving the pantry door open.

"Do the right thing, bro!" Frankie implored.

David ended the call, stepping out of the pantry and into his mother's shadow.

CHAPTER 23

School?

I watch the last light in my neighborhood go out at 12:10 a.m., but I'm not the least bit tired. There are so many unsettling thoughts swimming through my head that sleep is out of the question.

I decide to give myself a midnight manicure. In trying to cope with my arrest, the betrayal of my boyfriend, and the wicked Instagram account, I've completely destroyed my nails. They're nothing but chewed-up stubs—ragged reminders of my miserable existence. I sit at my desk and rip open a do-it-yourself nail tips kit Carrie had given me for my last birthday. Running my gaze over several rows of brightly colored tips, the iridescent purple ones catch my eye.

As I dot a thick white glob of glue onto my left thumbnail, my dad pokes his head into my room. "Baby, you need to try to get some sleep. I know this has been a grueling day, but if you stay up any later, you'll never be able to get up for school."

I whirl around and glare at him. "*School?* I'm not going to school ever again!" Then I spin back to my nail kit.

My mom must've been right behind him because in a couple of seconds they're both in my room, plopping themselves on my bed. Snowy is already there, sprawled across the covers like a king, his large black head resting regally on my pillow.

"You need to go to school," my mom says, her tone strong and emphatic. "This whole thing will resolve itself before you know it, and in the meantime, you can't miss your classes. You need to go right back there with your head held high and ignore whatever anyone says. You know you didn't do anything wrong."

My dad picks up where she left off, speaking in the persuasive, scholarly voice he uses when he tries to reason with me. "You've worked too hard and come too far to quit. Whether you decide on medicine or engineering, you've got an incredibly bright future ahead of you, and you can't just throw it all away. You're way too smart for that."

I twist my neck until I connect eyes with both of them. "Excuse me, but did you not see that fake Instagram account? The entire school—all my teachers, every kid—saw me get arrested this morning. And if they missed it in person, then I'm sure they saw it a thousand times on Snapchat or Twitter. I'm not going back there. *Ever!*"

It's my mother's turn again, and she doesn't back down. "The people who put up that page are not the kind of kids you want to associate with anyway, so just ignore them. And your teachers know you—they know you wouldn't do anything illegal. I'm sure they feel terrible about what happened, so don't worry about them."

I shake my head. "I just spent the last three years ignoring all the bad kids and the horrible things they've said. This year I had David, so I thought finally...finally things would be different. The nasty people who've made my life a living hell would leave me alone now, and I could go to school without hating every minute. But then look what happened? I couldn't even get through homeroom. Not five lousy minutes of peace. And you want me to go back there?" I swing my head from side to side. "Never."

I don't tell my mother or father about what Chloe Esposito's boyfriend did to her, but it's always at the front of my thoughts. That poor girl. If there were sex videos made of me, I'd have plastic surgery and hide in another continent.

My parents exchange a worried look. I guess they weren't expecting me to be so difficult.

"We had no idea what was going on in your school until this afternoon, when we saw that phony Instagram page and your friends filled us in on that ridiculous Class System and those vicious girls," my dad says. "You should have told us about this your freshman year—we could've stopped it before it got so out of hand."

"Oh, please!" I cry. "What could you have done? Sent the *nice police* after them?"

"Honey," my mom breaks in. "These girls are bullies, and there are policies against the exact kinds of behavior they've been exhibiting. They're no better than street gangs who use their numbers and power to intimidate people. They need to be stopped."

My chest heaves up and down. "And who is going to stop them? You?"

"We'll certainly try," says my dad. "No one should be subjected to their antics. Your school board is required to provide a safe environment for you to learn, and it's readily apparent that they've failed. They need to fix that."

"But what do you expect them to do?" I howl. My parents are being naive in their oversimplification of the problem, and I don't know how to make them fully grasp the reality of popularity politics at Westberry. I decide to start with the basics. "The school board can't magically make these girls unpopular and tell kids to stop idolizing them. David told me that when he went out with Krystal, she had over ten thousand followers on Instagram. I've never figured out why, but people worship her."

"There are still adults in the building," my mom interjects.

"They could control this girl."

I let out a pitiful laugh, which makes Snowy pop one black eye open and stare at me. "Are you kidding? The teachers *love* her! She knows exactly how to play them—she oozes charm in front of them. She's always sucking up and flirting. And the principal thinks she's the most amazing person in the entire school because she's the class president *and* the editor-in-chief of the yearbook. And have you forgotten that her father is Westberry's friggin' technology director, not to mention the varsity ice hockey coach who just came off an undefeated season?"

My father clears his throat before responding. "Look, it doesn't matter how much they like her. If she's been doing all these horrible things, she needs to be stopped and she needs to be punished. And if we can link her or one of her Things— as you call them—to this fake profile, then all the rest will fall into place."

I compress my lips. "I'm not holding my breath."

"Just so you know," my dad continues. "I've already contacted the Instagram Help Center and requested that they delete that profile and assist us in tracking the IP address of the fake account holder."

"How long will that take?" I ask with a skeptical tone. It's not that I'm ungrateful, but things haven't exactly been going my way lately.

"I don't know," my dad admits. "That's why I asked one of my paralegals, Aryana, whose an absolute whiz on computers, to help us out. She told me it'll be no problem for her to find the IP address of the original sender and to use an online tool to perform a location lookup. She should have an answer for us by tomorrow."

I nod and turn back to my nail kit. I place the last tip on my left pinky and admire my handiwork. At least one hand looks presentable now. I start to dab glue on my right thumb when I realize it's too quiet. My parents are obviously waiting for me to say something. I know it's not going to be what they want to hear, but I summarize my thoughts for them. "I'm still not going to school. Everyone saw me get arrested, and David made a total fool out of me. I'm never going back there."

My mom releases a long, drawn-out sigh. "I'm not entirely sure what's going on with David, but you should know that he called several times tonight and left messages apologizing over and over, saying that he didn't send anyone that picture."

I slam down the tube of nail glue and whirl back around. "Then who did? A ghost?"

She frowns. "In one of his messages he said he couldn't tell you who sent it, but he wanted you to know it wasn't him."

"He's such a liar!" I bellow. "I can't even stand listening to this!" The uncontrollable rage that flared up during the day overtakes me again, and I vault from my chair, storm out of my bedroom, and stomp down the hall. Snowy comes flying after me, his doggy toenails scraping against the wood floor as he scurries to my side.

From down the hall I hear my dad say to my mom in his deep lawyerly voice, "She's right, you know. He's trying to save his own hide, but he's a bad liar and we're going to prove that."

DAVID

◆

CHAPTER 24

The Dilemma

David stood on the edge of his mother's shadow, one hand still clutching the pantry doorknob. He cleared his throat while averting his eyes. "Um...did you hear anything I said?"

She planted her palms on her hips. "Every word."

He blanched the same porcelain white as the ceramic kitchen tile. His secret was out. Part of him was mortified, but a bigger part surged with relief. It had been so hard keeping the truth from his mother, watching her patient, loving eyes flood with disappointment every time he'd turn away or evade her questions. "So, do you believe me now that it wasn't me who sent that picture?"

She nodded. "I've always believed you. I couldn't fathom that you'd do that to your own girlfriend, and I think I know you well enough to tell when you're lying. I just didn't know who you were protecting...until now."

"Well, now that you know, what do you think I should do? Frankie says if I tell on him, he'll go to jail for life because he has all these other arrests and two convictions."

His mom's eyebrows shot up. "Two convictions? For what?"

David released the doorknob and shuffled over to a kitchen

chair. He sank down onto the floral seat cushion, wishing he were someone else. No one in particular—just an ordinary high school senior with ordinary problems.

His mother filled a tall mug with boiling water, dropped in an herbal tea bag, and slid a chair close to his. She stirred in two teaspoons of raw honey as she waited, alternating her gaze between her steeping tea and her pensive son.

It was difficult for David to start, but once he got going, the truth poured out of him like rushing water. He couldn't talk fast enough, filling her in on everything. She listened intently, nodding at first, then shaking her head and cringing at the deviant acts of her son's closest childhood friend.

"I knew Frankie would have trouble adjusting to a new school in the south, but it sounds like he went off the deep end." The edges of her mouth curved downward into a deep scowl as she stirred her tea, cinnamon-apple steam swirling between them. "I can't believe this is the same kid who used to hide behind his mother when he was young. He was so quiet and shy."

David half smiled. "Yeah, I remember that."

"So, what are you going to do, keep protecting Frankie or take care of yourself?"

He absently fingered the pile of paper napkins in their clear acrylic holder, flipping up the corners like he was shuffling a deck of cards. "I don't know what to do. It's not fair for me to take the blame for something I didn't do, but how do I rat him out knowing he'll go right to jail?"

His mom pushed her mug aside and shifted forward until her face was only inches from his. Her eyes narrowed into the critical, probing look he hated. "You wouldn't be ratting him out. You'd be telling the truth."

David twisted his lips as he gripped the armrests of his chair. "I'd be throwing him under the bus, and you know it!

Could you do that to your best friend?"

His mother blinked hard and exhaled, worry lines overtaking her pale skin. "I agree you're in a difficult predicament, but you have to think of your own future too, not just his. Do you really think schools are going to give you scholarships if you've got a criminal record? You've worked too hard for too long to give up your dreams."

"I know," he mumbled, every feature on his face crumbling.

"And without those scholarships there's no way I can pay for you. I'm barely making it now—the child support from your father doesn't go very far."

He nodded. "Every time I talk to Dad, he says the same thing, 'Thank God you're so athletic or I don't know how you'd go to college.'"

His mom gazed at him with such intensity it made him shudder. "You need to think long and hard about this. If you end up in jail, you won't be going to college at all."

David slumped against the cane backing of his chair, the weight of the world making him feel far older than his seventeen years. "I lose no matter what I do."

His mother's eyes watered as she watched her son try to sort through a tidal wave of emotions that no child should ever have to bear. "I don't envy you right now, but I'll give you some time to make the right decision." She tousled his short spiky hair. "Not too much time, though. I'm not going to let you go down for somebody else."

He pouted like he did as a small toddler, his head flopping over to the side. "I wish I wasn't me."

She kissed him on the cheek. "No matter what happens, I'll always love you."

CHAPTER 25

An Unexpected Visitor

"**O**h my God!"

I pull back my sleep-tangled mess of red curls and stare in horror at the bathroom mirror. It's the day after my arrest and I can't believe what I'm seeing. I've woken up looking like I have a terrible case of chicken pox. My smooth, clear skin has disappeared and been replaced by multiple alien lifeforms. My face has literally exploded into the surface of Mars, with unsightly red mounds of all shapes and sizes, and even a juicy cold sore sprouting across my top lip. I gob on mountains of cover-up, but know I'm going to have to buy out the entire acne aisle at the drugstore before I can be seen in public.

Thank God my parents decided to let me stay home because I think I'd rather be dead than let anyone see me like this. I was hoping today would be better—I mean, how much more bad stuff can I take?—but one look in the mirror reaffirms that I'm deep in my nightmare. The incredible stress I feel on the inside is fully visible on the outside.

At least I'm not alone. My mom took the day off from work—purportedly to keep me company, but I suspect it's to make sure I don't do anything stupid like jump off a bridge or slit my wrists. Teen suicides are constantly in the paper, and now that I've hit rock bottom, she probably thinks I'm a likely candidate.

The fact is, I'm not the least bit suicidal, but I do have a strong urge to run away. Far, far away. I'm giving serious thought to heading out west, getting a job at a ski resort, and completing high school online. Basically, starting a whole new life someplace else where no one has ever heard of Blair the Mare, Class C Loser.

I do love to sleep late, but being home while my friends are all at school is not so fun. There's nothing for me to do, nothing I want to watch on TV, and nothing else I can think about other than my total humiliation, the indignity of my arrest, and the dreadful Instagram account. And, of course, my backstabbing ex-boyfriend. I try watching a movie, then reading a book, but I can't concentrate on anything. My piano sits dormant because the last thing I feel like doing is practicing, and today is certainly not the day to start. My mom suggests going to the animal shelter, but I can't even force myself to go there.

When the house phone rings at 11:30 a.m., I pounce on it. "Hi, Dad. Did Aryana find the IP address?"

"Yes, baby, she did, but unfortunately it's not going to help us."

My hopes are instantly crushed. "Why not?"

"Because when she went to track it, she found that it's an unapproved IP address."

"What does that mean?"

"It means that whoever created the fake account must've hacked in or done something I don't fully understand. We can't tell you exactly how they did it, but this IP address isn't going to help us."

I throw myself on the couch, kicking the pillows with my heels. Damn it! This was my shot at getting the Ice Queen, and now it's gone. "Isn't there anything the Instagram administrator can do?"

My dad harrumphs. "I can't even get a response back from them, so I did something I really didn't want to have to do—I filed a complaint with the police so they can investigate this."

My heart skips a beat at the mere mention of police. I grumble, "Oh no."

"Oh yes. Let them do something useful instead of arresting innocent kids. Let them go find the real culprits. I talked to Uncle Marv about this, and he said that in this state it's a crime to impersonate someone else for the purpose of benefiting yourself or injuring another. I think this fake Instagram account might fit into that identity theft category."

I think about this for a moment. "Well, it won't matter what kind of crime it is if we can't find out who did it. Did the police say whether they could help us since the IP address is unapproved?"

"All they said is that they'll investigate."

The frustration in my father's voice isn't lost on me. He's trying not to say what we're both thinking: This will be another dead end.

"Thanks for trying, Dad, but the police will be about as useful here as they were in trying to find out who forwarded my picture to them in the first place."

"That's not fair, baby. Whoever sent that picture used one of those pre-paid burner phones you buy at Walmart— there's no way the police could track them down."

I heave a sigh of exasperation. "Since the damage is already done, it really doesn't matter anyway, does it?"

"Stop it, baby. That Instagram page was only up for a few hours, so it wasn't as bad as you're imagining."

"No, it was worse."

"Blair—"

"I'm gonna go for a run now, Dad. I'll talk to you later."

"Just do me a favor and stay close to home this time."

I hang up and set out to find my sneakers. I don't really want to run again, but I don't know how else to deal with all the anger and frustration that's roiling inside me. As I pass through the entry foyer, I catch a glimpse of the top of someone's head over the front bushes. Seconds later the doorbell rings.

"Who is it?" I call out.

"It's David."

I freeze. I never would've answered the door had I thought it might be him, but now it's too late to pretend I'm not home. "What do you want?"

"I need to talk to you."

The rage that I've been struggling to contain fires back up, and my fingers ball into fists. "Well, I don't want to talk to *you*."

He raps his knuckles against the wooden panels. "Can you please just open the door? I really need to talk to you."

"No!"

"I'm not leaving until you open this door." He knocks and rings the bell at the same time, non-stop. Snowy joins in the commotion, his loud bark mixing with the ringing and pounding.

"Honey!" my mom shouts from her office down the hall. "Can you get the door already?"

I steady myself and yank the door open. I know my face is a total disaster, but I guess it doesn't really matter at this point. I won't be seeing him again after today.

As I step outside, Snowy—who's been extraordinarily clingy to me the last two days—stays glued to my side, protecting me in his own special way.

David stares at me before speaking, his chocolate-brown eyes ringed with dark purple shadows. He seems to have gotten less sleep than I have.

"I can't even begin to tell you how sorry I am about this whole thing," he says, stepping forward. "I wish I could turn back time and reverse everything, but I can't, so I'm going to do whatever I can to make this up to you."

"Make this up to me?" I cry. "I was arrested, handcuffed, and fingerprinted on the first day of school, and now I'm facing thirty years in prison! How are you going to make that up to me?"

"Because if anyone's going to jail, it'll be me—not you. I won't let that happen. Not when it's all my fault. I should've erased that damn picture when you asked me to."

"*Hello?*" I cut in. "Aren't you forgetting the part about texting it to everyone you know? Sending it to the police?"

David jerks his head back like I've slapped him. "I never did that…that wasn't me. And I certainly didn't send it to the police. Why would I do that?"

I have no patience for his pathetic lies. "If you didn't send it, then who did?"

"I don't know who sent it to the police, but I do know who texted it from my phone. You have to believe me when I tell you it wasn't me. I would never do that."

My eyes burn into his. "So who was it?"

He dips his chin. "I can't tell you."

"That's because it's her!" I bellow. "Isn't it? You gave the Ice Bitch your phone to ruin my life!"

His head snaps back up. "It wasn't her. And *my* life is ruined too!"

I dig my fingertips into my waist and jut my face forward until it's only centimeters from his. "If it wasn't her, then who was it? You better come up with a really good lie, because the police are going to have to believe it too!"

"I'm not lying to you. It wasn't Krystal."

"Then who was it?" I repeat, my cheeks searing hot.

"Who?"

My eyes dare him to answer. He turns away, toward the shrubbery, as though the rhododendrons can help him. When he spins back, his shoulders are drooped and he looks utterly defeated, his entire body sagging like a wilted flower. "I can't tell you."

"Because it was her!" I roar, thick tears washing over my cheekbones. "I know it was! You've been together this whole time, and you just used me—pretended to care—so you could set me up!" I'm so choked up I can hardly breathe. "The two of you humiliated me—ruined my life—"

"No!" David yells, shaking his head, his arms reaching for me.

I back away in horror, like he's trying to kill me.

"I would never do that!" he wails, his face collapsing, caving in on itself.

I can't bear to see him anymore or hear more of his lies. I run into my house, screaming, "I hate you! I hate you!"

I slam the door and watch through the glass sidelight as he sinks down onto the front stoop and cries harder than I ever thought a guy could cry.

CHAPTER 26

Expelled

Early in the evening another ring of the doorbell brings more disheartening news. One look at Uncle Marv's troubled features as he steps into the living room tells me my problems aren't going away anytime soon. My father hands him some type of mixed drink as they settle into a pair of chestnut-colored leather recliners by the fireplace. My mother and I opt for the sofa.

As Uncle Marv stirs his cocktail, the heavy silence in the room becomes unbearable. "Stop fidgeting," my mom instructs.

I sit on my hands so I don't rip off my fake nails, but I can't stop tapping my feet. Snowy crawls out from under the baby grand piano near the rear sliding glass door and saunters over, stretching his long, black curly-haired body over my toes. You know your life has hit an all-time low when you're envious of your dog. He thumps his powerful curved tail against the hardwood floor, probably thinking about who is going to walk him next or whether we got him any new treats. I'd trade places with him in a heartbeat.

When Uncle Marv stops swirling his drink and finally speaks, he delivers the latest blow to my existence. "The president of the Board of Education called an emergency meeting that convened late this afternoon. I was just informed of the result."

"A meeting about Blair?" my mother asks, the corner of her right eye twitching.

"And David," Uncle Marv adds. "They're obviously the hot topic in the news right now, and all the buzz hasn't sat very well with the Board of Ed folks."

"What are you saying?" my dad presses.

Uncle Marv is slow to answer. He twirls his white mustache, smooths out his thick beard, then clears his throat. "I'm saying that they caved from all the pressure from loud, crazy parents and scared school administrators." He turns toward me. "They voted not to allow you and David back into the high school. You've been expelled."

"*What?*" my father cries.

"*Expelled?*" I stare at Uncle Marv with incredulity, like there's nothing more outrageous he could have possibly said.

My mom can't stop shaking her head. She leans forward to study Uncle Marv's face, then says, "You're not joking, are you?"

My dad is on his feet, towering over Uncle Marv. "What happened to innocent until proven guilty? They've only been charged, not convicted, for Chrissake! There's no basis for expulsion!"

My poor mom looks even more distraught than she did at police headquarters, both eyelids fluttering rapidly, her nose twitching nonstop. "We can't let them get away with this, Marv."

My lawyer rises, places his glass on the fireplace mantel, and faces my distressed family. "I don't intend to let them get away with it. This is a travesty of justice, and I have one of my partners working on a motion for injunctive relief right now."

"Injunctive relief?" I repeat. "What's that?"

Uncle Marv switches to plain English. "We're going to try to get an injunction so the Board of Ed can't expel you. In other words, we're going to ask the court for an order to let you back into school right now, because otherwise their action will cause you immediate harm and result in a gross injustice. Look at it this way: If your neighbor wanted to chop down your trees to make their driveway bigger, you'd run to court to get a restraining order to stop them, right?"

I nod.

"Well, that's a type of injunctive relief. If the court waits too long to make a decision and doesn't give you an injunction against your neighbor right away, then it will be too late— your trees will be gone forever. In this situation with the Board of Ed, we need the court to order them to overturn the expulsion immediately, because every day you miss from school is gone forever and will cause you permanent, irreparable harm."

"Uncle Marv is doing it this way," my father explains, "because if we brought a regular lawsuit against them to get you back into school, by the time the lawsuit was resolved, your senior year would be over. But the court will decide a preliminary injunction right away."

My mom folds her arms and narrows her eyes at Uncle Marv. "Can a school expel a child because of something that happened off school grounds? And wasn't this picture taken and sent before school even started this year?"

Uncle Marv grins. "Exactly. And that's only *one* of the grounds we have to fight this. The major thing we have going for us is that there's no current legislation in this state that allows public schools to expel students for sexting. Without any law allowing the Board of Ed to expel these kids, the Board has hung itself out there with no legal legs to stand on. I personally can't see the court letting them get away with this, but that's just my opinion. We have to see what happens."

"How soon can you file the papers?" my dad asks.

"I'm going to hand-deliver them myself tomorrow morning. Then hopefully we'll hear something by the end of the week."

I push my breath out in a big sigh. "I wasn't planning on going back to school anyway, but that was *my* choice. I can't believe they expelled me! I've only seen kids get suspended, not expelled."

Uncle Marv perches himself on the arm of the sofa to talk to me face-to-face. I get a whiff of his sandalwood cologne that I can remember since I was a baby. "Sweetie, there's something else I need to explain to you so you understand why I'm doing it."

"Okay," I mumble, afraid of what's coming next. I want my old Uncle Marv back. The one who cracks corny jokes and teaches me magic tricks. Not this one.

"I want to call David's lawyer and ask him if he'd like to be included in our motion for injunctive relief. My firm is doing the legal work anyway, and strategically I think it would be a good idea to work together as much as we can. I'd like to keep the lines of communication open between us, and I think this would be a good way to do that—and it's no skin off my back."

I furrow my brow. "Why do you need to communicate with them? He's the one who did this to me."

"Yes, he did, but as your attorney I need to look at the big picture. If there comes a point in time when the prosecutor's office is making him a deal or trying to play his side against ours, I want to know about it. That can only happen if we're on good terms. And offering to include him in these papers is an excellent way to hold out an olive branch early on."

I glance over at my mom and dad to gauge their reactions. Both are nodding in synch like two bobbleheads.

I shrug, knowing that I can't allow my personal animosity toward David to get in the way of my legal defense. "Do whatever you need to do."

CHAPTER 27

The New Dog

The following morning, I drag myself to the animal shelter. My mom convinced me that staying at home would only make me feel worse, and I know she's right. I always feel better when I help my furry little friends, feeding them, taking them for long walks, tossing them balls and sticks.

Of course, I really don't want to answer any questions about my school expulsion or legal problems, and thankfully, I don't have to. There are only a couple of older ladies at the front counter who glance up from their paperwork as I walk in. One comments, "Didn't school start already?"

I smile and say, "It did, but high school seniors can take community service days to fulfill college application requirements."

They buy it and I slip into the back.

I haven't been here for over a week and see that we're flooded with new dogs—mostly puppies—a few adult mixed breeds, and an older German Shepherd. I spend an hour with the puppies, getting them socialized and freshening up their cages. Six of them haven't been named yet, so I run through a mental list of rock stars, movie stars, and famous athletes, searching for a good fit. I'd gotten lucky a few weeks ago with Judge and Jeter for a pair of six-year-old pit bull mixes that were rescued from North Carolina, but I can't think of a group of six sports stars.

Since I'd stayed up ridiculously late last night after

Uncle Marv left binge watching *Friends* re-runs, the show's characters are fresh in my mind. I settle on Ross, Rachel, Monica, Chandler, Phoebe, and Joey, making a sign that says, "Please adopt in pairs." Hopefully, that will work to move them out quickly.

Next, I move on to the new adult dogs, Cosmo, Lola, and Max. I read their charts to make sure they're friendly before greeting them. There's limited information on the German Shepherd, Henry, since he arrived the day before, so I don't know enough about his temperament to take him out with the others. I leash up the three mixed breeds and usher them on a brisk group walk.

When I return, I give them all fresh water, and they happily collapse, grateful that someone helped them to escape confinement, even for a little while. I'm not sure if anyone gave them treats yet today, so I slip them each a few.

I shift over to the German Shepherd. His chart reads: "Name: Henry. Age: 11 years. Sex: Male. Spade/Neutered: Yes. Breed: Purebred German Shepherd. Known illnesses/ medical conditions: None. History: Owners both became ill and died within two months of each other. None of their children want the dog. They say Henry loves people but can be aggressive with certain breeds, especially smaller dogs. Current on all vaccines."

Henry has been watching me closely while I read his chart, arching his head up and locking onto my face. He's a beauty: mostly tan with exquisite black markings, and a long, glossy coat that's wavy at the tips. As stunning as he is, what strikes me is the intelligence in his big, light brown eyes—they're bright and insightful. I'd swear he's waiting for me to explain to him why he's here. The only other dog I've known that gave me such a strong feeling like this was my grandparent's dog Vonnegut.

I take Henry on an extra long walk and spend the rest of the morning grooming and playing with him. He's so appreciative he keeps licking my hands and face and wags his large, fluffy tail non-stop. It's clear that he's been very well trained and well loved. He knows all basic commands, a host of tricks, and is super affectionate. I imagine he's always had premium dog food and treats, as he's surprisingly energetic and spry for an eleven-year-old.

"It's so sad when a dog like that ends up here," I hear my supervisor say as she strolls by pushing a cart full of pet food and supplies.

Caroline is a middle-aged widow with the biggest heart of anyone I've ever met. After her husband died at a young age, she devoted her life to helping shelter animals. Almost every week she takes long road trips to kill-shelters all over the country to rescue her fur babies, as she calls them.

I bob my head. "He's so beautiful, though. I think he'll find a home really quick."

Her short, dark hair shakes from side to side. "Not at his age. No one's going to want a dog that old."

I don't want to hear that. "But he doesn't act old and there's nothing wrong with him. He's healthy, smart, and full of energy...someone can instantly have the perfect dog."

A doleful smile breaks over her face. "If only people thought the way you do, but they don't. They'll look at his life expectancy, which is only a couple more years, at best, and pass him right by."

I know the answer to the question that pops into my head, but I ask it anyway. "Can we make him a little younger?"

"You know we can't do that."

"What if we change his name to something that older

people would want, like Elvis or Elton John?"

She purses her lips and blinks at me. "You can't change the name of a dog at this age. And I don't even think it would help. The reality is that older dogs have a greater likelihood of getting sick and needing more care and expensive medications. Just like people."

My eyes slide back and forth between Caroline and Henry. Coming here was supposed to make me feel better and distract me from my own problems, but hearing the hopelessness in her voice cuts right through me, drawing out my own misery. I feel the blood drain from my face.

I hand her Henry's leash and clutch the top of one of the giant dog food bags in her cart to keep my balance.

"Are you okay?" she asks, her features heavy with concern.

"I just need some water, that's all."

She races off to get me a cold bottle, then escorts me outside and insists that she drive me home. I accept the ride, but rest my head against the seatback and stay quiet the entire trip. Caroline is the one person at the shelter I could confide in, but everything that's happened to me is still too fresh and raw. I'm not ready to talk about it yet—I need more time to process it all.

Of course, if I knew what was in store for me at home that afternoon, I would've stayed at the shelter.

CHAPTER 28

Splenda

L ater that same day, not fifteen minutes after the end-of-school bell rings at Westberry High, my house is graced with a visit from Splenda and her well-meaning mother. The news of my expulsion must've been too irresistible for my artificial friend, sending her whizzing home from school to grab her mother and head straight to my doorstep.

I hear her voice from my bedroom window as she and Mrs. Levine approach the front door. I'm firing off instructions to my mom before they press the doorbell. "Get rid of them fast! Don't tell them anything! Say I'm not here!"

I bound down the basement steps, purposefully leaving the basement door open a crack to eavesdrop. It's only a few seconds before my mother invites the Levine ladies into the entry foyer. From where I'm stationed, I can hear everything.

"Alyssa called me from school and told me what happened," Mrs. Levine says, sounding truly sympathetic. "I am so, so sorry. It's unbelievable how they could do that to a student like Blair. I wanted to tell you how shocked and appalled I am."

"Thank you," my mom responds. "We're pretty shocked and appalled ourselves."

"I didn't know what to do, so I baked this for Blair— for all of you. I know how much she loves my brownies, so I thought this might make her feel better."

"Oh, thank you so much," my mom says. "That was really

thoughtful of you."

"Is she here?" Splenda asks.

What nerve! If I was at school, you would've totally ignored me, you witch. Now that I'm expelled, you come to my house to gloat!

My mom doesn't miss a beat. "She's taking a nap. I'll be sure to tell her you stopped by."

Thank you, Mom!

Splenda is in full phony form. I may not be able to see her, but I can clearly picture the masquerade of concern on her face as she says, "I just wanted to tell her how bad I feel about what happened. Everybody does."

You are so full of shit!

"Well, thank you," my mom says, gracious as always. "It's nice to know she's got such good friends."

How does that saying go...with friends like you who needs enemies?

"Are Blair and David still together after this?" Splenda asks in her super sappy, I'm-so-phony-my-face-is-about-to-crack voice. "It has to be so hard for them right now."

Yes, the real reason you're here comes out. You're a nosy bitch fishing for gossip!

My mom fields the question perfectly. "Why don't you call her later or stop by again, and you girls can talk about all that stuff."

After the nasty Instagram ordeal, I finally came clean with my mom about Splenda and all the others who've been so rotten to me. Now that she's armed with the truth, she can safely suggest that Splenda call me, knowing it will never happen.

But Splenda doesn't want to leave without any gossip fodder. "Do you think their relationship can survive this? I mean, he sent around all those obscene pictures of her."

Again, my mom comes shining through. "I don't know where you're getting your information from, Alyssa, but you have to be very careful with rumors. They're almost never correct."

Splenda doesn't give up. "Well, I *saw* one of the pictures, and David *was* the one who sent it, so it's not a rumor."

My mom has learned from her attorney husband that in difficult situations it's always better to stay on the offensive and be the one asking the questions. "Which picture did you see?"

"I saw the one where Blair was posing in her underwear."

Posing? You bitch!

"How did you see that?"

"Uh...everyone's seen it."

"You said David sent around all these obscene pictures. How many are there?"

"Other kids said they saw a whole bunch of them."

"Which kids said that?"

"Well...uh...I don't remember exactly who. Just a whole bunch of people."

"Are those the same kids who created that malicious Instagram account of Blair?"

Splenda's voice drops a few octaves, from high soprano to low baritone. "Uh...I don't know what you're talking about, Mrs. Evans."

Some actress!

Now Mrs. Levine interjects. "What Instagram account? I haven't heard anything about an Instagram account."

"I'm asking Alyssa what she knows about it," my mom replies.

"Um...I don't know anything," Splenda sputters.

I'd like to take a picture of your wretched face right now and put it on Instagram!

"Well, maybe you can do me a favor and find out who was behind it. I would really appreciate your help," my mom says in her own syrupy-sweet voice.

"Um...uh, yeah, of course," Splenda responds. "Whatever I can do."

They exchange small talk a few more minutes before I hear my mom say, "Thanks for coming," and the door latch clicks.

As I climb the basement stairs, I yell out, "They're gone, right?"

My mom swings the door back and nods. "It's such a shame Alyssa is so different from her mother. It was more than obvious she was lying. When I asked her pointed questions, she was so uncomfortable she could barely talk."

I bob my head. "Now you see what I've been dealing with."

She smiles. "Not anymore. Once you know who your real friends are, you get rid of the trash."

I can't help but smile too. "Yeah, trash. A big pile of stinky trash."

DAVID

◆

CHAPTER 29

Seeds of Doubt

David dribbled, spun, then took a three-point jumper. Missed.

The ball hit the rim and bounced into the bushes.

He'd been shooting hoops by himself for two hours, desperately trying to pass the time while Westberry's varsity soccer team played their first home game of the season. Being expelled meant he was also banned from all extracurricular activities, and he was fairly certain he wouldn't be welcome if he showed up as a spectator. So here he was, relegated to his lonely driveway, practicing shots, layups, and rebounds by himself.

Since Blair couldn't go to the game either, it would've been a perfect night for them to go out together without worrying about bumping into anyone. Boys' soccer was really big at Westberry, and most of the student body was at the game. But she still wasn't talking to him and might never again.

He'd called Frankie every couple of hours and begged him to confess his role in the sexting fiasco, but his childhood friend always had the same answer: "Any punishment that you get will be a thousand times worse for me." And without Frankie coming forward, Blair would never know the truth and would never trust him.

He was so miserable he couldn't sit still. Besides skulking around feeling sorry for himself, he spent his days working out, playing with Lady Gaga, and doing menial tasks like mowing the lawn and staining the deck. He'd planned to take the SATs or ACTs one more time that fall, but the thought of studying made him even more depressed. How could he prepare for college when he'd been kicked out of high school?

This was all Frankie's fault, and as his mother kept saying, he was caught between a rock and a hard place. Nevertheless, she kept pushing him to go to the police and tell them what Frankie did. But if he did that then how could he live with himself? Not that he could live with himself anyway.

Just the thought of going to jail sent his insides into spasms. And if he could somehow stay out of prison but go to college with a criminal record, he was certain he'd lose his athletic scholarships. No matter how he sliced it, he couldn't win.

He checked his watch: 8:03 p.m. The game would be over within the next few minutes, and then his hockey friend Ricky would swing by to pick him up. He may not have been allowed on school property, but he could certainly go to postgame parties at private homes.

At 8:10 p.m. he heard the blare of a horn coming up the street.

"Hey, David," Ricky called from his souped-up Mustang. "You ready?"

David climbed into the shiny red convertible. "Game over?"

His friend frowned. "No, without you scoring we got totally crushed. I couldn't take it anymore and left before the end of the last quarter."

David was happy that his team needed him, but agitated that the reason he couldn't help them was because he was accused of something he didn't do.

"Mind if I stop for something to eat?" Ricky asked. "We've got some time to kill before the parties start."

"Sure," David said. "I'm kinda hungry too."

Ricky pulled into a drive-up burger place where the food was delivered by servers on roller blades. While they waited for their order, Ricky took the opportunity to fill David in on what his ex-girlfriend was up to.

"You know, Krystal has been so upset about what happened that she started a petition to get you back into school."

David spun toward Ricky. "*What?*"

"Yeah man, she and her friends are trying to get everybody in the school district to sign it. I think she said she's got over a thousand signatures so far, including teachers, and at tonight's game they were passing it around, trying to get a few hundred more."

Caught off guard, David mumbled, "That's really nice of her."

"It is," Ricky agreed. "And she's been saying really nice stuff about you too."

"She has?" This didn't sound like the same girl who'd broken up with him at the end of junior year and changed his Class status from A+ to C-.

"Yeah, she has. She's saying that the whole fight you had before the summer was a big mistake, and she never should have let you go." Ricky nudged his hockey teammate with his elbow. "She wants you back, man."

David stared out the windshield. Nothing in his life made sense anymore.

"You might want to get back with her. You know she

still cares about you. She wouldn't be going to all this trouble if she didn't."

Their sliders came, and David busied himself eating so he wouldn't have to talk. He'd really fallen for Blair this past summer and hadn't even considered getting back with Krystal. But now Blair was out of the picture, and, for whatever reason, Krystal was trying to help him.

Even more confusing were the things his lawyer was telling him, like: "Stay away from Blair; she's going to try to save her own hide at your expense. Anything you tell her, she'll use in her defense against you. She's no longer your girlfriend—she's as much an enemy to you as the prosecutor, even worse. She'll make a deal so you go to prison and she walks away...."

His brain was churning with far too many things right now. Adding Krystal back into the mix only made the hailstorm in his head worse.

Ricky stuffed the crumpled wrappers from their burgers into a paper bag and tried to restart the conversation. "So, what are you going to do, man? You gonna give Krystal another shot?"

David finished the last of his fries and thought about how to answer. "I really don't know what to do about anything right now. But I guess it couldn't hurt to talk to her."

DAVID

◆

CHAPTER 30

The Seduction

Later that evening David discovered that Krystal wanted to do way more than talk. By the time he and Ricky arrived at the second post-game party, she and her friends had changed into skimpy halter tops and were noticeably wasted. As soon as she saw David, she sprang out of her chair and leapt on him like a mountain lion latching onto its prey.

David gently pried her off. "Hey, we need to talk."

"Sure," she agreed.

They grabbed a couple of beers and headed out back onto a covered wooden porch. She pointed to a white wicker love seat near the house, but he steered her toward a far corner where they could speak in private.

After they settled into a pair of cream-colored mesh deck chairs, he began what he hoped wouldn't be too uncomfortable a conversation. "Krystal, it's really nice to see you again, but we haven't been together for months. Last I checked you broke up with me in front of half the school. You yelled that you hated me and dropped me to Class C. Now you're acting like nothing happened. What gives?"

Krystal placed her left hand on his forearm and gazed at him with an earnestness he hadn't expected. "That was a

huge mistake, breaking up with you. It's the biggest mistake
I ever made. I was really, really sorry about it all summer,
and I planned on getting back together with you when I got
back from camp." Her warm palm slid up his biceps, over his
shoulder, and onto his neck. She began stroking his hair, his
ear, his cheek.

"You know," she went on, "I've really missed you." Her
roving fingers dropped to his torso and ran up and down his
chest. Then, in barely an instant, they found their way to the
waistband of his shorts. "And I can tell you've missed me too.
What we had was—"

He snagged her wrist. "Krystal, listen to me. We can't
just go back to what we had before."

"Why not?"

"Because stuff happened."

"Oh, you mean *her?*"

"I mean a lot of things, and yes, *her.*"

"I heard you broke up."

David sighed. "Where'd you hear that?"

"From a lot of people. Don't tell me it's not true? After
what she did to you, you can't still be with her?"

"What do you mean, 'what she did to me'?"

"She got you arrested! How much worse can you get
than *that?*"

"Blair didn't get me arrested. That's not what happened."

"Well, that's what I heard." There was a slight slur to
her words as she set down her beer and took both his hands
in hers. "And I've been so upset about what happened to
you...getting expelled too. It's just so awful, I needed to do
something. Did you know that I'm trying to get you back into
school?"

He flashed a grateful smile. "I do know. I heard about
the petition. That's really nice of you."

She guzzled up his compliment, tilting her chest over the armrest of his chair so that her breasts brushed against the bare skin of his arm. "I would do anything for you. I love you." Her moist lips grazed his earlobe. "We're great together. You know what I mean."

David sucked in air as she slipped one hand under the waistband of his shorts again and caressed his inner thighs with the other. He had always loved her touch, and she was certainly right about what she'd said—they were great together. Sex had been the best part of their relationship, and it was something he really missed. Blair kept saying she wasn't ready yet, and not wanting to push her, he waited. But now Krystal was back, and she knew exactly what to do. In seconds, she was fully on top of him in his chair, straddling his lap.

"You and I belong together. We're perfect for each other," she purred, trailing wet kisses down his neck. She knew his vulnerable spots and exploited every single one of them, her agile hands moving faster.

David knew he should stop this, but couldn't. Or maybe he didn't want to. Maybe this was just what he needed.

"I bet *she* couldn't make you feel like this," Krystal whispered against his lips. "There's no way that loser would know what to do. I'm the only one who—"

"Hey!" David heard himself exclaim. It was like someone had flipped an off switch and catapulted him back to reality. He pulled his mouth away from hers and clutched her shoulders. "Watch what you're saying! I don't like it when you're mean."

"Okay," she said in a low slur. "I don't want to talk about that freak anyway." She lowered her lips to his. "Now, where were we?"

He stiffened and pushed at her shoulders until she drew

her lips away. "We can't be doing this right now. It's not that I don't want to, it's just that the timing is wrong. I need to figure things out."

Krystal didn't move. She just said, "What's to figure out? We both know what we want, so let it happen. Stop thinking so much."

David used all his strength to lift himself out of the chair with Krystal clinging to him. When he was upright, he carefully lowered her to the ground and peeled her off. She looked hurt and puzzled, her bottom lip jutting out in a childish pout.

Trying to ease the rejection, he said, "Look, it's not that we didn't have a great relationship, and maybe we still could. But right now, I really need to figure things out."

"Are you saying there's still a chance for us? You know we'd be the perfect prom queen and king."

"I'm saying I'm confused about everything right now. My life is way too complicated. I might not even be at the prom. I could be in jail by then."

She wrapped her arms around him and squeezed. "Nope. I'm not going to let that happen. I'm going to finish the petition to get you back into school, and then I'm going to do whatever it takes to make sure you don't go to jail."

He hugged her back and rested his chin on the top of her head. "Thank you. You don't know how much that means to me."

She snuggled into his chest. "I'll always be there for you."

CHAPTER 31

The Betrayal

It's my seventeenth birthday, and I'm having brunch with my parents and grandparents at my favorite diner near my grandparents' house. I drove us here in my brother Brett's car, a five-year-old silver Subaru Forester, which will be all mine while he's away at college. First thing Monday morning, when I'm supposed to be in school, I'm going to head down to the Department of Motor Vehicles to take my road test. I've been waiting so long I can practically see my license in the front plastic window of my wallet.

We've only had our food about two minutes when my father excuses himself to take a call. It could be his office, but I suspect that, more likely on a Saturday afternoon, it's about me. When he returns to our booth a few minutes later, I learn that I'm right.

"That was Uncle Marv," he announces as he eases back into his seat. "David's lawyer finally called him back this morning."

"And?" my mom asks with visible trepidation, the corner of her right eye twitching the way it does when she's really nervous.

"And he's taking a different tactic than we would've hoped."

My mouth goes dry, and I instantly lose interest in my omelet. "What does that mean?"

"It means that his lawyer believes he's better off acting alone than collaborating with us. He said he's already prepared his own motion papers to nullify the expulsion, so he doesn't need ours, and he doesn't want to do anything jointly because he believes we're on opposite sides."

My grandparents are up to speed on my horrendous predicament, and my grandpa, a retired lawyer himself, can't help putting in his own two cents. "Isn't this attorney being a bit shortsighted? Yes, Blair will maintain she didn't give permission to have that picture taken, and, in fact, she demanded its destruction, but David's in the same exact position regarding the expulsion."

My father swallows a bite of his tuna melt and dabs the edges of his lips with a napkin before answering. "Actually, Dad, he's telling a very different story about the picture." He catches my eye before continuing. "Hold on to your seats when I tell you this: His lawyer is claiming that Blair asked for David to take a photo of her, posed for it, then instructed him to send it to her, but he somehow inadvertently sent it to others during the transmission."

"*What?*" I shriek, my hands flying sideways, almost knocking over my water glass.

My dad frowns. "You heard me. His lawyer created his own version of the facts."

"But he's lying!" I cry.

"Welcome to the practice of law, my darling," my grandfather says. "The best defense is a good offense."

My mother smirks. "Now, where have I heard that?"

"But his offense is a lie!" I shout.

"Shhh, lower your voice," my mom instructs, pressing her forefinger to her lips.

"You think David will go along with this? He *knows* that's not what happened!" I'm so livid I want to take every glass and plate off the table and fling them at the back wall.

My grandpa hooks an arm around my shoulders to try

to calm me down. "Maybe that's what David told his lawyer. And even if he didn't, he'll do whatever his lawyer says to stay out of jail."

I still can't accept his answer. "Even if it's a lie?"

"Years behind bars are a strong motivator to say whatever you have to," my grandpa explains.

"But I'm not lying about anything. And isn't the truth supposed to set you free?"

The whole table chuckles, except for me.

"Only in a perfect world, and our world is far from perfect," says my dad. "The reality is that our justice system is flawed, and sometimes innocent people go to jail and guilty people get off scot-free. It's hard to determine exactly what the truth is when you're the judge or jury and you're hearing conflicting versions of the same incident. You'll see when you get a little older and you get called for jury duty. It's a hard job."

I shake my head back and forth. "I can't believe David would go to court and lie like that about me."

My mom releases a long sigh. "Honey, he already broke your trust by not deleting that photo and then sending it on to other people. And he lied and told you it wasn't him who sent it, yet he won't tell you who really did. I know you don't want to think he could make up a bogus story and tell it to a jury, but I don't want you to delude yourself into believing he's this honorable boy when he's already shown he's not."

My grandfather squeezes me closer and says, "Your mother is correct. If our privacy laws had caught up to the digital age, then David would be faced with an additional charge: violating your digital privacy. Don't ever forget or excuse the fact that you're the victim of his bad behavior."

"That's right," my dad adds. "And David is really lucky that the revenge porn legislation that's currently pending hasn't been enacted yet, or he'd be facing even more criminal charges, and we'd be bringing a civil suit against him."

"What's revenge porn?" my mom asks.

My dad picks up the second half of his tuna melt and waves it around as he speaks. "It's nonconsensual pornography— essentially when someone posts sexually graphic images of another person online without their permission. Distributing pictures or videos of a minor can carry steep penalties too."

"One picture is bad enough," I murmur. "If he shared videos of me, I'd have to move to Alaska." I don't say anything out loud, but can't help thinking about Chloe Esposito and her boyfriend's secret sex tapes.

My grandpa bends his lips into a smile. "See, there's a bright side for you. It could've been much worse. Now, eat that omelet before it turns into a Frisbee."

He releases me and grabs a roll from the breadbasket in the center of the table. My grandma snatches it out of his hand before it reaches his mouth. She may be a petite, frail-looking woman, but she's deceptively strong. "You've already had two," she chides. "That's enough carbs for one meal."

My dad chuckles.

"It's not funny," my grandma says, the creases between her eyebrows deepening. "Your father's put on ten pounds since we lost the dog. We need to get another one because walking him was the only exercise he got."

"I don't want another dog," my grandpa protests. "No one can replace Vonnegut."

I feel the exact same way. Vonnegut was incredibly special. Not just because he lived to be seventeen, but because he was the smartest dog you could ever imagine. When you talked to him, you'd swear he understood every single word.

"We wouldn't be replacing him," my grandma argues. "We'd be—"

I tune her out when my new phone pings with a message. Since the prosecutor's office confiscated my real cell phone, my parents bought me this throwaway at CVS.

It's a text from Kayla: "Rumor going around—heard from 2 dif peop—Yak made out with IQ last nite at Thing 3's house. If true u were rt about him. So sorry...P.S. Happy Bday!"

Yak made out with IQ last nite....

Her words reach me in slow motion, first drifting upward, then swirling around the front of my brain, gradually creeping in...and then *wham!* Full impact. They burn into me.

What the hell? Was this the same guy who'd just cried his eyes out on my front steps?

My mom is right. There's nothing honorable about him.

CHAPTER 32

Torn

A fter having the worst birthday of my seventeen-year existence, I have the best Monday morning I can ever remember. At 6:38 a.m. I'm the second person in line at the DMV, and by 8:05 a.m. I'm bursting out of the building, clutching my very first driver's license. I may be going to jail, but at least I can drive until then.

Next stop, the courthouse.

My parents and I meet Uncle Marv at the Westberry Justice Center to fight my expulsion. I must be riding a lucky wave, because at 10:32 a.m. we march out of there with a court order in hand that says I can return to school immediately. I still have to deal with the criminal complaint filed against me for the sexting charges, but for the moment I have one legal victory on my side.

The judge's words—after hearing oral arguments from my lawyer and David's— replay in my head like the lyrics of a great song I want to listen to over and over: "I am persuaded by several key points the defendants have raised, most notably the fact that no legislation currently exists that allows public school administrators to expel students for sexting. And I agree with Mr. Sherman that without a hearing, an investigation, or any type of due process, the Westberry Board of Education's hasty expulsion has violated the defendants' civil and constitutional rights. But perhaps the most compelling argument I've heard this morning is that the alleged acts of the defendants occurred off school premises. This Court does not believe that the Westberry Board of Education has the authority to impose penalties on children for non-school-related actions. Therefore, I am ordering the Westberry Board of Education to pay a $10,000 fine and permit the defendants to return to school at once."

I am, of course, extremely happy with the judge's decision. It should be *my* choice whether or not I decide to go back to school. But being in the same courtroom with David was unnerving. He kept trying to make eye contact with me, and I kept turning away, unwilling to look at the guy who betrayed me so badly.

Out in the parking lot, he comes running up from behind, calling my name. I whirl around and hiss, "Get away from me!"

But he doesn't take no for an answer and follows me. I excuse myself from my parents and Uncle Marv and circle behind a row of cars, where I can let him have it in private.

"How dare you even try to talk to me, you son of a bitch!" I spit out. "You are the lowest form of human scum on the planet and you don't deserve to talk to me—ever!"

"Blair, stop it!" he cries. "You have to listen—"

"No, I don't, you bast—"

"Can you just stop yelling at me and listen? I know the rumors that are going around, so I know what you must be thinking."

My eyes are squinted, shooting lethal darts at him. "Oh really, what am I thinking?"

"I'm sure you heard about me and Krystal, and you think we're back together, but—"

"But what? You're going to lie to my face and tell me you're not?"

"No, I'm not. She did come on to me at this party the other night, and she has been circulating this petition to get me back into school, but we're not back together. *You* are my girlfriend."

I snicker, emitting a sharp, scornful laugh. "No, that ended when you teamed up with that bitch of yours to send my picture to the police and get me arrested!"

"*What? Are you serious?* You think I teamed up with her to get you arrested? Why the hell would I do that? To get myself arrested too? Think about what you're saying—it's crazy!"

"Oh, that's right, you're gonna tell me again that you didn't send that picture—but you can't tell me who did?"

David runs his fingers over the crown of his head and paces back and forth. "I wanted that picture for *me*. I was never going to send it to anyone else, but a friend of mine borrowed my phone and *he* forwarded it. Not me."

"So now it's a *he*?"

"It's always been a *he*."

"But you still won't tell me who *he* is?"

David bites down on his lower lip. "I can't."

I throw my hands up in exasperation. "Of course not!"

"It's not that I can't tell *you*, I can't tell anyone—not even my lawyer. And if I did tell him, then I could get out of this whole mess and go free, but my friend would go to jail."

This was getting harder and harder to believe. "So you're going to go to jail for your friend?"

David draws a deep breath. "I don't want to, but how can I throw him under the bus?"

"The same way he's throwing you under the bus! A good friend wouldn't let you take the rap for something he did."

"It's not that simple. He has his reasons, and frankly, I can't blame him."

I have no idea who he's talking about, let alone whether he's even telling the truth. "Well, why don't you pin it on him anyway, the way you're pinning the picture you took on me!"

David scrunches his face in confusion. "What are you talking about?"

"I'm talking about how you told your lawyer that I asked you to take that picture and send it to me, and then you mistakenly sent it to other people."

"Are you deranged? I never said that."

"Well, your lawyer said you did!"

My former boyfriend shakes his head, then buries his face in his hands. "This is out of control!"

He's right about that. Both of us have lost control of our lives, and we have no idea what will be hurled at us next. I, for one, am completely overwhelmed and perplexed by everything that's happening around me.

I step closer to study him. "Look at me right now and tell me the truth—about Krystal, about the picture, about your friend, about your lawyer. You've done more than enough to me already, but no matter what, I deserve the truth."

He slides his fingers off his eyes and gazes at me intently. "I've been telling you the truth, but if you want me to, I'll say it again. I'm *not* back together with Krystal. The only person I want to get back with is *you*. I love *you*. And if you give me the chance, I'll show you that. I would never do anything intentionally to hurt you, and that includes telling my lawyer that you wanted me to take your picture. I never said that. I hope you believe me, because it's true. And I can't rat my friend out for sending your picture, because he'll go right to jail. I don't want to go to jail either, but he'll definitely go, and he'll go for a long time because he's done other things that have gotten him into trouble before. They have this three-strikes-you're-out rule or something."

That's the most information he's given me so far, and I don't know what to make of it. Yes, I desperately want to believe that he loves me and hasn't schemed behind my back, but can I trust him? A few minutes ago, I thought he was the biggest slimeball who walked the earth. Were the rumors I'd heard about him and the Ice Queen fooling around true? Does he really have a friend he's trying to protect who'd be in worse trouble if his identity were revealed?

He must sense my uncertainty because he reaches for my hand. I let him take it. I'm torn inside because I know full well how horrible it is to be called a rat. In my case the accusation was unfounded, but what if David really did rat out his own friend—what kind of person would that make him? And if he continues on this noble course, hiding the truth from me and the police and even his own lawyer, then what kind of person is he?

I lift my face to his. Our eyes meet and hold. "I *want* to believe you, but how do I know you're being honest? How do I know you're not playing me for a fool?" My heart pulls for him as my doubts tear me away.

He blinks hard, his fingers enfolding mine. "Every word I just said is true. I haven't lied about anything. What I wanted more than anything was to take you out for your birthday and tell you how much I love you, but you wouldn't even talk to me. Please understand that I just can't tell you who my friend is. Believe me, I would if I could."

My eyes water over, and my lips quiver as though I'm suddenly freezing. "I don't know what to think anymore—I just don't know."

I can't take being so conflicted. I want more than anything to just throw my arms around him and tell him I love him too and live happily ever after. But it's just not that simple.

I pull my hand away and head back to where my parents are waiting. We each depart for school, not knowing whether there's any chance of a future between us.

CHAPTER 33

Back to School

As much as I don't want to go anywhere near Westberry High School after my humiliating arrest, expulsion, and fake Instagram account, I have no choice. Uncle Marv fought hard for my return, and the judge ruled in my favor. After obtaining the court order, I can't exactly announce I'm not going.

By the time I leave the main office after showing the judge's order to Mr. Scott, it's the end of fifth period. I stop in the ladies' room to touch up my acne makeup before heading to my sixth period class, International Foods. During my sophomore year Basic Foods had been my favorite class, so I'm looking forward to the international version. I'm excited that Rachel is in the class too, but not exactly overjoyed that so are three out of four of the Things.

After discreetly showing the Foods teacher a copy of the order permitting me back in school, I sit in the front corner watching my classmates enter. The three Things are the first to saunter in. They swarm around each other like the aimless worker bees they are, lost without their leader. Thankfully, they make their nest on the opposite side of the room, but once they spot me they can't stop their whispering, frosty stares, and finger pointing.

I'm super surprised when I see Hunter Hartman head down the center aisle of the cooking stations. I can't believe that Rachel never mentioned he was in our class. I grab my phone to text her, but then realize how trivial it must've seemed to her relative to everything else that's been going on in my life.

Hunter drops his backpack at a neighboring cooking station and comes over to talk to me. This is a first.

"Hey Blair," he says.

"Hey," I say back.

Out of the corner of my eye I notice that Hunter and I are the focal point of the Things' attention. Their three sets of eyes are riveted on us as they lean forward—like they're half bowing—trying to hear what we're saying.

Hunter flashes those adorable light green eyes at me. "You know, what happened to you and David really sucks."

I feel a rush of heat travel across my cheeks. "Thanks."

Even though I stopped obsessing over him when I started going out with David, I can't help being nervous in his presence. He's standing really close, and I feel very self-conscious.

"Well, nice to see you back," he says with a smile, before returning to his station.

Now I *am* going to text Rachel. But before I can type a message, she sidles up next to me, welcoming me back with an exuberant squeal and an enormous hug. Other kids come over too, and they seem truly happy to see me, like I'm a celebrity or something. With all the nice greetings, I feel insulated from the Things and block them out for the rest of the class.

I love cooking, and learning how to make homemade pasta is the perfect way to ease back into school. As I pull long, floury strands of fettuccine from the pasta machine, I whisper to Rachel, "I have so much to tell you."

Her eyes float around the room and she whispers back, "Later."

When the class ends, the cluster of Things hovers near

the door and we have no choice but to walk past them. I have a haunting flashback to the ladies' room scuffle at the fateful pool party, so I stay close to Rachel. We manage to make it into the hallway without a hassle, but I freeze at the sound of my name.

"Blair, wait a sec! I want to talk to you!"

I wish I'd heard wrong, but it's the Ice Queen. I'd recognize that dreadful, raspy voice out of millions of people if you tested me blindfolded. Rachel and I turn to see her heading down the hall directly toward us, closing in fast. A revolting bubble of musky rose and lavender reaches me before she does.

"Blair," she says as she stops in front of Rachel and me. "I just want to tell you how happy I am that you're back in school."

I cock my head to the side and squint at her. *Am I hearing right? Where's the death stare? The mocking laugh?*

"I think what happened to you and David is really lame," she continues. "And everybody's been saying that you two are the school's guinea pigs. We've all sent photos and messages that we now know we could've been arrested for, so what happened to you two could've happened to any of us."

All the Things are nodding furiously at their leader's insightful words, so I just nod too. It's the first time the Ice Queen has ever said anything to me that wasn't a nasty slur or insult, and I don't know how to react.

The Queen offers me a sympathetic smile as she delivers the rest of her speech. "It's got to be really hard coming back to school after you've been expelled, so I just want you to know that we all feel really bad about what happened, so you don't have to worry about what people are saying—we're on your side."

Stunned, all I can manage to reply is, "Uh...okay...

thanks."

"Cute shoes, Rachel," the Ice Queen declares as her parting words, strutting away with her posse.

Rachel whirls to me, drawing her blonde eyebrows together and wrinkling her nose. "What was *that*?"

I shake my head. "I have no idea, but if you didn't hear it too, no one would ever believe me."

"Why is she being so nice now? She hasn't said anything nice to either of us in three years...or ever, actually. All I've gotten from her are Bessie the Cow jokes. I think it was just last week she said, 'Got milk?'"

"I don't know, but I'm sure it has something to do with David."

Rachel digests my words, and says, "Oh, you think she's pretending to be nice to you now that she has David back... to rub it in?"

"That's what I need to talk to you about. I don't know that she *has* David back. I bet she's acting this way to try to *get* him back."

"Wait a minute, I thought she *was* back with him. Now I'm totally confused."

The next bell rings—seventh period classes are starting.

"I'll fill you, Kayla, and Carrie in on everything later," I promise, sprinting off to calculus.

CHAPTER 34

The Real Plan

The next two weeks are quite difficult for me on many fronts. Academically, it's a real challenge to catch up on everything I've missed the first week of school, plus keep up with the new material. I spend a lot of time studying and have to stay after school for extra help a few days.

I only stop by the animal shelter once after my expulsion, and that visit depresses me even further. Although all six of the *Friends* puppies and Lola and Max have been adopted, Cosmo and Henry are still there. I ask the other volunteers if there's been any interest in either of them, and they say just Cosmo. As Caroline accurately predicted, no one wants an eleven-year-old dog, no matter how great he is.

I can barely look at Henry. His head and tail hang low, and his eyes are so gloomy and despondent I want to cry. Does he somehow know this is where he's going to spend the rest of his life? I can't imagine what the poor dog is going through, losing the two people he loves, then being locked up in a primitive cell as though he's being punished.

I realize that I'm probably overly sensitive to Henry's plight because of my own pitiful predicament, which David makes even worse. He wants everything between us to go back to the way it was before our arrests, but I'm not so sure I can do that. Uncle Marv reached out to David's lawyer again, and he's still not cooperating. How can we have a normal relationship when our lawyers are battling each other? One of us could pin the blame on the other, and that other would end up in jail.

And my level of trust in him just isn't there, knowing that he made out with his evil ex-girlfriend after the first home soccer game. I wish he'd deny the rumors, but he doesn't. Instead, whenever I bring it up, he says, "She came on to me that night, but it stopped right there." I don't know exactly what that means.

My close friends and I still can't comprehend why Her Highness and her swarm of Things are being so nice to us. And it's not only the Queen who's put her wickedness on hold—the whole A-list crowd has been friendly and attentive. It's actually a pleasure to go to school and be treated like everyone else. But my friends and I know something is up and this is too good to be true. We just don't know what's going to trigger the ax to fall...or when.

It turns out the "when" comes all too quickly—during my third week back at school. Carrie shows up at my house unexpectedly one evening just as my mom and I are about to sit down to dinner. She's still in her field hockey uniform, various shades of dirt streaked across her face and legs like war paint, her hair matted with sweat.

"You are not going to believe this!" she exclaims as she kicks off her cleats by the front door. Bounding into our kitchen, she goes right for a cold Gatorade in the fridge. "I raced over here after my game so I could tell you right away!"

Her excitement is infectious even though I have no idea what she's talking about. "Tell me what?" I cry in anticipation. My mom stays with us in the kitchen, curious to hear what Carrie is so anxious to report.

"Here's what happened," Carrie says, her words flying out so fast her sentences run together. "I'm in the middle of my game, and my stick breaks. Some giant ogre from the other team smacked it so hard it broke in half, so I had to go to the equipment shed to get another one. I was really pissed, but it ended up being a good thing because while I'm in there, I hear the Ice Queen's voice. It sounds like she's right next to me, but no one's in the shed but me. Then I smell pot. I look around and see that there are two small, screened windows close to the ceiling in the back of the shed, so I realize she must be behind the shed smoking."

I can't wait for Carrie to finish. "Who was she talking to? What was she saying?"

"I don't know who she was talking to—I assume it was her Things while they were on a break from taking yearbook pictures—but she was bragging about how her plan was working perfectly."

"Her plan?" my mom interjects.

Carrie nods. "Yeah, her plan. She was saying how everything was working perfectly, and the best thing she ever did was send that freak's picture to the police."

"So it *was* her!" I scream, locking onto my mom's gaze. "I knew it!"

"Wait," Carrie says. "There's more. She was bragging about how you and David are right in her pocket, and how she's going to break you two up and win him back and then dump him again in public at some big event like the Halloween dance so she can teach him a lesson for picking you over her."

I have to repeat the last part to make sure I heard right. "She wants to get him back so she can dump him in public as punishment for going out with me?"

Carrie bobs her head. "Yep! Then she said he'll have no one, which is what he deserves."

My mom pipes up again. "What else did she say?"

Carrie looks a little embarrassed to relate the next part in front of my mother, but she does anyway. "She also said that she still can't believe how someone like David, a Class A guy, could go out with someone like her and then with a Class C loser like Blair. She said she can't wait until the two of them both get what they deserve, and if her plan continues to go perfectly, they'll both end up in jail."

Anger surges through my veins. "You sure she didn't see you and then make up this whole story?"

"I'm positive. No one saw me. They were already behind the shed when I got there, and they had no idea I was inside. My whole team was in the middle of a game, so they wouldn't have had any reason to think someone was in there listening to them."

"You're awesome!" I exclaim.

"And there's one more thing you should know. One of the Things asked her why she wouldn't go out with David again when she got him back, and she said now that he's been with you, he's like dirty laundry. He's soiled for life."

As Carrie's story sinks in, my anger is replaced by an unexpected serenity. A delightful calm, like a blanket of peace and warmth, envelops me as I settle back into my chair. "So David's been telling me the truth. The Queen acted on her own when she sent that picture to the police."

"And it sounds like this has been her plan for revenge all along," my mom adds. "As payback she wanted to get both of you arrested, then get David back so she could dump him again in a painful way. She sounds like a real sick pup."

"Hey," I caution. "If Kayla were here, she'd never let you compare the Ice Queen to an innocent puppy."

My mom grabs the kitchen phone from its cradle and announces, "I'm going to call Marv right now. I have no idea whether he'll be able to use any of this information, but I'm going to tell him everything you said, Carrie. Thank you so much."

"You're welcome. I knew you'd want to know this right away."

I smile—my first real smile in weeks. "I need to talk to David."

CHAPTER 35

Criminal Mindset

I don't want to be a lawyer like my dad and grandpa—
I'm far more interested in the sciences—but I definitely
want to be involved with as much of my own case as I
can since my life literally depends on it. Uncle Marv has been
great about sending me copies of all the legal documents he's
prepared in my defense and keeping me up to date on the
latest developments with the court and prosecutor's office.

His firm has done mountains of research on sexting
in the United States as well as abroad, and the results are
shocking. It seems like legislators around the world don't
know how to handle this new wave of "crimes" that are now
rampant in the twenty-first-century digital age.

Unfortunately, his research shows that in most American
states, minors caught sexting are prosecuted similarly to
those convicted of conventional child pornography. They're
subject to stiff prison terms and sex offender registration
requirements. It's amazing to me that I can be thrown into
the same category as a child molester or pedophile and face
similar punishment. No matter how many times my dad
explains the law to me, it still doesn't make sense. Not at all.

What I *do* understand is that some legislators are
pushing for counseling and educational programs to teach
first-time teenage offenders about the dangers and social
consequences of sending and receiving nude or seminude
images, but other legislators want criminal penalties. And
among those who press for criminal penalties, some think

sexting should be considered a misdemeanor, while others believe it constitutes a felony.

There's only one thing lawmakers and prosecutors nationwide seem to agree on: sexting on computers, electronic devices, and cell phones is a serious, growing problem that isn't going away. I saw one poll that showed more than one in four teens admits to being involved in some type of sexting. According to another study my mom found, over half of teens fourteen and older have participated in sexting.

I keep asking myself, with statistics that high—that involve hundreds of thousands of kids—why is it I'm being singled out? Why aren't thousands of other kids being prosecuted too? I can't get over the unfairness of it all, and some days I feel like I'm drowning in self-pity.

In Uncle Marv's latest package there's a report about a fifteen-year-old girl that sends shivers up my spine. This poor girl sent a nude picture of herself to her boyfriend, but after they broke up, the vengeful jerk sent it on to dozens of her family and friends. And guess who was convicted of sexting?

I'm so panicked my fingers can barely tap the right keys as I make an urgent call to Uncle Marv. I skip "hello" and say, "In that packet of research you just sent…am I going to end up like that fifteen-year-old girl who was convicted?"

"Calm down, sweetie," Uncle Marv placates in his combo voice, a fatherly and lawyerly mix I've come to know too well. "Your case is nothing like hers."

"Well, it seems like hers."

"Listen to me, it's not. That's a revenge porn case—you have a completely different set of facts. You weren't nude in the picture that was sent, you didn't send it, you had no knowledge it had been sent, and you never approved of it being taken in the first place."

I splay my hand over the paper about the convicted girl. "But don't I have to prove all that?"

"No, as a defendant, you don't. It's the prosecution who has to prove their case, but you certainly want to make sure the judge and the jury understand and believe your version of the facts."

I sigh super loud. "Well, that's going to be a problem, because it seems like I'm going to have a version of the facts that's different than David's. What happens if they pick his version over mine? Then what?"

"Relax, sweetie. I know David's lawyer has his own way of doing things, but you're getting way ahead of yourself here. I don't see this case going anywhere near a jury. In fact, I've been negotiating with the assistant prosecutor all week, and I think we might be getting close to a plea deal."

This is the first time Uncle Marv has ever mentioned any kind of deal. I scoot forward in my chair. "Really? They'll let me have a deal?"

"Yes. I wasn't going to say anything to you until we were a little further along in our negotiations since I didn't want to get your hopes up, but now that you've called me so upset, I thought I should tell you."

"What kind of deal? Is it one where I won't have to go to jail?" I squeeze my eyes shut and pray.

"That's what I'm working on. I finally found a reasonable assistant prosecutor who thinks like we do. She understands that teenagers like you and David aren't really child pornographers and that there are far better alternatives to dealing with the sexting problem than criminal prosecution."

"What kind of alternatives?"

"Well, since in your case you don't have a prior record, and you didn't have a criminal mindset when the photo was taken because your picture clearly shows you holding up an outfit you're contemplating wearing, and since you were unaware that sending the photo constituted a criminal offense—"

"But I didn't send the photo—"

"Please let me finish. You need to keep in mind that David's lawyer is alleging that you instructed David to send it, but that's not going to matter if we reach a plea bargain. I'm trying to get them to agree to put you into a course that will educate you on the unique nature of cyberspace and the consequences of sharing sexually explicit images. I think I've convinced the assistant prosecutor that this incident can be chalked up to a juvenile mistake that was nothing more than a lack of judgment and common sense—"

"But I didn't make any mistake other than not grabbing the phone and deleting the picture myself. And trusting David...that was my other mistake."

Uncle Marv clears his throat. "Ahem, if I can finish here, I think I've convinced her that taking an educational program on mobile device and Internet safety would be enough of a deterrent for you not to commit any future acts like this again, so probation and counseling won't be necessary. You don't exactly pose a public safety threat."

I'm aghast. "They could put me on probation? Like a criminal?"

"Sweetie, I just told you that I don't think that will be the case if the assistant prosecutor agrees to put you in a program teaching you to use technology responsibly. But there are still two significant problems right now. First, she has to convince her boss—the chief prosecutor—that an educational program is the best way to handle this situation, and second, she has to resolve David's case in a way that is consistent with yours. Unfortunately, I don't know the stage of negotiations with David's lawyer because the guy is a real ass—he won't confer with me at all—and the prosecutor's office certainly isn't going to divulge the status of their confidential discussions."

Out of everything he just said, all I heard was *two significant problems.* "So, what if the prosecutor won't put me in this educational program? Then what happens?"

"Then I play all my legal arguments, and I've certainly got a lot of them. For instance, I'll use one of the same ones that was successful in overturning your expulsion. I'll argue that the photo of you was a form of self-expression that was protected by the First Amendment, and therefore, as constitutionally protected speech, you can't be prosecuted. That same argument was used in another state to get an injunction—it stopped the prosecutor from charging a teenage girl under that state's child pornography statutes."

"Oh," I remark, really impressed. "That sounds good."

"I've got lots of good arguments, but I don't want to go through them all now. I'm hoping we can get you a nice plea deal, and then I won't need any of them. That would be the best thing."

"How much longer do you think it'll take to get a deal?"

"I can't say—that's why I didn't plan on mentioning this to you yet."

"Can I talk about it with David?"

"Absolutely not!" Uncle Marv says in a tone so sharp my head snaps back. "This has to be one subject that's off limits. You don't want to jeopardize any of the progress I've made so far or muddy the waters. His lawyer and I are each handling your cases separately, and it has to stay that way. If his lawyer was conferring with me, it would be a different story, but he's not."

"Can I at least ask him whether his lawyer is working on a plea deal for him?"

Uncle Marv's tone is even sharper when he replies, "No! You cannot speak to him at all about his case or yours—not about any part of it. This subject is off limits." He pauses for a brief moment before adding, "My best advice is for you to stay away from him completely right now and have no contact. I understand you don't want to do that, but that's what I recommend. No contact. That way you don't risk divulging anything you're not supposed to."

I need to end this call. I've had more than my fill of legal talk for the day, and my head is spinning from everything he's said. I have to get back to my AP Bio homework—something I can understand—but I do have one more question.

"Uncle Marv, now that we know for certain it was Krystal Cooper who sent the photo of me to the police, shouldn't she be prosecuted? I mean, she transmitted a picture of a minor too."

"If only it were that easy," he responds. "But we have no proof that it was her." All we have is your friend saying she overheard someone who she thinks was Krystal saying that she sent the picture, but this Krystal will never admit to it, and it will be word against word. And all the people who Krystal was speaking to behind that shed will be her witnesses, not yours."

I release a long, frustrated sigh. "The Ice Queen wins again."

"What did you say, sweetie?"

"Oh, nothing. Just thanks for all your help. I need it."

DAVID

◆

CHAPTER 36

A Balancing Act

Now that David had become aware of his ex-girlfriend's real plan for him and Blair, he had to figure out the best way to handle her. Of course, every ounce of him was infuriated after Carrie related word for word what she'd overheard in the school's equipment shed. Blair had insisted that he hear it directly from Carrie to make sure nothing was omitted or misstated.

As disturbing as it was, he had no reason not to believe Carrie. Everything she said made sense when he thought about the way Krystal had been behaving the past few months. She'd broken up with him before finals, stayed out of contact all summer, then, when she found out about him and Blair, sent the incriminating photo to the police. After the arrests she acted exceptionally nice to lure him back and tried to seduce him at the first opportunity. That part troubled him the most because of his own guilty role in her plan. If she hadn't called Blair a loser, he might've...

Damn, he had to stop beating himself up over that. He was pretty drunk that night, Blair wasn't talking to him, he'd missed playing in the home soccer opener, he'd been expelled, and he was facing jail time. How much can a guy take? Anyway, Blair had heard the rumors that he'd made out with Krystal, and she seemed to be getting over it. If only he could.

The fact was, as nice as it was having Krystal act so friendly, he knew it wasn't real and wouldn't last much longer. She'd plotted and schemed to get him and Blair in trouble with the law—which had worked quite well for her—and now she'd moved on to phase two: win him back with fake kindness, false promises, and raunchy sex so she could publicly humiliate him even more than she had the first time.

After experiencing Krystal's wrath firsthand, he had true empathy for what Blair had endured over the past three years. He still didn't understand exactly what had caused Krystal to hate her so much, but he realized that the truth was, Blair probably didn't do a damn thing. Anyone who could act so irrationally, the way Krystal had at the end-of-year pool party, and then formulate a malicious plan for revenge against someone she claimed she loved, was unstable and probably psychotic.

It was hard not to tell her off when he saw her in school, but he, Blair, Carrie, Kayla, and Rachel had all decided that until they came up with a plan of their own, he had to play along with Krystal's so she wouldn't suspect he was on to her. The real challenge was giving her a taste of her own medicine in a way that wouldn't cause any further problems for him and the girls.

No matter what happened with Krystal, he had to maintain a good relationship with her parents. His future depended on it. One call from Coach Cooper to broadcast his arrest and badmouth him to the schools that offered him sports scholarships, and he'd be ruined.

At least Mrs. Cooper seemed to genuinely care about him. Every time she saw him she'd gush about how handsome he was and how lucky Krystal was to be going out with someone so nice and smart and athletic. She came to all his hockey and soccer games and cheered him on like he was a family member. He really had to wonder if Mrs. Cooper had any idea what her daughter was really like.

Right now, he had to perform a balancing act, staying close to Krystal without letting her seduce him. It was far easier than he'd thought it would be, now that he saw her for who she really was: an evil witch. All he needed to think about was the click of the heavy metal door shutting behind him in the tiny jail cell at the police precinct to be able to look right through her and see the monster inside.

He wouldn't have called her the Ice Queen like Blair and her friends. That was way too kind. He would've picked a more fitting name, like Godzilla.

D A V I D

◆

CHAPTER 37

Surprise Guest

Friday night at 7:15 p.m., David was getting ready for a date with Krystal. He didn't want to go out with her, but Blair, of all people, had made him. "You have to pretend you're interested in getting back together," she'd instructed. "We need you to stay close to her until we decide what to do. But not *too* close."

As he dabbed on the cologne Krystal had given him for his seventeenth birthday, he thought he heard a car pull up his driveway. When he peered out his bedroom window, he saw Frankie getting out of his black Jeep.

What the hell?

Under the circumstances he couldn't exactly say he was glad to see him. Yanking open his front door, he muttered, "What are you doing here?"

Frankie shuffled toward his friend, knowing full well he wasn't high on the Woods' guest list. "I had to come up to see you," he said, his eyes downcast and brimming with shame. "I feel so bad about this whole thing...I can't sleep anymore, I can't concentrate in school...I can't do anything. It's taken over my life."

David scowled. "And what do you want me to say? My life's been great?"

"I know it's sucked—that's why I'm here. This whole thing is wrong, and I need to fix it."

"What do you mean?"

"I mean I'm going to tell the truth about what happened. I can't live like this anymore, feeling guilty every minute because of what you're going through." He stuck his hand out for David to shake. "You've been my best friend my entire life, and I'm not going to screw that up. I'm going to get you out of this right now, no matter what happens to me."

David accepted the shake and heaved a sigh of relief. "I almost gave up on you, man."

Frankie nodded. "I know. I should've just stepped up right away instead of acting like a damn coward. I hate myself, and I know you hate me too. I'd rather be in prison than be a coward."

"You have no idea how glad I am you're telling me this."

"Actually, I think I do. So, let's go to the police precinct right now and get it over with." Frankie slapped his childhood friend on the back. "Come on. I'll drive there, and you'll take my car after they arrest me." He spun around to head for his Jeep.

"Hey, wait a sec," David called after him. "Tonight isn't good to go to the precinct."

Frankie spun back. "Why not?"

"Because you won't be able to get a lawyer till tomorrow, you'll have to sleep in a dirty cell, and your parents will need time to get up here. And besides, I think my lawyer is close to a plea deal, so I won't have to serve any time or have a record. I'll probably just have to take a special course and do some community service. Let's just wait to see what happens with me before you put your ass on the line."

His oldest friend started to cry. The last time David had seen tears fall from Frankie's eyes, they were both seven and

Frankie had fallen off his mountain bike and ripped his knee apart on a jagged rock. Now all two hundred forty pounds of his massive frame were quivering, his face contorted with relief and gratitude.

"Thank you," he sniveled, enveloping his oldest friend in a heartfelt embrace. He sobbed on David's shoulder for several minutes before pulling back and swiping at his wet eyes. "You're the best friend in the entire world, and I'll never forget this. I don't deserve you."

"I'm just happy that you decided to come forward. It's been bad around here, real bad. Both my parents have been pressuring me to tell the prosecutor that it was you who sent Blair's picture, but I've been protecting you. The only reason they haven't said anything themselves is because my lawyer told them that even if I wasn't the one who sent out the picture, I'd still be facing other charges. He said that since I admitted to taking the photo and it was on my phone, I would still be charged with the creation and possession of child pornography and endangering the welfare of a minor."

Frankie used the hem of his shirt to dry his face. "I know you've been protecting me—that's why I'll never, ever forget this. If there's anything, and I mean *anything*, that I can ever do for you, just say the word."

David thought for a moment, then his lips broke into a sly grin. "Well, actually, there is."

He filled Frankie in on his plan on their way to Krystal's house.

CHAPTER 38

Three's a Crowd

At first Krystal was speechless when David showed up at her house for their Friday-night date with Frankie at his side. She blocked the entranceway with her body, her hand clenching the doorknob, her icy stare skewering them both.

"Uh...what's *he* doing here?" she finally managed, bouncing a wrathful gaze between them.

"Oh, Frankie just drove up from Richmond to surprise me," David replied with a cheerful smile, slapping Frankie in between the shoulder blades. "I couldn't just leave him at my house by himself, could I?"

Krystal couldn't contain her fury, her eyes narrowing and blinking fast. "So you're bringing him out with *us* tonight?"

"I just said I couldn't leave him by himself. What else was I supposed to do?"

"I don't know," she snapped. "Send him back where he came from." She pointed to someplace off in the distance.

"Richmond is over six hours away—"

"Seven with traffic," Frankie broke in.

"And he just got here. He pulled up right as I was leaving."

"Well, you should've just left him," she said through gritted teeth.

Frankie held up his palms in surrender fashion. "Hey, I'm not stupid. I can see that I'm not wanted, so if I can just use your bathroom, I'll be on my way and you two can go out alone tonight the way you'd planned."

David glared at Krystal. "You're not being very nice. I think you should apologize to Frankie."

Krystal shook her head, her lips twisted in anger. "No, you can't bring someone else along on our date and then tell me *I* should apologize."

David sighed and took a different tack. "Look, I have a lot on my mind right now, and the last thing I want to do is fight with you. And there's something I really need to talk to you about."

"What?"

"Let him go to the bathroom, and I'll tell you."

"Do you mind if I grab something to eat too?" Frankie asked, clutching his stomach. "I'm starving."

Krystal's jaw dropped, horror-struck. "You want me to feed you too?"

"No," Frankie said. "I wouldn't want you to go to any trouble. I'll fix something myself."

Krystal started to protest, but David cut her off. "He's got a long trip back home, so just let him get something to eat and then he'll hit the road."

She pushed out an exasperated sigh, but stepped aside to allow Frankie to enter her house. David pried her fingers off the doorknob and led her down the front walkway to the driveway. "I want to talk to you in private."

Before they reached the pavement, a strong gust of wind whipped Krystal's hair across her face and blew her shirt sideways. She folded her arms over her chest and spun toward the house. "It's too windy out here. Let's go back inside."

"How about we sit in my car?" he suggested, rushing to open the passenger door.

She turned toward the car, hesitated, then trudged

over. Once they were seated, she lowered the visor mirror to smooth out her hair. "So, what do you want to talk about?"

"Well," he began in a sullen tone. "I got some really bad news from my lawyer today."

She shifted in her seat to face him, her expression softening. "What kind of news?"

David released a long, slow breath and met her eyes. "My lawyer said it looks like I might have to spend some time in jail."

Krystal seemed to be visibly moved. She placed a comforting hand on his knee and shook her head. "I am so, so sorry. That's really awful."

He nodded. "It is awful, and I never thought it would happen. I mean, my lawyer didn't either. When I first hired him, he said I have no criminal record, I'm not a danger to society, and what I did doesn't amount to child pornography—it was normal adolescent behavior. He said I'm not a pedophile, and the prosecutors shouldn't treat teenagers like the perverts and sickos who really are manufacturing and distributing kiddie porn."

"He's right," Krystal said, a flicker of sincerity in her eyes.

David frowned. "Unfortunately, our county prosecutor doesn't see it that way. My lawyer said this prosecutor doesn't see the difference between bad teenage judgment and true criminals who exploit children. By grouping teenagers in the same category as criminals and giving us the same punishment, my lawyer says this prosecutor's misapplying the law."

She shook her head again. "That's so unfair."

"I know. It leaves me with only two choices: I can either accept some sort of plea deal or take my chances and go to trial. But if I go to trial and a jury agrees with the prosecutor, then I could be sent to jail for a long time. I'd have the right to appeal, but that's risky and costs tons of money."

"If you accept a plea now, how much time would you have to serve?"

He shrugged. "The way it looks now, it could be a few years."

"A few *years?*" she repeated, the last word infused with disbelief.

"My lawyer doesn't really know yet. He's been trying to get me no jail time, but the prosecutor's insisting that I serve some time because she doesn't want other people thinking they can get away with sending sexually explicit pictures."

"You know, I saw the picture," Krystal said, her tone sympathetic. "And I didn't think it was that bad. I mean, not bad enough to be child porn. And if you think about what happened to Chloe Esposito with those sex tapes, this is really pretty stupid."

"Well, that's just it. It *is* stupid, and everybody thinks so but this dumb prosecutor."

Krystal stroked his cheek, trailing the tips of her long black nails along his chin. "It's really so unfair. Maybe a jury will think it's stupid too?"

David's phone pinged with a new text. He fished it out of his pants pocket and saw that it was from Frankie: "Nothing good to eat."

As he'd expected, Krystal glanced down and saw it too. "Your friend is a real piece of shit!" she yelled, launching into a rant. "It's not nervy enough to crash our date and then ask for my bathroom and food like my house is a highway rest stop. No, now he's complaining that he doesn't like anything. How dare he!" She reached for the door handle. "I'm going to tell him to—"

David grabbed her forearm. "Please stay!" he implored.

"Just let him figure out what he wants, then we'll get rid of him faster. And I'm not done telling you what my lawyer said."

That last sentence quieted her down. She settled back into her seat and rested a hand on his leg again. "There's more?"

There really wasn't more, but David had to make up something fast before she tried to leave the car again. He'd sent Frankie on a recon mission to search Krystal's room for any kind of dirt he could find on her, and he needed to give him more time. Frankie's message "nothing good to eat" really meant that he hadn't found anything yet. If he'd written "feeling better now," then David would've known that the mission was a success. Until he received that last signal, he had to keep Krystal out of the house.

"My lawyer told me I'll probably have to register as a sex offender," he said, trying to sound as morose as possible. He hoped she couldn't tell that everything he was saying was a lie. "If that happens, I wanted to know if you'd still be friends with me—if you'd ever go out with me again. I mean, *you* know I'm not a sex offender."

Without hesitation, she said, "Of course we'd be friends. But we couldn't go out because you'll be in jail."

Yes, I know. That's where you tried to put me, you bitch! he thought. But what he said was, "Would you visit me?"

She smiled. "Of course. I need some more community service for my college applications, so I think that would look really good—making visits to prisoners."

Bitch isn't a strong enough word! He had to resist the impulse to strangle her—then her wish for him to be an inmate really would come true. Frankie needed to hurry, or this was going to get super ugly super fast.

"Krystal, you wouldn't visit me just because you wanted

to see me? It would only be for college apps?"

She ran her fingers up his leg. "Oh, you know I was just kidding."

No, I don't. In fact, I want to eject you from my car! "I hope you were just kidding."

Her fingertips climbed higher on his thigh. Now that he'd learned from Carrie what Krystal was all about, he was repulsed by her touch. But he knew he couldn't stop her, or she'd leave and walk in on Frankie.

"I need to ask you something else," he said, his voice shaky and distressed. He placed his hand over hers.

"What?"

He didn't have anything else to ask and needed to think fast. "Uh, well, this is kind of hard to ask you. But I really need to."

"What?" she repeated.

Suddenly, the perfect question popped into his brain. "Okay, here it goes…I think the hardest thing about everything that's happened is knowing that somebody out there hates me enough to want to put me in jail. I wanted to know if you would try to help me find out who that somebody is."

He eyed her closely, her spontaneous reaction priceless. If guilt was a tangible commodity, then it was oozing out of her—the eyes that averted his gaze, the hand that jerked off his thigh, the body that stiffened and turned away.

He wasn't about to let her off the hook. "Any idea who it might have been? Who the rotten scumbag was who could stoop so low to do something this horrible to me?"

She managed to compose herself with astonishing speed, but couldn't hide the telltale twitching of her eyelids as she shook her head and said, "Sorry, no idea."

"I'll tell you, if I ever catch that cowardly piece of garbage who ruined my life, I'm going to make them pay. They're going to wish they never met me!"

No sooner had he finished his last sentence than she was out of the car, moving at a brisk pace up her driveway.

Oh shit. Frankie!

David sprang out of the driver's seat, yelling, "Krystal, wait!" But she didn't listen. He raced after her, catching up to her as she swung open her front door.

He clasped her upper arm. "Why'd you run away? Do you know who it was and you're afraid to tell me?" He was shouting, hoping Frankie would hear him and know that his time was up.

"I told you already that I have no idea who it was. Now let go of me and don't ask me again!" she hissed, wrenching her arm free.

Inside the front vestibule she pivoted to the left, toward her kitchen, but stopped short as she caught sight of Frankie coming down the hall from the wrong direction.

DAVID

◆

CHAPTER 39

Close Call

W hat were you doing?" Krystal barked at Frankie, her eyes accusatory, her voice teeming with suspicion.

David froze, his breath caught in his throat. This was *not* supposed to happen.

Krystal's index finger shot to the left. "The kitchen is *that* way!"

"Yeah, I know," Frankie said, relaxed and unruffled. "I just spilled some juice, so I went to the bathroom to get a towel to clean it up." He pointed to the mint-green towel flung over his shoulder.

"Haven't you ever heard of *paper* towels?" she fumed. "There are plenty of them *in the kitchen!*"

He nodded. "Yeah, I saw them, but it's a big spill and I didn't want to use them all up. And I had to go to the bathroom anyway, remember?"

Krystal stormed into the kitchen and erupted into a tirade the instant she spotted a jumbo-sized glass of orange juice lying on its side on the dinette table. The pulpy liquid pooled over the blue-pearl quartz tabletop and flooded a good portion of the white oak floor below. "You are so lucky my parents aren't home, or they'd kill you!" she roared. "This is a brand-new floor!"

Frankie unfolded the bath towel he'd brought and draped it over the large orange puddle covering the oak planks. Then he squished the towel around with his foot.

"You are such a fucking klutz!" Krystal hollered, snatching fistfuls of paper towels to soak up the wet mess on the tabletop. "I can't even believe what a loser you are!"

When her back was turned, Frankie rolled his eyes and twirled his finger in a psycho motion. David suppressed a laugh, grabbing a sponge from the kitchen sink.

Krystal deposited a wad of saturated paper towels into the garbage can by the back door, then whirled around to glower at David. "This is all your fault for bringing him here!"

He tossed the sponge to Frankie and faced her. "Can you just calm down? It was an accident."

She crossed her arms, her mouth set in an angry line, her eyes two dark storm clouds. "Maybe I don't want to calm down. Maybe I'm too pissed to calm down!"

"So, what are you saying, you don't want to go out tonight?"

"What? With the *two* of you? Gee, *what fun!*"

David wasn't sure if she was backing out because of Frankie or because of their earlier conversation, but he didn't care. He had the green light to leave.

Back in the safety of his car, he spun toward Frankie. "Do you realize what a close call that was? I almost had a heart attack!"

Frankie put a hand on his heaving chest. "You're telling *me*? *I* was the one who was almost nailed!"

"I tried to signal you from the front door. I was practically screaming."

"You were supposed to signal me *before* you came back into the house."

"Yeah, I know, but you saw who I was dealing with. She ran back inside before I could stop her."

Frankie slipped on his seatbelt and drew a series of deep breaths. "I still can't believe I let you talk me into doing this. When I said I'd do anything for you, I didn't mean criminal stuff. I'm in enough trouble."

"I think my plan was brilliant. You acted like the annoying, needy friend, and I distracted her while you searched her room."

"Except you left out the part where she came back early and I got caught."

"Well, that didn't happen, did it?"

"A bit too close of a call, bro. I almost shit in my pants when I heard you two back inside. I had to put the stuff I was looking at back the way I found it and get out of her room in like five seconds."

"So, how'd you get the towel so fast?"

"Oh, that was actually some strategic thinking on my part. First thing I did was go into the kitchen to get some food since that's what I was supposed to be doing. I had to show her that I ate something, right? Then, when I poured myself a glass of OJ, I almost knocked the glass off the counter, and that's what gave me the idea to do it on purpose—to make a big mess so I'd have to go to the other end of the house to get a towel. It worked perfectly—she thought I was coming from the bathroom, not *her* room."

David couldn't help but smile. "I can't believe you planned that out in advance. That's impressive."

"Hey man, I may not do great in school, but that doesn't mean I'm not smart and can't think on my feet."

"So, after all that, did you find anything?"

Frankie launched into a detailed description of his efforts canvassing Krystal's room. He started with her computer, which was a dead end since it was password protected, moved on to the myriad of personal female items stuffed into her drawers, and ended with the piles of old papers, school projects, toys, and albums shoved into the back of her closet.

David sighed with disappointment. "So, you're telling me you found nothing?"

Frankie's lips spread into a wide grin as he whipped out an old photo from the side pocket of his cargo shorts. "If you call this nothing."

He held up a grainy color picture of a chubby, dark-haired young girl, maybe eight or nine years old, with thick black-rimmed glasses and a V-shaped gap the size of a teepee between her protruding front teeth. She also had on a light pink top two sizes too small that forced her round, fleshy belly to pop out below the shirt's hemline.

"Don't tell me that's Krystal?" David said, his eyes wide with disbelief. He snatched the photo from Frankie's fingers for a closer look.

"You don't recognize your own girlfriend, bro?"

"*Ex*-girlfriend," he corrected, studying the picture. "I can't believe this is her."

"It's all her. All three hundred pounds," Frankie joked.

David couldn't tear his eyes away from the unflattering image. "It's crazy that someone who used to look like this could have the kind of attitude she does."

Frankie leaned over to gaze at the photo again. "Yeah, you'd think she'd be a wee bit more humble. What are you gonna do with it?"

David thought for a while. "I'm not sure. I'd love to give her a taste of her own medicine. The only thing is, this picture is so bad I don't know that anyone will believe it's Krystal."

"Would another help?" From the same shorts pocket Frankie plucked out a second childhood photo of Krystal.

In this one she and her older sister were standing by a homemade lemonade stand, pointing to a crude cardboard sign scrawled in crayon. Krystal wore a pale yellow dress that was also way too tight and accentuated her belly rolls. Her hair was parted straight down the middle and pulled into two long braids, further highlighting the gap-toothed smile and hideous glasses.

"This is beautiful! Frankie, you're the man!" David held out his fist, and the two bumped knuckles. "I gotta tell you, if I were her, I would've burned these instead of hiding them in my closet."

"Can you imagine the poor schmuck who has kids with her?" Frankie mused. "He's gonna say, 'What the hell? Where did these ugly little bucktoothed porkers come from?'" The two laughed so hard David had to pull over onto a side street until he could hold his lane again.

When Frankie caught his breath, he turned to David and said, "Uh, I was just thinking, have you ever seen Blair's baby pictures? You don't want to dump one ghastly girlfriend for another."

David grinned. "Blair's childhood pictures are all over her house. She's always been exactly the way she is now—adorable."

"You know," Frankie said, bobbing his head. "This just taught me that when I get serious with somebody one day, I'm gonna ask to see her baby pictures. I don't want any surprises like this."

"Me neither," David nodded.

"Seriously, if my kids looked like that, I'd demand a paternity test and pray my wife cheated."

They both chuckled, and Frankie tucked the pictures back into his shorts. "Where are we off to now, amigo? Looks like you're going toward the mall."

"I am—we need to grab something to eat. But first I have to stop and show these pictures to the one person who'll appreciate them as much as much as we do—maybe more."

CHAPTER 40

The Confession

I can't stop staring at the two childhood photos of my nemesis.

"These are priceless, just priceless," I keep repeating, clutching one in each hand as though they're rare treasures. "Those bushy eyebrows alone are worth a small fortune!"

David and Frankie rushed over after their recon mission at the Ice Queen's house, and the three of us stand in my dining room, enjoying the less-than-flattering pictures of Her Highness under the bright glow of the crystal chandelier.

"Yeah," Frankie agrees. "These are the kind of things people use as blackmail."

David's eyes light up as he turns to me. "There's an idea—want to blackmail her?"

The corners of my lips invert. "What would we blackmail her for? There's nothing she's got that I want. Besides, she's already done her damage."

Frankie's voice grows serious as he says, "I am really, really sorry, Blair. If I hadn't texted that picture of you, none of this would've ever happened."

I can't believe what I just heard and whip around to face my confessor. "It was *you*?"

Frankie's head snaps backward, seeming struck by the shock in my voice. "You didn't know?"

"No," David explains. "I didn't even tell Blair. I protected you so you wouldn't go to jail."

Frankie clasps David's bicep in his enormous fingers.

"You are the best friend anyone could ever have. I told you before and I mean it: No matter what you ever need, I'm here for you, bro."

David chuckles. "Even if it's more breaking and entering?"

Frankie holds up his palm as if he's swearing under oath. "I did not break in. I asked to use the bathroom, and she let me in. It was the food thing that really pissed her off." He breaks into a hearty laugh. "Did you see her face when I asked for something to eat? I thought she was gonna shoot me!"

That image of Krystal makes David laugh too, but I'm still stuck on the revelation that Frankie's the one who sent out my picture. I narrow my eyes at him and lock my jaw in a tight scowl.

"Uh, Frankie, I'm so sorry to interrupt your fun, but why did you do that? Did you know that by sending that picture you got us both arrested and expelled? We could go to jail because of you!"

Frankie stops laughing, and his large body shrinks to half its size as his chin drops and shoulders sag. "Believe me, I know. That's why I'm so sorry. I never meant for anything bad to happen—Davey is my best friend. I just remember thinking that it was a really hot picture and I wanted to share it. Problem is, I was drunk off my ass and didn't pay attention to who I sent it to. I obviously sent it to Krystal, and believe me, if I could take it back a trillion times, I would."

I need to verify the story David told me, so I ask, "Are you the one with the criminal record who's afraid of that three-strikes rule?"

A deep flush pulls across Frankie's cheeks, and his eyes plead with mine. "Please, please promise me you won't say anything—not yet, anyway. I came up here today to turn myself in because I can't do this to Davey anymore. It's been killing me—letting him take the heat for this—and I just figured enough is enough. I drove up here to go to the police and tell them the truth about what I did, even if they lock me up. Only when I got here tonight, Davey told me to wait because his lawyer is working on a deal he thinks will keep him out of jail, so he said I shouldn't say anything yet."

Now I turn to David. "Is that true? They're giving you a deal so you won't have to go to jail?"

David nods. "But my attorney told me not to talk to you about any of this because he said you have your own lawyer and we're not on the same side. I don't agree—I think we're in this together and we *should* talk about it. I mean, this only happened to you because of me and Frankie, so if I don't go to jail, there's no way you should."

"My lawyer told me not to talk to you about it either, but shouldn't we both know what's going on with each other? I don't want to find out afterward that you got something better...or worse."

"Me neither. If you ask me, our lawyers are stupid and we should tell each other everything that's going on."

I lay the photos of Krystal on the dining room table and extend out my hand. David shakes it, both of us proclaiming, "Deal!" Then we kiss and hold each other in a long embrace. Now that I know for certain it wasn't David who sent the picture, I let myself go, melting against his strong chest, sighing in contentment.

"Hey," Frankie intrudes. "Don't forget, I'm still here."

We pull apart, but remain holding hands.

"Krystal's pictures?" Frankie reminds us, pointing at the photos. "Now that you forced me to raid her bedroom, what do you want to do with these beauties?"

My mouth forms a wicked grin. "I'd love to make posters

of them and hang them all over school."

David grins too. "We could put 'The Real Krystal Cooper' across the top."

"Let's go do that right now," Frankie suggests. "How many copies do you want?"

I cross my arms, contemplating his offer, but ultimately shake my head. "I wish I had the nerve to do something like that, but I can't. It would be stooping to her level."

Frankie lifts his eyebrows. "So you're going to waste these beautiful hippo shots?"

"It's not a waste," I say, scooping them up and handing them to him. "They made my day. And from now on, every time I see her in school, I'll just picture her in these photos and it won't matter what she calls me—I'll just laugh at her."

David nods, the edges of his mouth curved upward. "Me too. I'll never get these out of my head."

DAVID

◆

CHAPTER 41

Payback

"You're not really going to waste these pictures?" Frankie asked from David's passenger seat. "I mean, I killed myself to get them, and they're so damn funny, it would be a travesty of justice to bury them in a drawer somewhere."

David glanced askew at his friend. "What are you suggesting...make posters?"

Frankie gazed at the two photos of Krystal, a mischievous grin spreading across his lips. "I have a better idea. Did you get your computer back from the police yet?"

"Nope. They've still got it."

"Then head over to the library at the community college. You know, the one on Willow Street."

"Sure. You going to tell me why?"

"It's payback time. After everything you told me Krystal did to Blair, I think she deserves to experience a page from her own playbook."

"I like the sound of that, but is it going to be legal?"

Frankie smirked. "Nothing's illegal if you don't get caught."

David shook his head. "I'm so close to getting a deal that I can't do anything that could risk it."

"Don't worry—I know exactly what I'm doing. I learned how to use VPNs in juvie from this hacker guy."

"What are VPNs?"

"Virtual private networks. They allow you to send data through encrypted channels. We can find an open computer on the second floor of the library and set up our own Instagram account for Krystal without anyone ever knowing."

"Shouldn't we just use an untraceable IP address—like the one Krystal used for the finsta of Blair?"

"Nah, with VPNs you don't need to do that. The beauty of VPNs is that the actual physical IP address will be replaced by the VPN provider, bypassing the content filters."

David crunched his brow. "Not following you."

"In other words, the VPN allows you to spoof your actual location, so it looks like you're someplace else, like Brazil or Australia or Japan. No one will ever be able to trace what we're about to do back to us here in Westberry."

"Are you one hundred percent sure? You can't exactly risk getting caught either."

Frankie pressed his back against his seat, a confident smile across his face. "I've done it before, and it works perfectly. You'll see."

Less than an hour later, The Real Krystal Cooper Instagram account featuring the Ice Queen pre-braces, pre–contact lenses, pre–eyebrow waxing, and pre–Weight Watchers, went live. David sent follow requests to at least a hundred kids from Westberry, making the account public so anyone and everyone could check out her new Instagram.

After peeling out of the college library parking lot, David turned to his partner in crime. "You did that fast."

Frankie beamed. "Yeah, I got real good at typing in juvie. I'm always so bored, I spend a lot of time on my computer."

"I think my favorite part of her new profile—even better

than the pictures—is the Bio. I wish I could see her face when she reads it."

Frankie laughed as he pulled the scrap of paper with his notes from his shirt pocket. He did his best imitation of a girl's voice as he read: "'Hi, I'm Krystal. As you can see, I've inherited my daddy's bushy eyebrows, my Aunt Martha's buck teeth, and my Grandpa Joe's pot belly. If you know me now, then you know that my parents spent a lot of money fixing me up. They had to. When I was younger, Santa wouldn't even come to my house because I scared him off. When I ran away, no one would come looking for me. I cracked the camera lenses, and airbrushing didn't help. Finally, I had an extreme makeover, but it didn't completely work. As you know, I'm still chunky and bitchy and there's no way to make me smarter. It's okay, though. I've got a whole bunch of people who are even dumber than I am that follow me around.'"

David grinned ear to ear. "That is too funny no matter how many times I hear it. It was a great idea you had to include myself in the follow requests, because now she won't suspect me as the one who did this."

"I told you, I'm real good at thinking on my feet. It's sitting in a classroom and taking tests that I hate."

"And you're absolutely positive we can't get caught?"

"Bet my life on it. Literally."

David took a hand off the steering wheel and patted his old friend on the shoulder. "You've been a huge help to me this weekend."

"Do I even have to say that it's the least I could do?"

"I just hope she doesn't figure out that you're the one who stole her pictures last night."

"Even if she figures it out, what's she gonna do, call the police?" Frankie switched back to his girlie voice and pretended to talk into his phone. "Hello officer, I'd like to report a theft. My ex's best friend snooped around my room and stole two of the ugliest pictures you've ever seen from when I was a child. No, officer, I can't prove anything. No, the pictures have no value. No, they're not collector's items. It's just that I look so ugly in them, I want them back. You understand, don't you?"

David laughed so hard he could barely hold the wheel straight. "Bro, you have no idea how much I've missed you."

Frankie answered with a light punch to his friend's thigh. "Same."

CHAPTER 42

David and Krystal

Back in school on Monday, the Ice Queen makes it crystal clear that she thinks David and I are behind her new Instagram. It could be because she knows David sent Frankie into her home, or because she thinks I retaliated for the Blair the Mare finsta, or because David had figured out she was the one who'd sent my underwear photo to the police. Whatever the reason...the bottom line is, she knows. And she's enraged.

The false niceness that she'd used as part of her masterful plan to win David back is gone. I'm a freak again with a capital "F," and my friends and I are back to Class C, less-than-dirt status. The Things have returned to their normal mean-spirited selves, hissing their nasty taunts—Blair the Mare, Bessie the Cow, Kimchi Kayla, Half-and-Half—and knocking into us as we pass by.

The big difference for me now is that I don't cower or run away. I face them head-on and laugh when they chant their demeaning Brainy Bunch lyrics and hurl their spiteful barbs. It's truly amazing, but their insults have lost their sting.

They're not prepared for my new defiance and get louder and more hostile as I snicker back at them. After everything I've been through—the catastrophic fallout and humiliation from the sexting photo and phony Instagram, the arrest and expulsion—there really isn't anything worse they can do to me. I'm just not scared of them anymore.

David, however, is a different story. The Ice Queen and her cronies completely ignore him. Her Highness obviously learned the hard way that her brilliant plan didn't work, and there's no point in pretending she wants him back. But David doesn't let on for a second that he knows anything's up beyond the fact that Krystal's still upset with him for bringing Frankie on their date and making a mess in her kitchen.

Outside of the cafeteria, I watch from a short distance away—slightly down the hall and around the corner—as he confronts his ex-girlfriend. He rests a hand on her shoulder and gazes at her earnestly. "I know you've been ignoring me, but I want to apologize again. I had no idea Frankie was going to pop in this weekend. I'd texted him the night before about how my lawyer had said I'd probably have to go to jail, and he felt so bad he just got in his car after school on Friday and drove all the way here to cheer me up. He didn't know I had a date with you."

The Queen's eyes bore into his like lethal laser beams. "*That's* why you think I'm upset?"

"No," he replies. "I know it's because he destroyed your kitchen too. He's such a big, clumsy thing. I'm really sorry about that. He's always been a klutz."

"You are so full of shit, you know that!"

David edges away, taking mini steps back. "Uh, I'm trying to apologize here. Why are you being so nasty?"

She's ablaze, spewing fire. "You know damn well why I'm so pissed, and don't pretend you don't, you son of a bitch!"

He raises his palms. "Whoa, hold on a sec. What's going on with you? You're acting insane!"

"Excuse me? *I'm* acting insane? After what you did, you're lucky I don't find a way to get you arrested again!"

He stops cold, peering at her in shock. "*Again?* You mean

you're the one who got me arrested?"

What an actor *he* is! He could give Splenda some lessons. The Queen's mouth freezes in its open position, her guilty face blanching as she realizes her blunder.

Two Things are loitering close-by and exchange nervous glances at their leader's slip up. I'm enjoying the entire scene, glued to it like a bad soap opera.

David continues staring at the Queen in feigned disbelief, making her squirm under his harsh gaze.

She tries to recover and says, "No, of course I didn't have you arrested. I meant that I'd find a way to get you arrested a second time."

I'm so proud of him at this moment, because he doesn't let her off the hook. His eyes are cold and hard as he closes the gap between them and slants his face downward until it's intimidatingly close to hers. "No, that's *not* what you said. It *was* you, wasn't it?"

"I…I didn't do anything," she stammers. "That just came out wrong."

"How could you?" He glowers at her, shaking his head. "After everything we had. You told me you loved me, and then you had me arrested?"

"But you didn't love *me*," she retorts, her index finger poking her own heart. "You couldn't have, or you wouldn't have gone out with *her!*"

David's eyes widen as his lips curl into a contemptuous sneer. "What are you talking about? You broke up with me and cut off all ties. We didn't see each other or talk for months. Why couldn't I go out with someone else?"

"You weren't supposed to go out with anyone else—you were supposed to wait for *me*! And then you picked *her*! You know how much I hate her!"

Every feature on his face hardens as his eyes drill into

hers. "So you had me arrested?"

She shakes her head repeatedly, but he backs away, his mouth twisted in revulsion. "I know it was you."

He spins on his heels and heads down the hall in my direction, and she runs after him. I definitely don't want to be in the middle of their drama and drop back a few feet, ducking into a doorway.

"It wasn't me!" she shouts. "But you're a son of a bitch for what *you* did!"

He stops walking and whips around. "What are you talking about—*what I did?*"

"You know what I'm talking about—the pictures you put on Instagram that you had your friend steal from my house!"

He glares at her with unconcealed contempt, recoiling as she approaches. "You destroyed my life—ruined my entire future—and you accuse *me* of putting up stupid pictures?" He shakes his head and emits a low, guttural laugh. "You're crazy. Just stay away from me."

CHAPTER 43

Celebration

Rachel, Kayla, and I clink glasses over the hibachi table at our favorite local Japanese restaurant, Fuji Fusion. We typically don't go out on school nights, but this Thursday night is a wonderful exception. We have major cause for celebration, and it's about me. I only wish Carrie were here too, but her field hockey practice ran late, and she needed to do homework and study for a French test. Same with Annie. School and sports always come first for her, so getting her to socialize is near impossible.

Kayla watches me pop a piece of sushi in my mouth and wash it down with raspberry iced tea. "So, this is really it," she says, her eyes gleaming. "You're free now. No jail, no sex offender registry, no trial. You get to take that course on responsible digital citizenship, do some volunteer work, and you're done. "

I toss her a thousand-watt smile and nod. "That's what my lawyer says. Next week we put the agreement on the record, and then I don't have to ever worry again about being in a cellblock. David and I both told our lawyers about the plea deals we were each being offered, so they finally started working together and it put an end to this whole nightmare. I can apply to biomedical engineering programs now, and actually go if I get accepted."

Rachel raises her glass for another toast, and Kayla and I jump right in. "To the best week you've had in a long, long time, a bright future, and sweet revenge." We click glasses again, and she adds, "I never would've believed you were capable of something like that, but you really cut the bitch down to size."

I lean in toward my friends and say in a super low voice, "I didn't do it."

Kayla gasps and shouts, "Who then...David? Frankie?"

My eyes fly wide open as I whirl around to see if anyone is listening. Thankfully, the restaurant isn't crowded, and we have the hibachi table all to ourselves.

"Shh!" I caution. "You can't talk about this in public. None of us need any more trouble."

Rachel drops her voice to a whisper. "I thought it was you too, but no matter who did it, it was awesome and everybody's talking about it. I mean, no one knows for sure if it was you, but I think they all suspect it was after what she did to you first."

"But she's denying it's even her," Kayla chimes in. "I heard she's claiming that those are pictures of someone else—like her sister's friend."

I burst out laughing. "Yeah, I've heard that too. It's a great excuse if you think about it. 'I've never been that ugly. It must be someone else!'"

Both girls join in the laughter, and Kayla says, "I'd probably deny it too if someone posted hideous pictures like that of me."

Rachel hinges over the rim of the table and grins. "She is hideous, isn't she?"

We tap glasses one more time, and I say, "And she always has been. But what I really don't get is how she's had no problem making fun of your weight all these years when she was heavier than all of us combined."

"We'll just add 'hypocrite' to her long list of shining attributes," Kayla remarks, her lips crinkling into a smile.

"It comes right after her advanced knowledge of Asia—where she expertly lumps the people of Korea, China, Japan, Vietnam, Singapore, and the Philippines into one country."

I'm chuckling as I glance up to see our hibachi chef wheeling over a cart of fresh food he's about to cook tableside. There are plates piled high with wide noodles, mixed vegetables, and raw meats, alongside a colorful array of sauces and seasonings. We're in for a feast.

Before he starts, Kayla asks. "Do you think IQ has permanently given up on Yak, or do you think she's still trying to get her talons into him?"

"It doesn't matter," I reply. "He really hates her since he found out she's the one who sent that photo to the police. Even if I didn't exist, I don't think he'd want anything to do with her. Would you ever want to see someone again if you found out they tried to send you to jail?"

"Well, the truth," Kayla corrects, "is that she tried to send *you* to jail. He was just collateral damage."

I smile. "Collateral damage. You tell that to David. I'm sure it'll make him feel better."

The chef, a round-faced Japanese gentleman with a thin mustache and a contagious grin, turns on the grill and squirts out some cooking oil. "Would you ladies like to see a volcano?"

The three of us nod, and he proceeds to build a tall pyramid out of raw onion slices. Then he flicks his lighter and a brilliant orange flame shoots up, the sudden heat making us all jerk our chairs back.

"That is so cool!" Rachel says, her face aglow in the dazzling light, her blue eyes sparkling.

The proud chef takes a bow, and we reward him with enthusiastic applause. As he begins preparing our sesame noodle appetizer, Kayla angles toward me. "There's one thing that's really worrying me."

Uh-oh.

"What?"

"Well, have you thought about what IQ's going to do now that her plan is ruined? I mean, she's obviously the vengeful type, and now that she suspects you and David posted those awful pictures, she's not going to just let it go."

I ease back in my seat and cock my head to the side. "What can that bitch possibly do to me now that she hasn't done already? Make every day of high school a living hell? Ruin my social life? Make sure people who don't even know me don't like me? Have me arrested? Try to break up my boyfriend and me?" I draw checkmarks in the air after each question. "What else is left?"

Kayla furrows her brow, taps her ceramic plate with her chopsticks, and sighs. "I don't know, but I have this funny feeling that she's not going to let you put up that account and walk off with her boyfriend without doing something about it."

"But it wasn't me."

"But she thinks it was."

"So, what exactly do you think she's going to do?"

Kayla shrugs, her intense, almond-shaped eyes laden with concern. "I don't know, but it's going to be something big. And bad."

I turn to Rachel. "Do you think Kayla's right? She's going to do something else to me that's really bad?"

Rachel shrugs too. "I don't know what could be worse than what she's already done, but I agree with Kayla. Her first plan was ruined, and now she has to come up with something else to save face. I think we'd be deluding ourselves if we thought you got the last laugh."

Kayla nods. "She's never going to let you win."

"I don't want to win," I retort. "I just want to be left alone."

We stop talking while the hibachi chef sprinkles sesame seeds and chopped scallions onto the cooked noodles, then scoops them off the hot grill and divides them between us.

Rachel doesn't waste a moment before slurping her first bite. "I love these!" she says while chewing.

Kayla gives up on her chopsticks and stabs her noodles with a fork. "This is so much easier."

I clutch my own chopsticks in an iron grip. My mouth had been watering from the delicious smells a minute earlier, but now I sit quietly, watching my friends eat, thinking about what they've just said. Should I be worried? Is this witch going to do more to me?

Rachel points at my full plate. "If you don't eat them, I will."

Noticing my glum expression, the chef says to me, "Want to see shrimp fly?"

I force a thin smile. "Sure."

He taps the broad blade of his knife on the grill three times, then masterfully flicks his wrist, sending a jumbo shrimp spinning high above the table. With minimal effort, he stretches his neck forward and catches the shrimp in the top of his tall white chef's hat.

We all applaud and cheer.

I end up enjoying the rest of my celebratory dinner, but I lie in bed late into the night wondering what I should be afraid of next.

CHAPTER 44

New Evidence

The following week doesn't go quite the way I'd anticipated. It seems that my friends' predictions were dead-on: our celebration was premature. While David happily finalizes his plea deal and enrolls in the educational class and community service program that will fulfill his end of the bargain, the prosecutor pulls back on my deal, citing new evidence against me.

I learn this splendid news when Uncle Marv places an emergency call to me just as I'm heading to my locker after the last bell on Tuesday afternoon. He refuses to discuss the reason for the urgency behind his call, so I blow off my swim practice and zoom straight to his office, praying I won't get a speeding ticket tacked on to the rest of my charges.

Both my parents are entering Uncle Marv's reception area when I arrive, and they look as anxious and on edge as I feel. My mom's face is creased with worry lines, and my dad's jaw is tight with stress, the way it's been throughout this entire ordeal. We're ushered into the main conference room, where my lawyer quickly joins us. None of us bother to sit down.

My dad locks eyes with his old friend and slaps the shiny mahogany tabletop with his open palm. "What's going on? Why did you call us all here?"

I'm bouncing from foot to foot, unable to stand still as I wait for Uncle Marv to drop the latest bomb. I glance at my mom, who is a jittery mess, her right eye twitching nonstop.

She protectively loops an arm around my waist.

My uncle is clearly not happy about delivering bad news and tugs so hard on his snow-white beard it seems like he's going to pull it off. "I called all of you here," he begins solemnly, "because the prosecutor's office just let me know that your deal is off the table."

As he shifts his sight on me, his voice grows even more sullen. "They claim to have new evidence against you that voids their offer."

I feel my stomach lurch, convulse, then sink like a cannon ball. The familiar lump in my throat that mushrooms every time there's more bad news swells so big right now it constricts my airway. I clutch my neck with one hand and my belly with the other. I want to ask the dreaded question, the one that no one in my family really wants to know the answer to, but I can barely breathe and certainly can't talk.

My mother voices the words I can't get out. "What kind of new evidence?"

Uncle Marv averts his eyes. "More sexually explicit pictures of Blair."

"*What?*" I shriek, tumbling forward. He might as well have just told me I'm going away for twenty years. I catch the edge of the conference table with both hands, my mom intensifying her grip on my waist.

My dad's jaw springs open. "More pictures? Are you kidding?" He peers at me, searching for answers, but I'm staring dumbfounded at my uncle.

"What is going on here, Marv?" my mom implores.

"Come with me," he commands.

We follow him down a short hallway into his private office, a large square room lined with bookcases. There, a dark-haired, dark-skinned man in his mid-thirties is seated at Uncle Marv's computer. "This is Sunil, my investigator."

Sunil glances up at us, nods, then announces to his boss, "Got 'em."

My legs wobble knowing that whatever is coming next is not going to be good. I want to tear out of here and go anyplace else, but I know I have to see these new photos. I just can't imagine what they are, when they were taken, or who took them.

In a moment I don't have to wonder any more. Sunil pivots the wide monitor toward my family, and a color photo of me in my new powder-blue silk cami set flashes on the screen. In the photo, I'm standing in my bedroom facing my front window, my hair half-wet, a red wide-toothed comb in my right hand.

"Who took this?" my father demands, his eyes blazing.

I stammer out the truth. "I...I don't know."

"It was him again, wasn't it? He took more pictures of you that you never told us about—didn't he?"

I hate it when my father's inner litigator comes out and he falls into cross-examination mode. He grills you like you're on the witness stand at a trial, speaking only in accusations.

"No," I whimper. "David never took a picture of me in that."

"Then who did?" He glares at me in his accusatory way that says, "I don't believe you."

"I told you, I don't know. But it wasn't him."

"Then who?" my father repeats, pounding Uncle Marv's desk with each word.

My mother stares at me expectantly, both her eyes twitching like crazy.

"I don't know!" I cry. "I have no idea!"

My dad loses it. Every blood vessel in his neck and face bulges, and his skin turns a deep shade of crimson. "What do you think—we're stupid?" he hollers. "You're protecting him again, aren't you? That son of a bitch got you in all this trouble, and now he's free, and you're *still* protecting him? Why don't you just take your future and flush it down the toilet!" He can't contain his rage any longer and storms out of the office, slamming the door so hard the walls rattle.

Uncle Marv speaks to me in a much calmer voice, but it's obvious from his sharp tone that he shares my father's thoughts. "Are you protecting David?"

"No," I insist, gripping the lip of the desk as though my life depended on it. I'm having a hard time controlling my own anger at these unfounded, insane allegations. "He didn't take that picture. He couldn't have—he didn't even have a phone when that was taken. He said goodnight to me and left....I went to sleep."

My uncle raises a disapproving eyebrow. "Why were you wearing that with him in your room?"

I roll my eyes. Uncle Marv sounds exactly like my father.

Fortunately, my mom comes to my rescue. "That's what she wears to bed, Marv. Blair likes to sleep in these silky, satiny things. She always has—since she was a little girl. All her pajamas have always had to be soft and silky."

The skeptical look on Uncle Marv's face doesn't diminish, his mouth still pinched, his features pulled into hard lines. "Blair, without playing any games or protecting anyone, can you please tell me who took this picture?"

I shake my head. "Believe me, I wish I knew. But it wasn't David. And no one else has been in my room." I shrug. "I don't get this."

My uncle signals Sunil with a quick nod. The investigator hits a couple of keys, and the next picture pops up. This time I'm completely naked as I face my dresser, the camera shot capturing a side view. I must have just come out of the shower, because my hair is dripping wet and there's a smoky gray bath towel strewn on the floor behind me.

I'm too embarrassed for words—having my Uncle Marv and this man Sunil look at me with no clothes on is more than I can bear. Thank God my father has already left the room.

"Where did you get these pictures from?" I croak, my voice barely audible.

Sunil speaks for the first time. "The prosecutor's office."

"But...where did *they* get them from?" I stutter. "No one else was in my room with me. You can see I just came out of the shower."

"That's what *we're* asking *you*," Uncle Marv intercedes. "When were these taken, and who took them?"

My brain is swirling with confusion...and frustration. Two powerful forces that are impeding my ability to think. "That's what *I* want to know. This doesn't make any sense. How did the prosecutor get these pictures of me from when I was alone in my bedroom?"

At my last words Uncle Marv's entire demeanor changes. He scrunches his Santa face, his somber brown eyes flashing with understanding. "Blair, someone who doesn't like you wants you to go to jail. Are you positive it wasn't David? There's no chance he's still got a thing for his ex-girlfriend and they're working together on this—sending these pictures by cell phone?"

I stumble back a step. "Did you just say these were sent by cell phone?"

Uncle Marv strokes his long white beard and nods. "That's how they were forwarded to the police again. Anonymously, of course."

"There are more photos than these two," Sunil pronounces. "Want to see them?"

No, but he displays them anyway.

There are three more, to be exact. Five in total. I'm wearing a towel in two, the powder-blue cami set in one, and I'm stark naked in the other two. I couldn't be more mortified. Now, Uncle Marv, his investigator, the prosecutor's office, the police department, and God knows how many other people in the world are looking at me in my birthday suit, fresh out of the shower, in what's supposed to be the privacy of my bedroom. The first photo David took had been bad enough. These are unbearable.

I throw open the door to Uncle Marv's office and stumble onto the speckled carpeting in the hall. Gulps of air rush from my lungs as I force my feet to work. I bypass my father, who's talking to an older gentleman in the waiting room, and stagger outside.

I want to run. I want to punch someone. I want to scream at the top of my lungs and never stop.

Why is this happening to me?

The loud horn of a train blasts somewhere nearby. I could get on that train and never come back. I could move to the west coast and start a whole new life where no one knows me. Anything would be better than staying here and facing this humiliation.

I lean against a light pole, squeeze my eyes closed, and try to slow my breathing. The horrible reality is that it doesn't matter where I go: I'll never be able to show my face in public again.

D A V I D

◆

CHAPTER 45

Blair's Bedroom Window

David had no idea anything was wrong until he opened his gym locker after soccer practice. That's when he saw Blair's urgent text: "Come to my house NOW!" After everything that had happened between them following their arrests, he was afraid to find out what was behind her message. Nevertheless, he dashed to his car and blew the speed limit the entire way to her house.

When he pulled up her driveway, he found her standing alone on her front paver walkway holding a large aluminum stepladder. An early autumn breeze lifted her ponytail, fanning her red curls out sideways, a light drizzle coating her bare arms and white swim team T-shirt. She seemed completely unfazed by the weather, her pale blue eyes squinting in concentration as she contemplated where to place the feet of the ladder.

He jumped out of his car. "What's going on? Why'd you send me that text?"

"I'm trying to see if my theory is correct," she answered, her voice flat and impassive. He watched her maneuver the ladder around an overgrown azalea in the narrow mulch bed that ran along the front of her house.

Striding toward her, he asked, "What theory?"

She set the ladder down under her bedroom window and whirled to face him, miniscule droplets of the misty rain clinging to her lashes. "Before I tell you, I need to know if you took any more pictures of me while I was in my room—besides that first one."

"More pictures? No...why?"

"You sure?"

"Yeah—I would know, wouldn't I?"

"Remember when it was really late last Friday night, and you waited for me to take a shower and get ready for bed because you wanted to kiss me goodnight right before I fell asleep?"

He smiled. "Of course, I wanted your last thoughts to be of me."

"I need to know if you took any pictures of me that night when I came out of the shower...with nothing on."

David crinkled his brow and stuffed his fingers into the front pockets of his sweatpants. "That would've been great if I was there when you came out of the shower, but you made me wait in the hall, remember? When you called me into your room, you already had on that light blue thing and you were combing your hair."

Blair clutched the top step of the ladder with both hands while she blew out a long breath. "Well, I didn't see you take any pictures, but maybe you took them when I wasn't paying attention."

David stepped forward, raising his voice. "I did *not* take any more pictures of you. Haven't we had enough problems from the first one? And if you really want to know, I'm scared to ever take another picture of you again!"

Her conflicted expression told him she was still torn. The rain and wind picked up, and she swatted at some flyaway strands of damp curls that drifted across her face.

"How do I know you haven't tried to get close to me again so you could take more pictures and make sure I go to jail since the first time didn't work? How do I know everything you're doing and saying isn't part of Krystal's master plan and you're not just following her orders?"

He closed the space between them, stopping just short of her toes. "I hate her—maybe even more than you do. I'm not a puppet that just follows orders. I make my own decisions, and the person who I've decided to be with is *you*. Now get that through your head!" His eyes shifted to the stepladder, and he poked at the front side rail. "Do you mind telling me what you're doing out here with *this,* what pictures you're talking about, and why you sent me that text?"

She slicked her fingers along the second step, studying him as she spoke. "There are more pictures of me taken in my bedroom that were sent to the police. If you didn't take them, then the only theory I can come up with is that someone climbed up to my window."

David's eyes bugged out. "The police have *more* pictures of you?"

Blair nodded.

"When did *that* happen?"

"I just found out this afternoon."

"And you think someone used a ladder to get to your window?" he asked, pointing up toward her bedroom.

"It's the best theory I've got."

"You think Krystal?"

"Who else?"

He shook his head. "There's no way Krystal would dare to come to your house, climb up a ladder, and take your picture. She may be capable of a lot of things, but she'd never do something where she could be caught so easily."

"So maybe *she* didn't take them but had someone else

do it."

He kept shaking his head. "Who in their right mind would do that?"

"Hey, you went out with her, and the entire school follows her. You can't see how she could convince someone to take a few pictures? One of the Things? The next guy she's gonna sink her fangs into?"

"Maybe you're right, but you need to know that I had nothing to do with any of this." He angled his face toward hers, resting a hand on her rain-splattered shoulder. "What can I do to prove that to you?"

"For starters, how about holding the ladder?"

CHAPTER 46

Six Sleuths

Late Saturday morning, David, Kayla, Rachel, Carrie, and I sit on my bedroom floor in a tight semicircle around David's iPad. Frankie participates in our brainstorming session from Virginia via FaceTime. After his fearless foray into the Queen's lair and his skillful assistance with the Real Krystal Cooper Instagram, he's proven he's worthy of being part of our mystery-solving powwow.

"Okay," Rachel begins. "Here's what we know: First, a stepladder would be way too low for anyone to reach Blair's window, so they would've had to use a bigger ladder to get up this high—you know, like the kind house painters use."

From the rectangular screen on the iPad, Frankie lends his two cents. "No one walks around carrying giant ladders like that. You need a truck for one of those babies."

David nods. "And this doesn't seem like it happened just once. Blair says the new photos of her were taken on two or three different days."

"At least two," I confirm.

Kayla shrugs her shoulders. "So?"

"So," David continues, "someone either drove up in a truck or somehow carried a huge ladder through the neighborhood and set it up right in front of this house on at least two different occasions without anyone noticing. What are the odds of that?"

"Highly unlikely," Kayla agrees. "Unless it was an inside job."

Frankie picks up on her intimation and says to David, "Oh man, she thinks it's you!"

David turns to Kayla, his features tight. "I had nothing to do with this. That's why I'm here trying to help."

"Either that or you're a double agent," Kayla retorts with a laugh, even though I know she's not joking. Before anyone else arrived, Kayla had shared with me her belief that David was the culprit behind the new photos. She'd deduced that he was the only person—other than my family—who had been in my bedroom, and therefore it had to be him.

David starts to defend himself. "I am not a—"

"Let it go, buddy," Frankie directs from his viewing screen.

"No," David says. "I want to know why she thinks I'm a double agent."

Kayla doesn't hesitate. "Maybe it's because you made out with the Ice Queen not too long ago, and you're the *only* person who's been in Blair's room who could've possibly taken the new pictures. Not to mention that you *did* take the first picture."

"Enough," I break in. "David was never in my room after I came out of a shower, so I know it wasn't him. Can we please get back to figuring out who it actually was?"

"Well, first we need to figure out how it was done," Rachel corrects. "Then we'll have an idea of who did it."

Rachel may be a top contender for valedictorian, but she's missed the boat on this one. I blink hard at my friend. "Uh, we already know who did it. I've been in a cyber-war with her for weeks. And did you forget that little part where she got me arrested?"

Rachel shakes her head. "You tell me how the Ice Queen or one of her Things got into this room or climbed up to that window to take those pictures?"

Kayla uses this opportunity to shoot David an accusatory glare.

"You know," he says to her. "You're really pissing me off. I wasn't going to tell any of you this, but I tried on my own to get to the bottom of this."

I raise my eyebrows. "What'd you do?"

"I tried to call Krystal, but she wouldn't talk to me, so I went to Pam—who you call Thing 3. We've always gotten along really well, so I asked her if she knew about new pictures of you being sent around, or if she heard anyone talking about it."

"What did she say?" I ask.

"And when were you planning to tell us this?" Kayla adds.

David presses his lips together. "I didn't tell you because she said she didn't know anything about it, and she wasn't very kind to Blair."

I slant my head sideways. "What exactly does that mean?"

"It means she doesn't like you."

"Well, I know that already. Are you really not going to tell me what she said after everything I've been through?"

He sighs in resignation, rustling his fingers through his spiky hair. "Okay, if you must know, she said, 'I don't get why anyone would want to take more pictures of that freak anyway.'"

This revelation from Thing 3 doesn't bother me in the least. It's not exactly like I'm hearing it for the first time.

Our group grows quiet until Rachel breaks the silence with her next hypothesis. "I'm thinking this could've been done by someone from one of the houses across the street."

At that possibility, we all jump up and converge on my front window. I have a corner room, so there's also a side window, but the pictures couldn't have been taken from that one based on the angle of the shots.

"Hey, what about me?" Frankie calls out.

Kayla beats David to the iPad and holds it up so Frankie can see too. Her fast action isn't lost on me. Ever since Kayla met Frankie in person the previous weekend, when he stole Krystal's childhood photos, she hasn't stopped talking about how cute he is. Even though he's a huge football player and she's a petite gymnast, sparks flew between them. I tried to dissuade her from liking someone who's been in so much trouble with the law, but Kayla still has her crush. Jokes about the total mismatch of the little intellectual and the big inmate have had no effect. I ultimately let up on her now that I'm back to wondering whether I'm going to be an inmate myself.

"The only house that's close enough for anyone to see in would be that one," Rachel says, pointing to a white colonial with black shutters diagonally across the street.

"That's kind of far," Kayla remarks. "Those pictures look like they were taken by someone standing right in this room."

"Haven't you heard of a zoom lens?" David says with a snide edge to his voice.

"Don't you two start again!" Frankie warns.

Kayla flashes an innocent smile. "I wasn't implying anything bad, I was just making a point. Even with a zoom lens I don't think someone all the way over there could get those shots."

"Zooms can be really powerful," David presses.

I've been friends with Kayla long enough to know that she doesn't back down when she thinks she's right, and this is one of those times. "But look at the angle they would've been taken from," she argues, extending her right arm out forty-five degrees.

"You know," Frankie interjects. "From what I'm seeing, Kayla is right. The angle would be way off from that house... which could mean only one thing."

David turns to face the iPad. "What?"

From Richmond, the big guy raises his eyes toward mine and says, "Well, you're not gonna like it, Blair, but I bet someone took those photos of you with a drone."

I lean in toward the screen. "Did you say *drone*?"

"Yeah, drone. They're everywhere now. You can get a pretty decent one for only a few hundred dollars. And they're in toy stores too, really cheap."

The thought of someone hovering their drone outside my window to secretly take pictures of me is too sickening to digest. I want to puke up the protein shake I had for breakfast.

"Damn!" David cries. "You must be right! How else could someone have taken those pictures?"

Kayla shudders and backs away from the window. "From now on I'm going to make sure my shades are shut when I get dressed."

My eyes spring open at her statement. "The pictures aren't from a drone—they can't be. I always close my shades before I change at night. My mom taught me when I was a little girl that if it's dark outside and you put the light on, everyone can see in." I hold up the illicit picture of me in the towel. "See the wall sconce behind me—it's lit. That means my shades were shut, so even if there was a drone out there, it couldn't have taken these shots."

"Maybe that night you forgot to close them," Kayla offers.

"No," I say with conviction. "I *always* close my shades before undressing. It's like closing the door to the bathroom. It's something I automatically do."

Kayla licks her lips, then says, "Maybe the shade wasn't

fully closed."

I narrow my eyes at her. "I always make sure they're *fully* closed. And look at this picture—you can tell by the wide angle of the shot that it wasn't taken through a crack in the shade."

David tips his head back and sighs. "If it wasn't a drone, then we're at a loss."

Carrie, who hasn't said a word the entire morning, finally pipes up from her perch on the corner of my bed. "Maybe we're not." She moves to the center of my room and stops. "If we concentrate on the camera angle those pictures were taken from, it brings us right there." She points straight ahead—at my desk.

All eyes in the room swivel to my white laminate desk, book-filled hutch, and laptop computer.

David sidesteps over to my desk chair. "Carrie, you're saying someone had to stand over here to take them?"

She nods.

He glares at me. "*Who* would that have been?"

I instantly pick up on his insinuation and shoot back, "I had the whole hockey team up here, didn't you know?"

"Now *you two*?" Frankie bellows. "We have to stop letting this thing make us fight and work together."

Kayla beams at her crush. It's clear from her glowing expression that Frankie's peacemaking attempts are making her like him even more.

Carrie locks eyes with me as she extends her forefinger at my computer. "Blair, isn't that your school-issued Chromebook?"

"Yeah, why?"

She crosses over to it and taps the top of the monitor. "Well, it has a webcam, right?"

"Yeah, they all do. Why are you asking?"

"Because everything is pointing to the pictures being taken from right here," she says, directing my attention to the tiny circle at the top of my laptop. "If David didn't do it, and your room is too high up for someone to look in without a big ladder, and you say your shades were shut, then the pictures had to have been taken from right here. It's the only answer."

Kayla's mouth falls open. "Oh my God, she's right! Someone's been taking pictures of you through the webcam. It's gotta be!"

David and I exchange disbelieving looks, while Rachel throws her arms around Carrie. "You're a genius!" she cries.

Carrie grins ear to ear. "I was kind of mad that you all dragged me out of bed this morning, but now I'm really glad I came."

I fling my arms around Carrie too. "Thank you! I knew there had to be an explanation for those pictures!"

Frankie notices that Kayla isn't sharing in our excitement. "What's wrong, Kayla? Carrie solved the mystery, but you don't look so happy."

Kayla's face is a mask of concern as she stares at the tiny camera lens. "She only solved part of the mystery. The real question is...*who* is accessing Blair's webcam?"

CHAPTER 47

C-6

Our mystery-solving powwow moves down the hall to my dining room table, where we await my dad's homemade pizzas. He loves to treat our guests to his authentic Neapolitan creations, which he makes from all fresh organic ingredients, including his own homegrown herbs and handmade mozzarella. My friends and I are practically drooling from the tantalizing aromas wafting in from the kitchen.

Carrie tilts up her nose and sniffs the air. "Now that's worth getting up early for."

Kayla chuckles. "I know this is early for you, but its lunchtime for the rest of us."

"It's not early for me," I declare. "I already had a swim meet at eight, so I was up at six-thirty. Then I stopped by the shelter. I'm starving."

David nods. "Me too. I had to be at soccer practice at seven. Believe me, if I got to sleep till ten, I wouldn't be complaining."

Carrie scowls at him. "I get up at the crack of dawn all week, stay up really late studying every night, and go to church on Sundays. This is my only day to sleep."

"Well, this was the only time out of the entire weekend we could all meet," Rachel says in a clipped tone. "So, let's not waste any more time talking about sleep." She folds her arms and clamps her teeth together. "Can we get back to solving the rest of the mystery now?"

I know that Rachel will stop acting grumpy once we get some pizza into her. She doesn't normally eat breakfast, and by late morning she has protein crashes and turns into a grinch.

Kayla tucks a few strands of her long silky hair behind her ears and shifts forward in her seat. "There's no mystery. We know whose daddy the technology director of the school is, and the bitch got him to spy on Blair."

My dad pops out of the kitchen, his left hand wrapped in a silicon oven mitt. "Kayla, I heard what you just said, and I think you might be right. I got off the phone a few minutes ago with Aryana, the paralegal from my office who's my tech guru. She said that for a school-issued computer, the network administrator would absolutely be able to monitor Blair through her webcam because he'd have her IP address."

Rachel hugs herself. "Ooh, I have the chills. It's like Big Brother is watching."

"No," Kayla corrects. "It's Big Daddy who's watching."

David appears pretty shaken too, his lips compressed and his eyes blinking fast. He's super pale as he says, "You know, it may not be only Blair he's been watching—he has access to all of our computers. For all we know, he could have pictures of all of us."

"Well, that's a creepy thought," Carrie says. "It gives me goose bumps."

I bob my head. "But he could be right."

Rachel's blue eyes take on an eerie glow as she turns toward me. "He could've been watching us while we were in your room before."

Kayla pulls her arms into her chest and shivers. "I can't even imagine someone having a hidden camera in my bedroom. I feel so...so violated just thinking about it."

I can't believe my friend's insensitivity. "Ahem, how do

you think *I* feel? It's *my* pictures that have been sent to the police and plastered all over the Internet!"

Kayla's eyes roam over each of us until they settle on me. "But he could post pictures like that of any of us at any time. We're all sitting ducks."

"Listen, everyone," my dad interjects, waving his mitt. "Our focus now needs to be on how we can prove that Krystal's father was involved in this. We all seem pretty sure that there's no coincidence—he's the school's technology director, so it had to be him who took the pictures—but we're speculating. Without proof, we can't go to the police or the prosecutor."

I toss a skeptical gaze at my father. "And how are we supposed to get proof?"

The oven timer buzzes, and he spins toward the kitchen. "That's where we have to be creative," he yells over his shoulder.

As we devour the first set of his outrageously delicious pies, my father plants the seed for his idea to nail the Ice Queen's dad. Then he lets us kids brainstorm until we formulate a workable plan. We stay on FaceTime with Frankie while we flesh out our strategy, and Kayla is so excited to have him involved, she names our group the Cyber-Six, or C-6 for short.

We toast frosty glasses of fresh-squeezed lemonade—à la my mom—to our team's new name, and pick the upcoming Monday to put our ingenious plan into action.

CHAPTER 48

Showtime

George Cooper's technology office is on the second floor of Westberry High School near the physical sciences wing. It's situated in a busy corridor, and his door is almost always open. Today, we're counting on it.

Our C-6 team decided to use a code name for Mr. Cooper so no one could accidentally overhear or intercept any of our messages. Since everyone in school refers to him as Coop, we needed something different. After a couple of jokes about his henpecked status living in an estrogen-dominant household with the Ice Queen, her sister, and mother, we came up with Rooster.

With his balding head and round belly, Rooster has always reminded me of Humpty Dumpty, and now that I've seen the unflattering photos from the Queen's younger years, I can't help but think of her the same way. Whenever I get nervous about implementing our plan, I use a mental image of the horrible family sitting on the edge of a red brick wall to help calm my nerves.

After picking at my periwinkle blue nail polish and checking the time every five minutes since 7:00 a.m., Carrie and I are about to begin scene one of our C-6 production. She's volunteered for the lead role since she's always wanted to act, but has never had the time because of her commitments to field hockey and lacrosse. This is her chance to get dressed up and cinch the spotlight. Normally, she wears baggy sweats to school, but for her starring debut she's decked out in high-heeled black leather ankle boots and a tight, stretchy teal dress. She's also let down her ponytail and enhanced her catlike green eyes with smoky kohl eyeliner. I have to say, she looks great.

Carrie's curtain call is at the end of sixth period. With her medium-length, wavy dark hair swinging from side to side, she rounds the corner of the physical sciences wing and teeters down the hall past Rooster's office—which, thankfully, does have its door open. After passing two adjacent classrooms, her feet suddenly fly out from under her, and she careens headfirst into a bank of bluish-gray metal lockers, an ear-splitting smack reverberating outward in all directions.

This is where I enter the scene. "Oh my God! Somebody help her! Heeelp!"

As hoped, Rooster bolts from his office at my bloodcurdling screams and races toward us. The fallen girl is sprawled flat on her back, lying motionless, her books strewn across the floor. I'm bent over her, frantically shouting, "Carrie, are you all right? Look at me! Carrie, open your eyes!"

Her eyelids are closed, and she doesn't respond. Other kids run over and circle around us, but no one seems to know what to do.

"What happened?" Rooster cries, kneeling next to Carrie and me. I see the alarm in his eyes when he taps her cheek and she doesn't react.

"I don't know!" I wail. "I was coming from the other direction, and the next thing I know she went down, slamming her head into the lockers." I place my hands on Carrie's shoulders and shake her. "Wake up, Carrie! Wake up!"

"Don't do that!" commands a voice from above me. "She might have a spinal injury." It's Mrs. Ventura, a Latin teacher who also rushed over at the sound of the commotion. I start to whine. "A spinal injury—nooo!" Then I poke her arm. "You're going to be okay, aren't you? Carrie, wake up!"

There's a large crowd of kids looking on now, expressions of horror on their faces at witnessing Carrie lying corpselike on the floor. Rooster barks instructions up at them. "Someone call an ambulance. And get the school nurse—tell her we need a backboard. Now!"

He's white as a sheet and looks like he might faint when I cry out, "Oh my God, is that blood?" I slide my hand under Carrie's glossy hair, and when I pull it out my fingers are coated with dark red liquid. "Oh my God! Oh my God!" I scream in high-pitched hysterics, waving my bloody hand over my head.

"Can someone get some paper towels?" Rooster hollers, his voice a mixture of panic and fear. "*Now!*"

"I have some tissues in my purse," Mrs. Ventura volunteers, handing a wad to Rooster.

"I have some too," I whimper, rummaging in my bookbag with my non-bloody hand.

Seeing that we're focusing on cleaning up the blood rather than administering any type of first aid, a male voice in the crowd asks, "Is she breathing? Does she need CPR?"

Then a girl in the front remarks, "I think she's dead. She hasn't moved."

Rooster places an ear over Carrie's mouth. Relief sweeps over his features as he announces, "She's breathing!" Then he places his own mouth against her ear. "Carrie, can you hear me?"

Still no response.

I grab one of Carrie's legs and violently shake it. "Get up!" Tears rush down my face as I keep screaming her name.

"Carrie! Carrie!"

I catch a glimpse of Mrs. Ventura, who's standing with her hands crossed over her heart, her breaths coming in short puffs. She whirls her head around and yells, "Where is the nurse? Did anyone get her?"

"What about an ambulance?" Rooster adds, his voice quavering.

All of a sudden, Carrie's eyelashes flutter and her lips begin to move.

"She's alive!" a boy in a football jersey shouts.

"Carrie!" I call out. "Carrie, can you hear me?"

Her eyes open to thin slits and blink. She strains forward, like she's having trouble focusing. "Blair?" she whispers.

"Yes!" I shriek, snatching one of my friend's hands and squeezing hard. "It's me! Are you okay?"

"I don't know," she mumbles, her lips barely moving.

"Does anything hurt?" Rooster asks, his bushy dark eyebrows knitted together.

"I...I," she starts to say. Then she reaches behind her to touch the back of her head. When she removes her hand it's covered with fresh, gleaming blood.

"Oh dear," she mutters. "These stupid boots."

"Is that what happened?" Rooster asks, pointing to her feet. "You slipped?"

She nods as best she can. "Yeah, I'm not good in heels. Should just stick to cleats."

Nurse Lu finally arrives and uses her first aid kit as a shield to push through the crowd. "Let me through!" she commands. "Let me through!" Long before I see her face, I spot her mounds of bleached-blonde locks piled high above her head, secured by her signature ceramic butterfly clips.

Rooster scoots back to allow Nurse Lu to assess the injured girl. Her first task is to check Carrie's pupils and pulse. "Vitals are good," she pronounces.

Carrie's eyes open wider now, but her voice is low and weak. "Can I get some ice, please? My head really hurts."

As Nurse Lu retrieves an instant cold pack from her first aid bag, Carrie pushes herself up to a sitting position and leans back against a locker.

Mrs. Ventura yells, "She shouldn't sit! What if she has a spinal injury?"

Before Nurse Lu can agree, Carrie says, "I *don't* have a spinal injury. I just banged my head a little, that's all." She takes the ice pack from the nurse and rests it on the bloody area.

I get to my feet and try to gaze over the mass of onlookers to find David, but I'm way too short. If he's still outside Rooster's office, then Carrie and I need to drag this charade out a bit longer.

The seventh-period bell rings.

"All right, everybody, go to your classes," Rooster urges. "She's okay. Move along now."

I'm happy when the crowd disperses enough for me to see down the hall, but panicked to find David still stationed in front of Rooster's doorway.

This could get really ugly.

D A V I D

◆

CHAPTER 49

Plan Execution

The second after Rooster exited his office, Kayla slipped inside. While David pulled the door closed, Kayla eased into Mr. Cooper's chair and began to search the files on his desktop computer. The idea behind creating an emergency was to get Mr. Cooper out of his office without logging off or shutting down. C-6's plan could never work if his login ID and password were needed.

As it was, the plan might not work anyway. If the technology director had in fact taken pictures using Blair's webcam, he could be storing them anywhere. And if he were smart, he wouldn't be keeping them on the hard drive of his school computer. But right now, this was their best bet.

The odds were against them, but C-6 voted unanimously to go ahead with the plan. The only other option was to get inside the Ice Queen's house again and try to access her father's home computer, but neither David nor Frankie were eager to attempt that feat. After the debut of the Real Krystal Cooper Instagram, the Queen wasn't on speaking terms with David, and Frankie certainly wouldn't be welcome in her home.

David's heart raced as he watched Kayla click away at Rooster's computer. "Can't you go any faster?"

"No!" she snapped. "My hands are so sweaty my fingers keep sticking to the keys."

"Well, try anyway," he muttered, his own fingertips nervously tapping against his outer thighs.

Kayla's role in the C-6 production was taking much longer than it was supposed to. If she didn't hurry, they were all going to be caught and have nothing to show for their efforts other than a trip to the principal's office—and hopefully not the police station.

"Damn!" Kayla swore for the third time.

"You know," he said, "if you stopped looking up at the door and paid attention to what you're doing, it'd go a lot faster. Let *me* keep watch, and *you* concentrate on the files."

"I *am* concentrating. I already accessed Rooster's start menu and opened his pictures folder. I'm just blown away by the volume of subfolders he's got—there have to be hundreds of them. How am I supposed to figure out which ones have Blair's pictures when there are no names, only dates? And there's no time to open them all. He could be back any second."

David cracked the door, his eyes darting down the hall. "You still have some time. He's in the middle of the crowd with Carrie."

"He's got so many damn pictures folders, I don't know where to begin!" Kayla whined.

"Start with the most recent ones," David suggested. "The pictures he took of Blair are pretty new, so they're probably in one of the last folders."

"But we don't know how long he's been watching her. He could be just adding the recent pictures to a file he opened a long time ago."

The commotion in the hall grew louder, and panic flashed across David's face. Kayla jumped up and shrieked, "What do I do? I'm not done!"

"Just sit back down and finish—fast!"

"Let me know when he's coming," she cried, dropping back into Rooster's chair with such force the wheels skidded backward. "Carrie may have the biggest part, but she's not the one who's going to be expelled for breaking into a school official's computer."

David pushed the door all the way open and stood guard at the threshold. He braced himself against the doorjamb, pressing the heels of his hands into the hard metal.

"I'm doing what you said," Kayla murmured. "Opening the last files he created."

"What's in them?" he asked over his shoulder.

"The most recent has photos from the PTA-sponsored faculty breakfast on the first day of school. And the file before that has graduation pictures of last year's seniors, but the one before that has photos of the cheerleaders and football players from the home game three nights ago. Damn—he uploads files totally out of order!"

"Well, he's not exactly going to label it 'Blair's Webcam,' so you just have to search."

"Gee, why didn't I think of that!"

"You don't need to get testy. I'm trying to help."

"Well, you're not. And just so you know, I'm scanning through tons of his most recently created folders, but so far there's nothing."

The voices in the hall grew more animated, prompting David to peek around the corner. "You need to hurry. The nurse just got here."

Kayla slapped at the mousepad, tears flooding her eyes. "I can't do this. It's impossible!"

CHAPTER 50

Show's Over

Out in the hall, Rooster asks about an ambulance for the fourth time. Carrie shoots me a look that screams, "Get me out of here now!"

"You know, Nurse Lu," I say. "She looks so much better than she did before—I don't think she needs an ambulance."

"Uh, no. I really don't." Carrie smiles, tugs the hem of her tight teal dress lower on her thighs, and kicks off her high-heeled boots. "I'll be able to walk just fine without these stupid things. And I'm feeling so much better now that I'm sitting up."

"You were unconscious, my dear," Nurse Lu states. "That's extremely serious, and you need to get checked out in a hospital."

Rooster nods. "She's right. They need to make sure you don't have a concussion or internal bleeding. When any of my hockey players bang their heads, we always get them checked out, especially if they were unconscious."

Carrie gazes up at him incredulously. "I wasn't unconscious. I was just too embarrassed to open my eyes after such a klutzy fall. I wanted you all to just go away."

"*What?*" he exclaims, his eyes bulging. "You weren't unconscious? I was ready to give you CPR!"

Mrs. Ventura looks aghast too, her chin pulled all the way back into her chest. "And I was worried that you might have broken your neck!"

Carrie hoists herself to her feet with my assistance. "I'm

really sorry to have worried you all so much, but I'm fine. I think I'm just more humiliated than hurt." She removes the ice pack and holds it out to show the adults she's okay. "Look, the bleeding has almost stopped. It's just a little scrape."

"You should still sit back down and wait for the ambulance," Rooster directs. "I'm glad you think you're okay, but you gave us quite a scare."

Nurse Lu bobs her head. "He's right. You should sit and rest until the EMTs get here."

"Now that I know she's all right, I have to get back to class," Mrs. Ventura announces, backing away from our small group in the direction of her classroom.

Rooster turns to the nurse. "I've got to get back to work too. Are you okay waiting by yourself?"

I steal a peripheral glance down the hall. David is still loitering outside Rooster's office. I throw Carrie an anxious look, my eyebrows hiked all the way up my forehead.

"Uh, Mr. Cooper, do you think you can help me downstairs?" Carrie implores. "I just want to go home and need some help getting to my car."

"You absolutely should not be driving, young lady," he proclaims. "You need to get in the ambulance when it arrives." With that, he spins on his heels and heads back to his office.

We watch as David heads him off in the hall, but there's nothing we can do anymore. It's now up to David and Rachel to distract him.

"Okay, I'm out of here," Carrie declares, scooping up her boots and pushing off the wall of lockers. "Blair, can you drive me home?"

"Of course," I reply, sidling up close so she can clutch my shoulder for support. I've already tossed her books into my backpack, so there's nothing left on the floor except a smattering of blood and some stained tissues.

We start down the hall, but Nurse Lu trails close behind. "You can't just leave!" she shouts at Carrie. "We have an ambulance on the way!"

Carrie shakes her head. "Sorry, but I hate ambulances. I'm not going in one."

"Stop or I'll call your parents!" she roars.

"I'll have them call you or come in later," Carrie yells over her shoulder, picking up speed as we approach the nearest stair bank. We're practically airborne as we fly down the steps and sail out the closest exterior door. Nurse Lu is still in hot pursuit, her bleached hair out of its butterfly clips, billowing in a whitish-yellow cloud behind her.

We dart around the side of the building to the student parking lot at warp speed, our chests heaving. I know that I can get in huge trouble for an unauthorized departure from school, but honestly, after everything I've been through, I really don't care.

As I pull out the school exit in my Forester, the ambulance is turning in, its red and blue lights whirling, sirens blazing. In my rearview mirror Nurse Lu is at the mouth of the student lot, pounding the air with her fist. I can see her lips moving but, thankfully, I'm too far away to hear the expletives she must be spewing.

DAVID

◆

CHAPTER 51

Best-Laid Plans

David watched Kayla chew on her bottom lip as she stared at Rooster's computer screen. "What are you doing now?"

"Scrolling through the folders with three-digit numerals that increase in ascending order. The others have only two digits, but it seems that the ones with three digits contain photos of school events."

"So, what's in the two-digit ones?" David asked.

"I'm going to open some of them now. Let's see...there's photos of a Cooper family ski trip...a beach vacation—"

"Any chance he stuck Blair's pictures into one of those?"

Kayla shrugged. "I don't know."

A loud tinny ring catapulted her out of her seat like it had burst into flames. Seventh-period bell. She patted her heart and sank back down. "That scared the life out of me."

"Just hurry up," David said, resuming his post in the hall.

Half a minute later he backed inside Rooster's office, his face ashen. "Everybody's leaving. He'll be back any second!"

"I need more time!"

"You don't have it!"

"I don't want to be the one to blow our whole plan. I'm

just going to send some of these two-digit files to Aryana."

"You need to stop now!"

"In a couple of minutes. You and Rachel stall him!" She slapped Rooster's monitor on its side. "Why is this thing so damn slow? It's taking forever to load each jpeg file."

"Don't wait for each one to fully go through before sending the next," David suggested. He stepped back into the hall, readying himself for his C-6 acting role.

Kayla nodded. "You're right. I'm just going to fire them all off."

Moments later, as Rooster approached his office, David positioned his body so his back blocked the doorway and said, "Coach Cooper, can I ask you something?"

That was Kayla's cue to get away from Rooster's computer immediately. As David pivoted around, he caught Kayla vaulting over the corner of Rooster's desk into one of his guest chairs. Only a gymnast could have accomplished that move.

Rooster stepped over his door threshold to find Kayla waiting for him in front of his desk. She thrust her laptop at him. "Can you please help me, Mr. Cooper? I think my computer might have a virus."

No sooner did she finish her sentence than Rachel burst into the small office. "Mr. Cooper!" she cried. "I lost my entire English paper and I need your help quick!"

Clearly rattled from the nerve-racking ordeal with Carrie, the befuddled man crinkled his nose and alternated his gaze between Rachel, David, and Kayla, not knowing who to help first. But Rachel didn't let up.

"I spent the entire weekend writing it, only when I went to print it in the library, it's gone! All fifteen pages! The only thing on my flash drive is the first paragraph. I'm so sick, I'm going to throw up!" She clutched her chest and pushed out quick shallow breaths. "I think I'm having an anxiety attack!"

If Rooster's complexion wasn't ghostly white before, it was now. C-6 had hoped that he wouldn't allow the class valedictorian's English paper to disappear on his watch, and thankfully, they'd predicted correctly. He spun toward Rachel and said, "All right, let me take care of your problem first, that seems to be the most urgent." Then he addressed David and Kayla. "I'll help you two next."

"Thank you so much!" Rachel exclaimed, turning toward the door.

Rooster stayed planted, holding out his palm. "Let me have your flash drive."

Rachel spun back to face him, pointing over her shoulder down the hall. "It's in the library—in the computer."

The idea for this ruse to keep Rooster out of his office longer came from Frankie, who had experienced a similar problem with a European history paper. He'd finished it late at night but couldn't print it at home because his ink cartridge had run out, so he saved it onto a flash drive and brought it to school the next morning. Only when he went to print it in the library, his flash drive was empty.

After a brief pause, Rooster said, "All right, let's go."

"I have to get to my next class now," Kayla announced, moving toward the door. "I'll come back later."

David eased into one of the guest chairs. "I can wait, Mr. Cooper. I only have lunch now."

As soon as Kayla watched Rachel and Rooster round the corner, she darted back into the tech office.

"What are you doing here?" David hissed, his eyebrows shooting up. "Didn't you finish?"

"No, he's got a zillion files. I didn't have enough time to send them all to Aryana, so I gave her as many as I could, and I hope it's in one of them. But I need to delete all my emails to her that are in Rooster's sent log so he doesn't see them."

She dropped back into Rooster's chair and proceeded to delete her emails—thirteen in all.

David rose from his guest chair and stationed himself in the doorway again. After a couple of minutes, he leaned against the doorframe and said, "Aren't you done yet? How long does it take to delete some emails?"

"Since I didn't have time to open any of those other files, I'm trying to send Aryana some more now. The more I send, the better our chances."

"The more you sit in that chair, the better our chances of getting caught!"

"Can't you just be quiet and look out for him?"

"I really hope Blair is in one of those files, or this whole thing is for nothing," he grumbled.

Five minutes later David heard Rachel's loud voice echoing off the lockers. "Thank you so much, Mr. Cooper. As soon as I get home, I'm going to try that." She may have been out of view, but that was their final cue.

Kayla heard it too and stood, returning the mouse to the exact spot she'd found it. "I emailed forty-two files and deleted all of my transmission records," she whispered to David as she slipped out the door.

Before Rooster returned to his office, David was seated back in a guest chair, and Kayla was galloping down the hall to her journalism class.

CHAPTER 52

Mission Accomplished?

"Are you going back?" Carrie asks as we flee from the school.

We're about halfway to her house, and I'm still panting from our crazy escape. "I don't want to, but yeah, I guess I should. You?"

"You kidding? They'll throw me in that ambulance. I'll have one of my parents call and tell them I'm okay. I'll go back tomorrow when they've calmed down."

"Well, I've gotta tell you," I say with sincere admiration. "You really should be an actress. If I hadn't known you were faking, I would've been freaking out."

Carrie grins. "Thanks, but you're pretty good yourself. If I didn't know I was faking, I would've thought I was a goner based on your reaction."

"Let's just hope that Kayla found something. She was in there for a long time."

"She probably didn't, or she would've been out of there right away."

I frown. "Yeah, I was thinking that too. I mean, he *is* the tech guy. It would be really dumb for him to store pictures of me on his school computer."

Carrie holds up an index finger to make her next point. "Except for the fact that he would never think we'd figure out it was him and go looking for them. The tech guy is the one who always looks at everyone else's stuff—he'd never think anyone would go through *his* stuff."

I toss her a feeble smile. "I hope you're right."

Carrie's fingertips graze the back of her head. "I can't wait to get this fake blood out of my hair. I don't want it to get all matted and have to shave my head."

"I can't believe how real that stuff looks."

She nods. "It really does. And it was cheap too. Because it's almost Halloween, I found it at the dollar store with all the vampire stuff."

"You could squirt the rest on your face and go trick-or-treating at Rooster's house," I joke. "Can you imagine his expression if he found you bleeding on his front steps?"

"I'm so glad I'm graduating this year so I won't have to see him too much more," she chuckles, pulling out her comb. "I thought he was going to strangle me when I told him I hadn't been unconscious."

"And Mrs. Ventura too. Did you see her face?"

We both laugh now.

In another couple of minutes we arrive at Carrie's house. We stay in my car while I text Kayla to see if she found anything. She writes back immediately: "Not sure."

I angle my face toward Carrie. "What does *that* mean?"

She shakes her head. "I don't know, but it doesn't sound too good. I guess we'll have to work on Plan B after all."

Now I shake *my* head. "You really think David or Frankie will be able to get inside Rooster's house and get on his home computer? And even if they could, how would they get rid of the Queen and her family so they could search? We're gonna need a Plan C."

"Oh," says Carrie, separating the clumps of hair near the crown of her head. "I didn't know we had one."

"We don't," I lament. "That's the problem."

"It would be so much easier if you would just go to the police and let them do this."

I try to suppress my annoyance. "You heard my father. The police aren't going to just take our word for it that it was Rooster using the webcam. They need probable cause to get a search warrant."

Carrie squishes her lips as she considers my explanation. "I guess we're in a catch-22 then, because unless they do a search and find the pictures, they're not going to have probable cause to believe he took them."

I heave a deep sigh, my eyes welling with tears. "Something like that. This whole thing just sucks."

"Do you think your father would've been okay with our plan today?" she asks. "I mean, I know he told us not to do anything illegal, and not to tell him if we were even thinking of doing anything questionable—because he's a lawyer and all—but there really wasn't any other way."

Steady tears stream down my cheeks as I shake my head. "No, I'm sure he would've thought we went too far. Especially because we all could've been arrested if we got caught. He never would've approved of that." I grip the steering wheel so tight my knuckles glow a translucent white. "And it was all for nothing anyway. A big fat nothing!"

"You have to stop being so negative."

"How can you expect me to be positive when, every time I think I'm going to get through this, more bad things happen? No matter what I do, they just don't stop."

"It'll work out," Carrie says in a cheerful tone, wiping the fake blood off her comb with a tissue. "You'll see. Everything will be okay."

I swing my head back and forth. "No, it won't. You're all going to go off to college and have the time of your lives, and I'm going to end up in jail. I just know it!"

"Hey, that's not going to happen. Do you hear me? Not going to happen."

I bury my face in my hands. "I just want to die!"

Carrie scoots over and wraps her arms around me. She tries to soothe me by telling me wishful things like, "It's all going to work out," and, "Everything will be all right," but I know they're not true and sob harder.

I'm going to end up like poor Henry, trapped in a cage, helplessly viewing the world from behind ugly metal bars. No one can tell me differently—that's the way everything is heading. And how sad is it that I can't even help a dog, let alone myself? I'd begged my parents to adopt Henry, to give him a good end to his life, no matter how little or long it is, but my dad insists that his allergies are still too bad. I even suggested building a big doghouse in the backyard, but he said no to that too. I tacked up posters of Henry's beautiful face all over town, but no one wanted him when they learned his age. My heart breaks for Henry, for me, for anyone who is helpless and has no control over their own destiny.

I'm heaving in hoarse breaths, shuddering, my eyes too blurry to see, when both our cell phones beep at the same time. Carrie reaches into her purse to grab hers. Through my wet, foggy haze I make out the outline of her mouth spreading into an ear-to-ear grin as she reads the message. "This couldn't have come at a more perfect time," she says.

I don't know what she's talking about, and I don't care.

She shakes my shoulders. "Hey! You better not die just yet, because Aryana just sent C-6 a text saying, 'Mission accomplished!'"

I slide my fingers down my cheeks and tilt my disbelieving eyes toward hers. My throat is clogged with mucus and phlegm, but I manage to eke out, "Really?"

She holds up her phone so I can see for myself. "Really. You can stop crying now, because all those bad things you were talking about just came to an end. They're officially over."

I blink away pools of tears to read the two wonderful words: "Mission accomplished!"

CHAPTER 53

One Step at a Time

My dad sent Uncle Marv the incriminating evidence C-6 discovered on Rooster's school computer, and Uncle Marv in turn forwarded it to the Westberry Prosecutor's Office. I went back to school after I dropped Carrie at her house, and I'm jumping out of my skin waiting for a response.

I don't want to go to swim practice, but I already missed way too many practices when I was expelled and can't miss any more. I leave the pool four times during the hour-and-a-half session to check my phone, but so far, nothing.

When practice finally ends, I skip a shower, throw sweats over my wet bathing suit, and sprint to my car. My first call is to my father.

"Did you hear anything?" I holler over my Bluetooth microphone. I'm too jittery to drive, so I sit in the driver's seat with the engine running.

"Hi, Dad, how are you?" he quips, reminding me I've lost my manners.

But I have no patience for his etiquette lesson. "Dad, just tell me!"

He chuckles. "I hung up with your Uncle Marv about ten seconds ago. We've finally got some good news."

Good news? For real?

"*What?*" I screech.

"Marv got the assistant prosecutor to look at the file Aryana forwarded to his office. The prosecutor's office agreed to investigate the origin of the sender. In other words, they'll need to verify that the IP address of the computer from which Kayla initially sent the picture files belongs to the school and, specifically, is registered to George Cooper."

That isn't quite the good news I was hoping for. I wanted my dad to tell me it was all over, they'd confiscated Rooster's computer, and now he's the one going to jail—not me.

My dad picks up on my disappointment. "Hang in there, sweetie. This is going to happen one step at a time, but once it starts, it'll happen very fast. You'll see."

I push out a frustrated sigh, but it sounds more like a growl. "I really don't expect them to do anything that'll help me. Remember how they were supposed to find the creator of the fake Instagram account? I haven't exactly seen that happen. They seem to only want to put me in jail, not help me."

"Stop being so negative, baby. We just handed them the source of these pictures, and they can't ignore it."

"How can I not be negative?" I whine, slumping in my seat. "Somehow they'll say it wasn't him, or they don't have enough evidence to charge him, and they'll just keep prosecuting *me*. This isn't good news at all."

My dad's tone switches to the authoritative one I hear him use with his clients. "Listen to me. You and your friends went and did the hard part. All they have to do now is verify what you've provided—and they will. This Cooper guy has no idea he's even a suspect, or he never would've left those pictures on his computer. He didn't try to remove the incriminating evidence or cover up his crime, so it'll be really easy for the prosecutors."

I suck on my lower lip, processing what my father just said. "I hope you're right."

"Baby, I may not be a criminal lawyer, but I do know

that Cooper's ass is fried."

"What does Uncle Marv say?"

"He says that he's incredibly impressed with you and your super sleuth friends, and now it's just a matter of time for everything to fall into place. He says your nightmare is almost over."

I grunt like an unhappy bull, digging my fingers into the tops of my thighs. "I've been saying that to myself every day, but it never ends."

"A little longer, baby, and you'll see that your old man is right."

We hang up, and I back out of my parking spot. Somehow all the excitement of the afternoon vanished and zapped every ounce of my energy along with it. I can barely hold myself upright as I pull out of the school lot.

Will this nightmare really end, or will I forever be caught in this eternal, serial dream that's actually my miserable reality? At the moment I'm almost too tired to care.

CHAPTER 54

Rooster

A driving rain pelts my living room windows early in the morning as severe thunderstorms and gale-force winds sweep through the state. The dangerous winds have already knocked out power lines in neighboring towns, and there's a tornado watch in effect. But Kayla and Rachel and I are unfazed by the powerful storm. We huddle together on my sofa, our attention focused on the iPad screen resting on my lap.

My mom glides into the room with an ostrich feather duster and starts cleaning the glass photo frames on the coffee table. "I'm so glad your father was right," she says as her duster flies over each frame. "The prosecutor's office wasted no time investigating the source of the files which contained those webcam pictures. The evidence that your C-6 group uncovered yesterday led right to that awful man."

Rachel nods. "I heard that last night the prosecutors, local police, county sheriff's department, and FBI sex crimes unit raided both the school technology office and the Coopers' home. They confiscated all their computers, hard drives, tablets, and smartphones...everything. And then they took the Rooster into custody."

"Can you imagine what that must've been like for the Cooper family?" Kayla remarks.

I narrow my eyes at her, "Uh, yeah. I can."

Kayla covers her mouth with her hand. "Oh my God—I'm so sorry. I can't believe I just said that!"

"It's okay," I say with a sigh. "As long as they're going after the *right* person this time."

"Have you heard from your father or Uncle Marv yet?" my mom asks as she slides over to the handblown glass sculptures and pictures set atop the baby grand piano. "It's after nine, and the arraignment hearing should've started by now."

I shake my head. "No, not yet."

My eyes stay fixed for a moment on my neglected piano. I haven't touched it in almost a month. Week after week I've canceled my piano lessons and told my teacher that I've been too busy with the start of school and college applications to practice. The truth, of course, is that I haven't been able to make myself sit still long enough to focus on my music, and I haven't even looked at a college application yet. But how do I explain my sexting scandal to a woman who's at least seventy years old?

Rachel refocuses my attention, saying, "I'm so glad we're watching remotely from here. I wouldn't want to be face-to-face with anyone in the Ice Queen's family right now."

"Yeah," I nod. "As much as I'd like to be there in person as the witch's father answers for what he did, it's so much better to have Aryana live stream it to us."

"How does that work again?" my mom asks.

I explained this to her earlier during breakfast, but technology isn't her thing. "Aryana's sending live video feed to my iPad via FaceTime. We'll see the arraignment as it happens without being there."

She almost knocks over one of the glass sculptures as I'm talking, but catches it in midair. Carefully setting it back into place, she asks, "Did David go to the arraignment?"

"No," I snap, not hiding my annoyance. "His mother wouldn't let him. And she wouldn't let him come here either.

She said he can't miss any more school, and she doesn't want him to have even one late arrival added to his messed-up record. Now that he's accepted his plea deal, she told him they're done with lawyers and courts, and she doesn't care one iota about anyone else's legal problems."

Kayla has been busy texting this entire time, and she glances up from her phone to say, "Carrie wanted to come over too, but her parents overruled her. They're so mad about her part in C-6 that she's not allowed to have anything to do with our group ever again. She had to tell them the truth about our mission because she needed them to call the school to get her back in, and they were so angry they ordered her to stay away from us. They told her we lacked good judgment and we put her in a precarious position."

My phone pings with a text from my dad. I read it aloud: "Bad weather delayed start of arraignment. Downed trees and nonfunctioning traffic lights stopped key court personnel from getting here."

My mom lays down the feather duster and heads toward the hall closet. "In that case, I think I'll vacuum."

I chuckle and tell my friends, "She's been so uptight this morning waiting for the proceeding that's she's been cleaning like a mad woman. She's already scrubbed the entire kitchen, mopped the floors, *and* washed the windows. I don't think my house has ever been cleaner."

"Well, you've gotta admit this is pretty nerve-racking," Rachel says, twisting the tips of her sandy curls around her fingers.

I'm not really one to talk about nerves. The last half hour I've been chipping away at my silver nail polish and glancing at the time every thirty seconds. My shoulders tense all the way up to my ears when the wall sconces in the living room blink twice.

"Uh-oh," Kayla says. "Do you think we're going to lose power?"

I shrug. "I hope not. We have underground wires, so we don't usually lose electricity, but this storm is supposed to be off the charts."

The lights blink again. This time they stay off for several seconds before coming back on.

"You should get your flashlights and candles ready just in case," Kayla suggests, her eyes steeped with worry."

I flip on the TV to catch the most up-to-date weather report. The newscasters are showing the ominous-looking funnel of a tornado decimating a town about fifty miles inland. My friends and I are entranced by the fireball-red, electric-blue, and neon-yellow satellite images, but we all jerk our heads back to my iPad when another text pings and flashes on my screen: "About to start."

I mute the weather station and holler over the vacuum cleaner. "Mom, they're starting!"

From somewhere down the hall I hear the vacuum motor switch off and the metal handle crash against the hardwood floor. In less than five seconds my mom is scooting next to us on the sofa.

Based on our view of the courtroom, Aryana must be transmitting from the right rear corner. We see the backs of peoples' heads rise as the judge—a statuesque blonde-haired woman with glasses—enters, and then lower again when they're told to be seated. The Rooster sits at the defense table with his hands folded, next to his portly attorney in a shiny light gray suit.

From our angle I can't tell if the Ice Queen is one of the people sitting in the tightly packed row behind her father, but I imagine she is. The Things are probably sandwiched right in there with her. Aryana texted me that she can't zoom in any closer, so we have to settle for the panoramic view.

I feel fortunate that my own arraignment was handled in private, but my dad explained to me before he left for the courthouse that it could help to sway the judge's decision and lower bail if the defendant's family and friends are there to support him and show he has strong ties to the community. From the sea of dark maroon jerseys, it looks like most of the hockey team and half the teachers are there. The room is filled to capacity.

The defendant rises, and the formal charges are read aloud. I cringe as I hear many of the same ones I was accused of: "Endangering the welfare of a minor; possession of child pornography; production and distribution of sexually explicit photos...." But I bob my head emphatically at the ones addressing Rooster's illicit actions against me: "Official misconduct, pattern of official misconduct, cyber-harassment, stalking, Internet sex crimes, misuse of confidential information, invasion of privacy for secretly using a camera to view and transmit live images...."

"Oh yeah! Oh yeah!" Rachel cheers. "Now he's gonna get it!"

Kayla raises her palm for a high five. "It's about time!"

"I'll never understand how a grown man with a family—a career in education—could do something like this to a child," my mother says with indignation. "He's really sick."

The judge asks, "How does the defendant plead?"

Rooster lifts his head high and replies, "Not guilty, ma'am."

The judge starts to say something else, but Rooster interrupts her. "Judge Weiss, before we go any further, you need to know right now that I didn't do anything wrong." His voice is panicky, if not desperate, but his delivery is strong and convincing. "I'm not just *saying* that I'm not guilty, I'm not. I have no idea what any of this is about. I never spied on anyone with a webcam, I've never distributed any pictures—I have no idea what's going on!"

"Mr. Cooper," the judge cuts in. "This is not a trial, it's an arraignment. All this Court needs to hear from you right now is how you plead. A trial is the proper forum for you to—"

"But I don't have the time or money to go through a trial for something I didn't do! This is so unfair—that's why I'm telling you right now that someone must have put this stuff on my computer, or else you've mixed me up with someone else. I can't afford to lose my job, my—"

"Wow, he's saying so many of the same things I did when I was first arrested," I break in. "It's kind of unnerving to listen to this." It may be Rooster's arraignment, not mine, but there are still criminal charges pending against me and I feel like I'm reliving the traumatic courtroom experience all over again. My stomach is a lead weight, and familiar pangs of anxiety stick in my throat.

The judge slams down her gavel. "Mr. Cooper! You've made your plea. Now I'll hear from the attorneys if they have any remarks regarding bail, which I hereby set at $500,000."

Rooster screams, "*$500,000!*" and whips his head back and forth. His lawyer gently guides him back into his seat, where he shields his face with both hands. The image of Humpty Dumpty falling off the wall and going *splat* pops into my head.

His lawyer takes over, making several arguments as to why his client should be released on his own recognizance and in no way poses a flight risk. He cites Rooster's strong ties to the community, waving his hand over the large crowd as proof of the technology director's formidable support network. He rambles on about Rooster's tight-knit family, his dedication to his job, and the children he coaches.

To close, his lawyer argues, "Mr. Cooper is a solid, upstanding citizen who has no criminal record, has never broken the law and, in fact, has never even gotten a parking ticket. If he is not released on his own recognizance, then the defendant respectfully requests that his bail be substantially reduced to a more manageable sum."

The judge doesn't bite. She simply says, "Counselor, the defendant will be remanded to jail if he cannot post the requisite bond."

The gavel strikes again, and the hearing is officially over. A court officer rises and calls the next case.

CHAPTER 55

The Hearing

Hail the size of gumballs whacks the windowpanes as my mother and friends and I watch the end of Rooster's arraignment hearing. The loud wail of the winds and smacking of the hail make us nudge closer to one another on my living room sofa. Snowy doesn't like the scary sounds either and drapes himself across our feet.

"He is such a liar!" Kayla exclaims, her mouth pinched with disgust. "I know for a fact he took those pictures of you since *I* found them on his computer!"

My mom grimaces. "I'm afraid lying is the least of his transgressions right now."

A booming clap of thunder sends Rachel's head spinning toward the living room windows. "If this doesn't stop, I am *not* going to school today."

"But it would be so worth dealing with the storm knowing there's no Ice Queen to bother us," I say.

"True," Rachel acknowledges, "but I'm still hoping the school loses power or they call an early dismissal."

"Quiet, everybody!" Kayla shouts as she points to my iPad. "Look at what's going on!"

The four of us dip our faces toward the bright screen. There's a ton of commotion coming from inside the courtroom, but it's not clear why.

"I can't tell what's happening," Rachel says, as we all strain to get a closer look. "I thought the arraignment was over."

My mother nods. "It was, but it sounds like there was an objection from someone in the audience."

From the angle of Aryana's camera, all we can see is a partial side view of a very distraught lady in a flouncy green dress standing behind Rooster. "He's innocent!" she screams. "Let him go!"

"And who are you?" The judge asks, elevating her voice above the chatter-filled room.

"I'm his wife, Karen Cooper."

"Mrs. Cooper, this hearing is over. Please exit the courtroom at once," the judge directs.

"You don't understand!" she bellows, her arms thrust forward, pleading. "He's innocent! You can't do this to him! He'll be fired. We'll lose everything...and he doesn't even know what this is about!"

There was something about her last statement that made the judge stop and stare at her. It could've been the words themselves or the way she said them, but the judge doesn't instruct her to leave again. The spectators who had started to exit the aisles sit back down, and an unsettling quiet consumes the courtroom. I believe I spot Splenda and the Shape Shifters in one of the center rows. It looks like Enema is next to them.

"Mrs. Cooper," the judge says, drawing out each syllable. "Do *you* know what this is about?"

The hysterical woman first glances at her husband, then peers at her daughter. Now that most of her profile is visible, I can see that her face is contorted with the painful decision she is about to make.

This time when she speaks her voice is low and small. "I do, Your Honor."

"Can you tell me, please?"

Rooster is peering at his wife as though she's lost her

mind, his nose scrunched into a tight ball, his eyes flashing bewilderment. His lawyer's face is also a mask of confusion. There's an intense silence in the courtroom as everyone waits for the lady in green to speak. At my house we're holding our collective breaths, none of us able to wrench our eyes from the screen.

If my pulse was high before, it's in the stratosphere now. I'm on the edge of my seat, spellbound by the melodrama unfolding before me. The musical score of the storm is the perfect accompaniment to the unexpected turn of events in the courthouse: As the excitement at the hearing crescendos, so do the roaring winds and lashing rain.

"My husband is telling you the truth. He knows nothing about this," Mrs. Cooper finally says. "I'm the one who took the pictures."

"*What?*" Rooster cries, clutching his middle as though he's been sucker punched.

Surprised gasps from the audience resonate throughout the crowded room.

"I did it for Krystal!" she wails. "I needed to help her get rid of that horrible girl who's been destroying her senior year. You know, the scrawny redheaded mutt who stole her boyfriend!"

Scrawny redheaded mutt? I wince at the flattering description.

Kayla, Rachel, and my mother all gaze at me at once, the shock registering in their eyes. "This is unbelievable!" Rachel whispers.

"Unbelievable" falls far short of what I'm thinking. Outrageous is more like it. All these years I've suffered at the hands of the Ice Queen but kept it from my parents. Meanwhile, the very bitch who tormented me must have been complaining to her mother about me to such a degree that the woman tried to send me to jail. If that's not over the top, I don't know what is.

Mrs. Cooper continues with her confession. "That girl made the horrible Instagram profile of Krystal, she put up those awful pictures and told everyone they were of Krystal, and she harasses Krystal every day in school—she's made her so miserable, and no one's done a damn thing to stop it... so *I* had to!"

"Oh, Karen," murmurs Rooster, shaking his head from side to side. "You didn't?"

"It's her senior year," his wife explains. "She deserves to go to the prom with her boyfriend. They'll be the king and queen, the way they're supposed to. Everything will be right again when this girl is out of the way. You'll see!"

"Oh, Karen," Rooster repeats, his voice fraught with sorrow. "How did you get on my work computer?"

"From home. I figured out your password, and I logged on remotely. It was—"

"Don't say another word, Karen," Rooster's lawyer instructs, his open palm raised at her face like a stop sign. "You've already said too much."

"Bailiff," the judge directs. "Please take Mrs. Cooper into custody."

"No!" Krystal cries, wrapping herself around her mother, trying to protect her from the inevitable.

A new image of the Humpty Dumpty family pops before my eyes. They're lying at the base of the red brick wall, their shells shattered, their yellow insides oozing everywhere.

As the bailiff slaps handcuffs on Mrs. Cooper, Rooster tries to peel Krystal away. The frantic girl is screaming "No!" over and over in a piercing wail, clawing for her mother. She latches on to one of her mother's arms, wheeling her head in search of anybody in the courtroom who will help her.

At that moment, for the first time ever, I see panic and terror on the Ice Queen's face. I've never thought of her as human before, not until this very instant. This larger-than-life creature has always seemed to have the perfect existence: Everyone's always followed her, she's gotten away with whatever she's wanted at school, she's the epitome of popularity and, as far as I know, she's never had any problems. Basically, her persona has been that of a supernatural being.

But seeing her agony as her mother is taken away cuts right through me. Krystal Cooper is human after all, and she's just hit rock bottom. I know exactly what rock bottom looks like, because I've seen it far too many times in my own mirror.

I would never have thought it possible before this moment, but I actually feel sorry for the Ice Queen. Really sorry. The anger, bitterness, and jealousy I've harbored for over three years slips away.

The hearing ends for the second time as the courtroom suddenly goes black. All that can be heard over my iPad is the cacophony of shrieks and screams.

CHAPTER 56

The End

By midday the nor'easter is still going strong, and there are power outages, emergency school closings, impassable roadways, and major flooding statewide. If the local mall wasn't dark and underwater, my friends and I would be shopping our hearts out right now, but by default, my house—which miraculously escaped the town-wide blackout—is our home base.

Through Snapchat, Twitter, Facebook, Instagram, and texts, the stunning news about the Ice Queen's mother spread like wildfire throughout the student body. David and Carrie can't wait to get the details, and dash over to my house as soon as Westberry High loses power. Since Carrie's parents forbid her to be part of our group, I'm super surprised to see her come through the front door with David.

"What are you doing here?" I ask as she rushes over to give me a hug, reaching me before David. Her sweatshirt is saturated from the short hike up my front walkway, but I don't care.

"I told my parents I was meeting my field hockey friends at a diner that had a generator," she explains. "They don't know I'm here."

David impatiently breaks in to give me a hug too, one that is so tender and sweet I'm swept away by its genuineness. He's shrugged off his wet windbreaker, and his soft gray T-shirt is warm and dry. I linger in his arms, relishing the closeness of his body, his hot breath along my cheek. My lips brush against the tip of his ear. I whisper, "I love you," the words pouring from deep within my heart. He smiles and tightens his grip, pulling us even closer. We are one, melted together...so natural, so perfect.

My idyllic moment is broken by Carrie jabbing her finger into my shoulder blade. "Tell me everything!" she cries, bouncing up and down. "This whole thing is so crazy!"

Kayla recognizes that I'm a bit preoccupied and delivers the most up-to-date information. She's all smiles as she says, "Aryana sent us a text about half an hour ago explaining that the courthouse lost electricity from a downed power line, and Mr. & Mrs. switched places—he's free and she's in custody. Blair's been joking that Rooster is now free range and his wife—the Hen—is in the coop."

David and Carrie laugh, and I happily report the rest of the news. "My dad is there too, and he called to say that he and my Uncle Marv are using the sudden turn of events to demand an immediate meeting with the chief prosecutor. We're waiting now to see what happens."

"Blair, why don't you all come in here and sit down," my mother calls from the kitchen. "My snickerdoodle cookies are almost done."

"You know my mom," I say to my friends as we make our way toward the mouthwatering smell. "She hasn't stopped cleaning and baking the entire morning. It's how she channels her nervous energy."

"Well, since I channel *my* nervous energy by eating," Rachel quips, "I'm moving in with you."

We all giggle as we settle into chairs around my kitchen table. Kayla grabs her phone off the counter to FaceTime Frankie. It's the first time C-6 is together again since we completed our mission.

Although Kayla had called Frankie earlier to fill him in

on the surprise confession in court, he keeps saying, "Who could have predicted it was Krystal's mother—the Hen— behind those pictures? I never would've guessed that."

"*You* wouldn't have guessed it?" David chimes in. "How do you think *I* feel? I'm the one who knows her."

"I know you're pretty surprised too, bro," Frankie says.

"Surprised?" David repeats. "Shocked is more like it. She's always been so nice to me. And I've always been able to talk to her about other stuff too, like politics and global warming—you know, important issues, and she's seemed so well informed...so well-grounded. I can't wrap my brain around her doing this."

He steals a glance at me, and I turn away, uncomfortable with my designation as the scrawny redheaded mutt who ruined his relationship with his ex-girlfriend. I also can't help thinking back to our conversation in the café the night we ran into Mr. and Mrs. Cooper, when I tried to warn him that the Queen's mother might not be so nice. *I told you so* would be a bit of an understatement at the moment.

David continues talking about her. "This is just so screwed up. I mean, I can't believe she'd do this just so Krystal and I could be prom queen and king. Like, is it really that important? And why couldn't she get it that *her daughter* is the one who broke up with *me*?"

"Well, we don't know what Krystal's been telling her," Kayla theorizes. "It sounded to me this morning like Krystal has told her some massive lies, and she thinks everything Krystal did to Blair was done by Blair to her daughter."

While the Snickerdoodle cookies are cooling, my mother has moved on to making cheese blintzes. She sets down her mixing spoon and pivots toward Kayla. "I don't care what her daughter told her," she says, her eyes flashing with anger. "She's an adult, and there's no excuse for her actions. No matter what she thought Blair did, you don't secretly stalk a child online, take pictures of her while she's undressed, and then send them to everyone in the world. There's just no excuse for that!"

"That's why she's the one in jail now," Frankie says, stating the obvious.

I face Frankie on Kayla's phone screen. "The problem is, everyone is going to believe Krystal's lies and blame *me* for putting her mother in jail."

David throws an arm around me and reels me in close. "No, I'm going to make sure that doesn't happen. There's a reason the woman was arrested. She's the criminal here and you're the victim, and I'm going to make sure everybody knows that."

I twist my lips. "Get real. Krystal's been going around saying I stole her boyfriend, and now add to it that I've sent her mother to jail. You think I'll be able to show my face in that school again?"

"Honey," my mom breaks in. "You haven't done anything wrong...you never did. You have no reason to be ashamed."

"Uh, Mrs. Evans," Rachel says, her eyes locking onto my mother's from under her sandy mane. "You don't know our school. You don't have to do anything wrong, but if Krystal says you did, then you did."

My mom and Rachel are both right, and their remarks force me to think about everything that's happened—where I am now and where I go from here. Yes, I'm a victim—again. And yes, they'll be lots more gossip and rumors about me after today's arraignment. The question is, what do I do about it? Do I hide, or face it head on?

I shut my eyes and pull in a deep, reflective breath. I'm no longer the clueless freshman who strolled into Westberry High over three years earlier. I've been through hell, and I survived. And this morning, I learned that the one person who I thought was invincible isn't so invincible after all.

I open my eyes, and say with renewed conviction, "You know what, I'm not afraid anymore. The worst is over for me, and no matter what happens, I can handle it. I'm just going to live my life and be grateful for everything I have. And by that, I mean all of you."

Each of my friends slaps my palm, and David presses a light kiss on my lips.

"Let's eat to that!" Rachel announces as she rises from her chair, her eyes fixated on the cookie tray. "I can't wait anymore. They smell too good!" She piles a stack of the hot cookies on a plate and ferries them back to the table. Each of our hands shoots out like we've never seen food before.

My mother's gaze roves over our small group. "What I still don't understand—what none of you have ever fully explained—is how one girl can have so much power?"

"That's what we've been trying to figure out for years, Mrs. Evans," Carrie replies, her words coated with bitterness.

"It probably comes from her father being the head hockey coach and working in the school," Kayla offers. "And don't forget, her older sister just graduated two years ago, and I heard she was really popular too."

David touches the side of my chin with the tip of his forefinger and pivots my face toward his. "None of that matters if you and I are free and don't have criminal charges hanging over us. We'll be able to get through anything."

"Speaking of criminal charges," my mom says, tilting her head to the side. "I hear the garage door. It sounds like your father just got home."

I fly out of my chair and gallop down the hall so fast I almost careen into my dad. "*Well?*" I cry, grabbing on to the staircase banister to slow myself down.

He can't hold back his elation and hoists me high over his head—like he used to when I was a little girl—in a grand victory gesture. "You are free, my baby!" he exclaims. "It's all over!"

"Yes!" I shout, punching the air. "Yes!"

C-6 breaks into a raucous applause at the incredible news, and my mother joins my dad and me, tears of joy rolling down her face. Even Snowy is ecstatic, standing on his hind legs to wrap his large black paws around us and lick my face. It's barely a moment before everyone is enfolded in a giant group hug, laughing and crying at the same time.

"Hey, what about me?" Frankie calls from the bottom step of our staircase where Kayla had propped up her phone.

"Virtual hug!" Kayla yells, charging at the phone with her arms outstretched.

"We're gonna have to do this in person!" Frankie hollers back.

"Yes, we are!" Kayla says, her grin electric.

When we all quiet down, my dad picks up two large brown paper bags with Chinese menus stapled across the tops. "I didn't know if we'd lose power, so I made sure we wouldn't go hungry."

"Are you kidding?" I joke. "Mom has been cooking nonstop for hours, and she only started doing that *after* she cleaned every inch of the house."

My mother laughs. A merry, robust laugh straight from the heart. "I couldn't just sit here waiting all day. I had to do *something*."

My dad motions everyone toward the dining room. "Come on, let's go have our celebratory feast. After what you kids have done for Blair, I should be taking you out for lobster, but with this storm we'll have to rough it."

Once we're settled at the dining room table, digging

into cartons of scallion pancakes and vegetable dumplings, I glance over at my father. "So, can we get some details, Dad?"

He finishes spooning out his wonton soup and tosses me a devilish smile, his eyes sparkling with a playful glint I haven't seen in weeks. "That poor chief prosecutor. Uncle Marv and I marched into his office and refused to leave until he agreed to a fair plea deal for you. The office was running on an emergency generator and everyone was scrambling around in panic mode, but we didn't care. We wanted the paperwork drafted on the spot. After what came out in court this morning, they needed to end the hell they've put you through once and for all."

"What's a fair deal?" my mom asks, emptying a packet of Chinese noodles into her egg drop soup.

My dad's face lights up like the Times Square Ball on New Year's Eve. "A fair deal is attending an educational program, performing twenty hours of community service—which she can do at the animal shelter—and getting all of this expunged from her record when she turns eighteen next year."

I grin so wide my cheeks hurt. "And they can't change their minds again and take back their offer?"

My father displays a proud smile and shakes his head. "Nope. It's a done deal. The charges against you are formally dropped. Since you're a minor, I signed on your behalf and made it one hundred percent official."

"Thanks, Dad!"

David sets down his fork and furrows his brow. "How come I got stuck with sixty hours of community service, and Blair only got twenty?"

"I didn't see your lawyer in court this morning, but get in touch with him immediately and fill him in on what happened, if he doesn't already know," my father suggests.

"Maybe he'll be able to get your community service reduced too. Blair's uncle and I were extremely persuasive today. We made it very clear how ludicrous it was to prosecute a young girl as an adult sex offender when she engaged in normal teenage behavior. And in Blair's case, as you know, she never consented to having a picture taken of her, she had no intent to commit a crime, and she didn't even know a crime had been committed until she was arrested."

"The same with me," David whines. "I had no idea what was going on, and I didn't do anything wrong either."

We'd ended the FaceTime call with Frankie when we sat down to eat, but I wonder what he'd say if he was still on the call. Although my parents now know the whole truth about Frankie's role in the sexting scandal, they choose to remain silent.

Kayla clears her throat and turns toward David. "I guess I owe you an apology...a huge one. You know I had my doubts about you, but you've really proven yourself. I'm really sorry about those things I said."

David offers a good-natured smile. "Thank you, but under the circumstances I understand why you felt the way you did."

"You know, baby," my dad says, leaning over the table in my direction. "I have some other good news for you. I was saving it so you had something that would cheer you up in case things didn't go well this morning." He taps his cell phone several times as he's talking.

I can't even imagine what he's referring to, but I can tell by the way his eyes are dancing and the corners of his mouth are curving that it's going to be good. My mom seems more excited than me, and prompts, "Any day now, Sam...."

My dad laughs and raises his phone screen, his smile as broad as the table. "Your grandma and grandpa just adopted a new dog. Someone told them this was a good one."

I gasp.

It's Henry! The picture on my dad's phone is of Henry! I'd know those inquisitive eyes, gorgeous black markings, and large pointy ears anywhere.

"They really got Henry!" I bellow, grabbing my dad's phone for a better look. I'm so overcome with emotion, tears start budding in my eyes. "When?"

"Yesterday. They wanted to get him settled in before the storm hit. When it let's up, we'll go see him in his new home."

I'm at a loss for words. I didn't think I could be any happier than when I found out I was free, but this just propels me into another galaxy. I didn't plan on crying again for a long time, but I can't hold back the tears.

My dad has always said that we should never underestimate my grandma, and clearly, he knows what he's talking about. Somehow, she accomplished the impossible, convincing my stubborn grandpa to change his mind and get another dog. And not just any dog. I can't help but think about how amazing it is that Henry's luck turned around at the same time as mine, even when all seemed hopeless.

This is truly the best day of my life.

My mom tosses me a brilliant smile and passes around a fistful of fortune cookies, a giddy gleam in her eyes. "I know we usually open these after dinner, but I can't wait. Blair and David, you go first." She bounces in her seat like an excited child.

We both crack ours in half at the same time, but I read mine first: "'All the darkness in the world cannot put out a single candle.'"

"What's that supposed to mean?" Carrie asks. "Maybe that we should get candles ready in case you lose power?"

Rachel swallows the bite of General Tso's chicken she's

chewing and takes a stab at it. "No, I think it means that no matter how many bad things happen or try to get in Blair's way, they'll never stop her. She'll always shine."

"Wow, Rachel, that's so sweet...so profound," my mom compliments.

I nudge David. "Come on, read yours."

He smoothes out the thin white strip of paper. "My lucky numbers are thirty-two, twenty-nine—"

I rip the fortune out of his hands. "Stop being a clown!"

"Okay, okay," he says, snatching it back and flipping it over. "It says, 'Don't obsess over your reputation and you can do anything you like.'"

That draws a round of chuckles. Then Kayla reads hers. "'Make happy those who are near, and those who are far will come.'"

"Ooh," I tease. "That one's definitely yours."

Kayla's cheeks flush a dark burgundy. To avoid eye contact with any of us, she busies herself rolling up a moo shu pancake.

I glance at Carrie. "Your turn."

With a dramatic flourish, Carrie crushes hers against the tabletop and unfurls the white paper. "Failure is not falling down but refusing to get up."

Everyone bursts out laughing.

"Hey," she says with a defensive air. "It doesn't say anything about *fake* falling!"

Rachel waves hers over her head. "Me next. Mine says, 'The longer you wait, the more unexpected developments will occur.'"

"I'm so glad I didn't get that one!" I exclaim. "I don't want any more surprises for a long time."

"No?" David says, looking hurt. "I was hoping you might like this one." He slips his hand into the back pocket of his jeans and pulls out a skinny envelope. It's plain white with no writing.

I have no idea what it is, and I'm bubbling with curiosity as he places it in my hands. When I slice it open, my eyes nearly pop out of my head. I'm looking at two prepaid tickets for our first skydiving jump.

"Oh my God!" I shriek, launching out of my seat. "I can't believe you did this! We're really going?"

He nods. "After everything we've been through, there's nothing we can't do."

I throw my arms around him and squeeze with sheer delight. "Thank you! Thank you! When did you get them?"

"Last week, when those new pictures came out and the prosecutor's office took back your deal. I wanted to do something really special for you—show you that life is still worth living."

"Uh, what are those tickets for?" my dad asks, narrowing his eyes.

"Skydiving!" I squeal, holding them high in the air.

My mom morphs a pale shade of green. "I didn't just hear that."

I wave the tickets in front of everyone and circle my gaze around the table. "All right, C-6, are we all doing this together?"

My friends avert their eyes and mumble a chorus of different excuses—things like "afraid of heights," "hate flying," "too young to die."

I cradle my fingers around my boyfriend's neck. "Looks like it'll be just you and me."

Those warm chocolate-brown eyes with the honey-gold kaleidoscope specks smile back at me. "That'll be perfect."

Discussion Questions

1. Should sexting be a crime?

2. Do you think David was engaging in normal teenage behavior when he took Blair's picture?

3. Do you think Blair and David should have been charged with sexting crimes under child pornography laws?

4. Should adults caught sexting pictures or videos of minors be charged under child pornography laws? Should there be an exception if an adult is in a relationship with a minor?

5. If Blair and David agreed to sext each other, would it be fair to charge them under criminal laws?

6. If Blair sexted a photo or video of herself, should that be considered a crime?

7. Was it okay for Frankie to send the sexually explicit picture of Blair without her consent?

8. When people who knew Blair received the sexually explicit images of her, what should they have done?

9. Should the Ice Queen have been charged with revenge porn?

10. What should the penalty be for revenge porn?

11. Since teen sexting has become prevalent in our society, what should the law be regarding teen sexting?

12. Are social media and video game companies doing enough to combat cyberbullying on their platforms? What else can they do to stop/deter harmful conduct and promote positive behavior?

13. When Blaire was being cyber-bullied, what do you think could have been done to help her?

14. As the victim of sexting and cyberbullying, should Blair have had the right to have the hurtful/harmful/embarrassing posts removed?

15. What can you do if you are the victim of sextortion?

16. Should the legal, social, emotional, and psychological consequences of sexting and cyberbullying be taught in school?

Glossary Of Terms

Arraignment

Court proceeding in which the person charged with a crime is formally read the charges against them and expected to enter a plea

Bail

Security such as money, property, or bond imposed on a person charged with a crime(s) to obtain their conditional release from police custody and ensure they will appear in court at a future date

Child Pornography

Any visual depiction of sexually explicit conduct involving a minor

Cyberbullying

Repeatedly and intentionally harassing, mistreating, or making fun of another person through the use of computers, cell phones, or other electronic devices. Examples: mean comments, rumors, threats, hurtful pictures or videos, creating mean web pages.

Finsta

Fake Instagram account

Minor

Person who has not attained the legal age of adulthood (someone under 18 years of age under federal law and in most states)

Plea Deal	**(also Plea Bargain)** Agreement in a criminal case between the prosecutor and defendant in which the defendant agrees to plead guilty or no contest to a less serious charge(s) or reduced sentence
Revenge Porn	**(also Nonconsensual Pornography)** The distribution of sexually explicit images or video of individuals without their consent and for no legitimate purpose
Sexting	Sending, receiving, or forwarding sexually explicit material over cell phones, computers, or digital devices. The sexual material includes nude or partially nude photos, videos, video links, texts, and messages.
Sextortion	Type of cybercrime threatening to expose sexual images or intimate personal details of the victim in order to force them to do something, such as pay money or send more sexual images
Vindictive Sexting	Sexting that is done spitefully or vengefully with the deliberate intent to hurt others

Acknowledgements

It is with the utmost gratitude that I thank all of the people who had a part in helping me bring this story into the world, starting with my family, for being there at every stage of the process, my ever-supportive friends, my editors, designers, and readers, and everyone else whose valuable contributions factored into the final product, with a special shout out to Evelyn Pentikis, Pat Padden, Cooper Critchley, Katie Martinez, and Asya Blue.

Made in the USA
Middletown, DE
15 December 2020